BOOK
OF THE
NIGHT

BOOK
OF THE
NIGHT

The Black Musketeers

Oliver Pötzsch
Translated by Lee Chadeayne

amazoncrossing

Previously published as *Die Schwarzen Musketiere—Das Buch der Nacht* by bloomoon in Germany in 2015. Translated from German by Lee Chadeayne. First published in English by AmazonCrossing in 2016.

Published by AmazonCrossing, Seattle

www.apub.com

Amazon, the Amazon logo, and AmazonCrossing are trademarks of Amazon.com, Inc., or its affiliates.

ISBN-13: 9781503938427
ISBN-10: 1503938425

Cover design by Edward Bettison

Printed in the United States of America

PROLOGUE

November Eighth in the Year of Our Lord 1620, outside Prague in Bohemia

There was a crash as the door to the church flew open, and the old nun knew that death had come to take her.

The noise of battle could be heard through the shattered windows, the deafening sounds of muskets and cannons, the neighing of frightened horses, the cries of dying men.

Of many dying men.

The Battle of Weißenberg had been raging now for more than an hour. The army of Bohemian rebels had dug in atop the supposedly impregnable hill, but the imperial soldiers had been attacking furiously, and their battle cry *"¡Santa Maria!"* could be heard in nearby Prague. The legendary General Tilly was at the head of nearly thirty thousand soldiers attacking the rebels who had turned against the German Kaiser and elected their own king. With pikes, lances, and swords, they defended themselves bravely, but nonetheless the rebels were being slaughtered one by one.

The old nun could tell that the soldier was a Spaniard in the service of the Kaiser's army. His breastplate was battered, and his helmet sat askew atop his head, hanging down over his unshaven face. With murder in his eyes, he grinned as he approached her, making a swishing sound with his sword as he almost playfully swung it through the air.

"Where is it?" he hissed, suddenly raising the weapon and pointing it toward her, bringing it closer and closer until it nearly touched the old woman's throat.

"Where is what?" the nun replied in a calm voice.

As the abbess of the oldest cloister in all of Bohemia, the venerable Mother Agatha was just as wise as she was brave. She understood, of course, what the man wanted from her. He had tried again and again to wrest the powerful object from her control, but until now the Saint George Cloister adjacent to the Prague Castle had always been a place too safe, too well watched for any theft. Unfortunately, those times were now past—now that chaos and war were raging in Bohemia—and one of the most evil monsters in the war, a broad-shouldered mercenary more than six feet tall, was standing before Mother Agatha with raised sword. He would stop at nothing to get his hands on the abbess's most valuable secret.

A demon incarnate with a huge, bulging scar across his right cheek.

"*¡Dámelo!*" the man demanded in Spanish and came a step closer, but Mother Agatha didn't budge. If she gave up now, then all her efforts would have been in vain. She had to remain strong to the bitter end. This was the final task God had given her—she had to protect the secret.

As it became increasingly clear that the Bohemian rebels would lose the war against the Kaiser, the abbess had decided to have the mighty object removed from the city. Along with her most loyal servants, she had escaped through a small, secret gate into the neighboring forest. Nevertheless, someone had noticed, and mercenaries had appeared from all sides and chased them like animals. Here in the church it seemed that Mother Agatha's attempted escape had come to an end, and without taking her eyes off the soldier, she prepared herself for her imminent death.

"I don't know what you are speaking of," she said, her voice still calm and firm.

"You know very well, old woman," the Spaniard growled, reverting to broken German. "We have been watching you for a long time. Did you think you could escape us?" The point of his sword was now pressed directly against her throat. "So, where is it? Out with it! And where is the young nun who was with you until just recently?"

Mother Agatha smiled as she gestured with her withered hands toward the destroyed interior of the church. "Did you really think I would be so dumb as to run into this trap if I didn't have a plan? Blinded by hate, you followed me, you and your bloodhounds. Ha! The girl is long gone." She briefly pressed her lips together. "The girl, and also what you have been pursuing so relentlessly. You can tell your master he will never get his hands on it. Never will he be able to use it to bring misery to mankind. It is well hidden."

"You . . . devil woman! *¡Bruja!*"

Without further ado, the mercenary ran her through with his sword, and with a moan the old abbess fell to the floor.

"Your master is the devil . . . not I," she struggled to say. "You . . . have failed."

Her eyes glazed over, and a peaceful smile spread over her face.

"*¡Maldito!*" The Spaniard kicked the lifeless body with the tip of his boot, then turned away. He knew he'd made a mistake. He should have forced the old woman to tell him where the other nun was. Perhaps now he'd never find what he was sent to get.

His master would be very, very angry.

The soldier stepped out into the November fog that still hung over the abandoned church like a cloud of gunpowder. Outside, his comrades-in-arms were sitting on their weary horses, watching him with curious eyes and waiting.

"Go look for this young woman!" he ordered them. "She must be somewhere nearby. And be sure you bring her to me alive, damn it! She's the only one left who can tell us where to look." He spat on the ground and stuck his bloody sword back in its sheath.

Suddenly, there was an infernal commotion somewhere in the fog. The flashing of the cannons up on the mountain looked like distant lightning, and the noise, mixing with the screams of the soldiers, sounded like the howling of a thousand-headed monster.

"*¡Santa Maria!*"

The imperial forces had won the battle.

I

Eleven Years Later . . .
September 25 in the Year of Our Lord 1631, at Lohenfels Castle near
Heidelberg in the Palatinate

The blow caught Lukas on the side, on his temple. He staggered, fell back a few steps until he was relieved to feel the solid trunk of an oak tree behind him. Moments later, he pulled himself together and went on the attack. His blows were precise—feint, attack, parry, high cut, quick retreat, a second lunge, and then a sudden thrust forward, causing his opponent to stumble and almost fall backward.

Lukas was preparing a final blow when his opponent's weapon struck him on his sword hand. With a cry of surprise, Lukas dropped his stick as tears of pain welled up in his eyes.

"You . . . cheated, Father!" he gasped. "You just pretended you were falling back."

With a laugh, Friedrich von Lohenfels tossed his carved wooden weapon into the bushes and patted Lukas on the shoulder.

"In a battle, nothing is ever fair," he finally said with a grin. "That's one thing you still have to learn. It's only about who wins."

"But we are knights!" Lukas protested.

"You, a knight?" His father roared with laughter. "I'm afraid before you become a knight, you'll have to eat a few more haunches of venison. At present, all I see before me is a skinny twelve-year-old kid."

Lukas clenched his lips. He hated it when his father teased him because of his small stature. Among boys his age, he was in fact usually the smallest, but the most adept at wielding the stick and the dull foil. It had been a long time since any of his friends had dared to call him a kid. Lukas's hot temper was well-known, as was his skill. Whenever his father had time, he practiced with Lukas in the courtyard of their castle or in the nearby forest, just like today—his birthday.

"I'm thirteen today," he said, turning angrily to his father. "Have you forgotten?"

Friedrich von Lohenfels raised his hand apologetically and then bowed dramatically. "Excuse me. You're right. Well then, noble knight Lukas von Lohenfels, may I invite you after this mock battle to my humble castle for a cup of apple cider?"

Lukas laughed as his father took a few comical bows. His anger had passed. The two had been walking in the forest all day. First they had hunted deer, with some of his father's servants, but then Friedrich led the boy to a lonely clearing, where he taught him a few more sword-fighting tricks. For over two hours, they had practiced attacks and defense; like two dancers, they'd collide into each other again and again, and then spring back, until sweat ran down Lukas's face and every muscle in his body ached.

It had been his finest birthday present.

His father didn't often have an entire day to devote to him. Usually, Friedrich was busy with administrative duties on behalf of the Kaiser in the castle, which lay in a rather isolated region known as the Odenwald Mountains, a day's ride from Heidelberg. Or he was far away, fighting for General Tilly and his Catholic League against the accursed Protestants.

As long as Lukas could remember, wars had been raging somewhere or other in the German Empire. It had all started long ago in distant Bohemia, where the Protestants revolted against the Catholic Kaiser and threw his representative from a window of the Prague Castle. Afterward, the Protestants had been slaughtered in the Battle of Weißenberg, and ever since then, war had spread like wildfire through the German Empire. Lukas's mother once told him that the war was every bit as old as he was himself, and sometimes it seemed to Lukas that the conflict would never cease. For as long as he lived!

"You've really made good progress in sword fighting," his father said as they walked together through the forest. It was early fall, and the leaves on the beech trees and oaks shone in many colors. "Especially feinting, but also your low cut is much improved. Now I can tell you that I actually stumbled briefly." Friedrich von Lohenfels shook his head. "But don't tell anyone. If word gets around that my own thirteen-year-old son outwitted me, Tilly won't take me on any more expeditions."

"So much the better, then you'll stay in the castle with us," Lukas replied with a grin. "With me, Mother, and Elsa, and you can teach me more tricks."

His father sighed. "I'm afraid I can't do that, lad. Now that the Swedes have attacked the Reich, I'll probably have to head out to war again soon."

"Then take me along!" Lukas begged excitedly. He straight-ened up so he would look bigger. "You said yourself I'm a good swordsman, even a very good one. I . . . could fight in the Black Musketeers, just as you used to. I can start out as a simple baggage servant, and then—"

"Enough of this nonsense!" his father interrupted brusquely. "War is no children's game. Be happy that until now you've been spared. You may be a good fighter with the stick and the foil, but real fighting is something entirely different. Real blood flows, and I don't want it to be the blood of my son. And now no more of that!"

As they trudged silently through the dense forest, listening to the singing of many birds, Lukas thought about all the tales he'd overheard when grown-ups talked about war. Lukas had long ago stopped trying to understand who were really the bad ones and the good ones in this eternal conflict. Catholics fought against Protestants; some German electors—the princes entitled to take part in choosing the Kaiser—actually fought against the Kaiser; and foreign powers such as the Danes, Spaniards, and, recently, the Swedes were in search of the spoils of war in the Reich. The Palatinate, where Lukas and his parents lived, was for now in the hands of the Bavarian elector, but the soldiers had so far spared Friedrich von Lohenfels because he stood on the side of the Kaiser, and thus the Bavarian Catholics.

For many citizens of the Palatinate, Lukas's father was there-fore a traitor. Lukas had often been in fights with boys his age and older who secretly cursed and mocked his father. All of them had come to regret their words later.

"If I can't go off to war with you, then at least tell me about the Black Musketeers," Lukas grumbled after a while, as their home appeared from behind the trees. Lohenfels Castle was a gloomy-looking building with high walls perched on a rocky promontory above the Neckar River. Around the castle were a few fields and simple farmhouses, and far below, the roaring of the wild river could be heard.

"Very well," his father grumbled back, "just so you'll stop pestering me, even if you've heard the story a thousand times before." His voice was deep and calm, reminding Lukas of the many times his father had told him bedtime stories. "The Black Musketeers were the best fighters in the Reich," he began, "trained in the use of all sorts of weapons and feared by everyone. They served as bodyguards to the Imperial General Wallenstein—"

"Under whom you served in the war against the Danes," Lukas interrupted. "You were one of them, weren't you?"

"Who's telling this story? You or me?" His father pressed his lips together grimly before continuing. "Yes, I was one. We fought and shot like the devil, with swords, pikes, daggers, muskets, and pistols, and drove the Danes and their allies back across the Elbe River. God knows, I never saw better fighters than these old-timers all dressed in black, like shadows in the night and phantoms by day. But the Kaiser dismissed Wallenstein, and the Black Musketeers were scattered to the winds. They don't exist anymore. They belong to the past." Abruptly, he clapped his hands to indicate the discussion was over. "Now let's go and see if the servants have finished roasting the wild boar on the spit. I'm dying of hunger. You should eat something, too," he said, winking at Lukas. "If you want to become a warrior someday that everyone fears just as much as they did the Black Musketeers, you've got to put a little meat on your bones."

As his father disappeared into the kitchen, Lukas climbed a worn stone staircase to the second floor of the living quarters. There in the so-called knights' hall—the only large, heated room in the castle—his little sister, Elsa, came toward him. Her eyes were flashing with excitement.

Unlike the dark coloring that Lukas had inherited from his father, Elsa had freckles and flaxen hair that always looked a bit tousled. She was also an impudent whirlwind who sometimes got on Lukas's nerves. He often wished he had a brother with whom he could practice stick fighting or slip away to the nearby river to go fishing.

"Mother said I can go hunting with you and Father tomorrow," she announced triumphantly. "And I can try shooting the crossbow."

"You want to shoot?" Lukas responded with a laugh. "When you tramp through the forest, you'll scare the animals all the way to Heidelberg. It would be better for you to stay home and stick your nose in a book, or knit something."

"Wouldn't that suit you just fine! I'm supposed to sit here like a good girl while you and Father go out and have all the fun? Just wait till I tell Mother."

Tears of anger glittered in her eyes, and Lukas sighed. Father had promised to take him along tomorrow on the great hunt, and the thought that Elsa would be clinging to his shirtsleeve the whole time noticeably dampened his spirits.

"Suppose instead I read you a good story tonight," he suggested in a conciliatory tone.

"You can't even read," Elsa sneered. "You always just pretend. I watched very closely the last time."

Lukas blushed. In fact, he was far better in stick and sword fighting than in Latin, grammar, and penmanship—in stark contrast with his sister, who, even though she was just nine years old, could flawlessly recite the work of the Roman poet Ovid.

"Even if you're right," he grumbled, "you're not coming on the hunt. It's just for men."

"I had no idea you were already a man," said a soft voice behind him. Lukas turned around and discovered his mother standing in the doorway. She was smiling. "Have you perhaps already found a woman you would like to take for a wife?"

"I saw him in the barn with the tavern keeper's daughter," Elsa crowed. "They kissed!"

"That's not true!"

Lukas jumped at her, and soon they were scuffling under the big table in the middle of the hall.

"Stop right now, you two!" their mother cried, pulling Lukas gently to her. "It's surely not asking too much to let Elsa go along just once on a hunt, so do be a bit understanding."

Lukas slipped out of her embrace. "You're always on her side," he whispered between clenched teeth. "Even on my birthday."

"But that's not so," his mother replied. "You are both my children, and I love you both the same. Just in a different way," she added after a pause.

Sophia von Lohenfels had friendly, intelligent eyes that made her look older than her thirty or so years. Despite her position as lady of the castle, she usually wore a simple linen dress like that of a farm woman. Her husband sometimes scolded her for this, but Sophia liked being among the common folk and in the small towns, where she was recognized as an experienced healer. Some people whispered that she had magic powers. They also spoke of her miraculous healings, flowers blooming in the middle of winter, and soup that suddenly appeared in an empty kettle.

Once, when Lukas was very young, it almost came to a court trial, as the lady had aroused suspicions of witchcraft. But naturally, that was nonsense, as Lukas knew.

"Let Elsa go with you on your next trip to the villages," Lukas suggested. "Someday she'll surely be a great healer like you, and I'll be a great fighter and hunter like Father."

"Oh-ho! It sounds to me like someone doesn't want to do his Latin lessons," Sophia replied, waving her finger playfully at her son. "Until you finish them, you're not going anywhere, young man."

Lukas rolled his eyes, and his mother gave him a kiss. "So we'll wait and see what happens tomorrow," she reassured him. "But now let's go and eat."

Lukas hadn't eaten a thing since morning and suddenly realized how hungry he was. Shortly afterward, the servants brought in steaming platters of leg of deer and wild boar and hot, fragrant loaves of bread. His father also came and took a seat. Then they all joined hands and gave a prayer of thanks while Lukas was absorbed in thoughts of the next day's hunt. Would he shoot a wild boar with his crossbow? Or perhaps even a large stag?

It took a while before he realized how sad his father looked. Silently, the great man sipped wine from his chalice. Something seemed to be bothering him.

"Are you all right?" his wife asked as she pushed a platter in front of him with a large piece of meat. "Have you received some bad news?"

Friedrich nodded. "Indeed. Over in Saxony, the accursed Swedes have dealt a disastrous defeat to Tilly's army. A messenger just arrived with the news, and he says we have lost more than twelve thousand men."

"Does that mean that Tilly will lose the war?" Lukas asked between bites. A slight wave of anxiety came over him. Along with the Catholic Kaiser, it had been General Tilly who until then had held his protective hand over Lohenfels Castle and its inhabitants. If he was defeated, or even dead, what would happen to them?

"Tilly is a tough customer," his father replied, "but I'm afraid I shall soon have to return to the war. The army now needs every man."

"Then are you going to leave us again?" Elsa asked quietly.

"Eventually, yes." Friedrich sighed, then a smile suddenly spread over his face. "But not today, and not tomorrow, either." He raised his glass of red wine as he pushed the jug of sweet apple cider across the table to his children. "And now let's all drink together. To the best kids and the best wife that can be found in all of the Palatinate."

The cups and glasses clinked, and Lukas's fear subsided with each delightful sip. Father would protect them, as he always had. They were the Lohenfels family, loyal friends of the Kaiser. How could anyone do them any harm? Here in their castle, they were safe.

His mother's eyes sparkled as she served the dessert—cheesecake with hot raspberries, his favorite.

"Happy birthday, Lukas." His mother smiled.

Lukas spooned up the warm, sweet compote while behind him a fire crackled in the fireplace, and he felt warm and secure. He didn't know this was the last evening he would spend in the company of his family.

Soon after, Lukas lay awake in bed, watching the flickering shadows cast on the wall by the tallow candles.

In the second bed lay Elsa, leafing with fascination through a dog-eared book she had taken from the castle library, full of colorful drawings of the strangest animals—dragons with three heads, sea serpents with wide-open mouths, and lions with the tail of a scorpion.

"What is that, for heaven's sake?" Lukas asked after a while, yawning. The day had been long and strenuous, and he was having trouble keeping his eyes open.

"This? A book about animals in far-off Africa," she told him. "It's rather exciting, and there's a lot you can learn from it."

"But it's in Latin!" Lukas replied, shaking his head. "How can anything be exciting when it's written in Latin?"

"It isn't really so difficult. I already know most of the words from our schoolbooks—*leo*, for example, that means lion. And a *mantichora* is—"

"Oh, just stop!" Lukas interrupted. "It's enough that Mother torments me with that. I don't need to hear it from my little sister, too."

"Then it's your loss. Just stay dumb. But don't come begging me for help when a horrible manticore attacks you."

Elsa became absorbed in her book again while Lukas tried to think of some smart reply. But he couldn't think of anything. Sometimes his sister really made him furious, but then there were other moments when he loved her more than anything in the world. Lukas could remember how he'd held Elsa in his arms when she was an infant. She was so tiny and fragile! He'd held her hand when she took her first steps, and fed her, and sung her to sleep. In all these years, a bond had grown between them that occasional quarrels could not destroy.

Still, he was furious beyond words that Elsa wanted to take part in the hunt the next day. Who was he, anyway? Her nursemaid? Fighting and hunting were for men, not for women, especially a woman who tormented him with Latin words.

At the same moment, it occurred to Lukas that he hadn't done his Latin lessons. His mother had made it clear he wouldn't be allowed to go on the hunt until he'd finished his exercises.

"Elsa?" he asked hesitantly. "Uh, I have a proposal for you. You can go on the hunt with us tomorrow if—"

"I'll help you with your Latin lessons before breakfast," Elsa interrupted with a yawn. "Is that what you wanted to say?"

Lukas was shocked. Sometimes Elsa really seemed to be clairvoyant, a gift she had probably gotten from her mother.

"Ah . . . yes," he replied. "Would you really do that for me?"

"Yes, but only on one condition. That you let me sleep next to you." She laid the book aside and looked over at him nervously. "These stories about manticores and fire-spitting dragons are more gruesome than I realized."

Lukas nodded with a smile, and Elsa crawled into his bed, where she soon fell sound asleep, her little body gently cuddled against his own. He could feel her warm skin against his shirt, and then, finally, he drifted off to sleep as well.

Sometimes little sisters could be a nuisance, but sometimes you needed to have them there.

II

When Lukas awakened the next morning, he noticed at once that something was wrong. Father was standing straight as an arrow alongside his bed, and his face looked dark and tense. He was staring through the little window that opened onto the courtyard with a look that suggested he felt the presence of something infinitely evil lurking outside. It was still early morning, and the sun had not yet risen.

"Quick, wake your sister and go over to the keep," his father ordered. "I want you to hide down below in the dungeon. That's the safest place to be, do you understand?"

"In the dungeon?" Lukas replied, confused and rubbing his tired eyes. "But why—"

"Don't ask, just do what I tell you," his father interrupted harshly. "And stay there until you hear from me." Without another word, he turned and left the room.

Immediately, Lukas was wide-awake. He had never seen Father like this. It almost seemed that the brave warrior was terribly afraid of something. When Lukas hurried to the window, he saw in the dim light about two dozen strangers on horseback in front of the castle. Could they be enemy soldiers? Were they the Swedes his father had spoken of?

Quickly, he put on his shirt, leather jacket, and trousers, and then he wakened Elsa, who was still sleeping soundly beside him.

But his sister just turned aside, groaning. "We've got until the next cock's crow," she mumbled. "The sun isn't even up yet."

Lukas bit his lip. Father had ordered him to seek refuge in the keep with Elsa as soon as possible. If he got into a long discussion now, it might be too late; so he decided to try a trick.

"Come, we'll play a game," he said, trying to sound calm and cheerful. "We'll hide in the dungeon, and Father will have to come and look for us. How about it?"

"Hide in the dungeon?" With sleepy eyes and tousled hair, she sat up in bed. Now she'd become curious. "I thought we were going hunting today."

"Ah, yes, but not right away. We have to wait for the beaters to get here from town."

Elsa grimaced. "Ugh, it stinks in the dungeon, and there are rats. I don't want to go down there."

"But it's the best hiding place in the whole castle," Lukas whispered. "Father will never find us there. Come on, sissy."

"Oh, very well." She looked at him suspiciously. "But don't think you can lock me up there and go hunting alone with Father. I'm not that stupid."

Reluctantly and still half asleep in her nightgown, Elsa let Lukas lead her out of the room. Down in the courtyard, a few excited servants had already gathered in the semidarkness while Friedrich von Lohenfels stood in their midst giving them orders that Lukas couldn't hear. Two of the watchmen were already lowering the drawbridge and preparing to open the gate.

Clearly, the men arriving at the castle aren't Swedes, Lukas thought. *So why then all this excitement?*

"What are the servants doing?" Elsa asked.

"They're letting the beaters in. Now come, before Father sees us."

A few minutes later, Lukas and Elsa had reached the keep. The tower, with its three-foot-thick stone walls, was the safest part of the castle. It was here that the residents withdrew during a siege. A steep wooden stairway led along the outside to a massive door about thirty feet above the courtyard. Inside the tower was a trapdoor and a ladder leading down into the stinking dungeon. The stump of a torch was still burning in a bracket close to the opened trapdoor.

"Down that way," Lukas ordered and reached for the torch. "Hurry!"

He climbed down the ladder with Elsa and quickly shut the trapdoor above them. The torch cast a faint light only about four or five feet ahead of them, and somewhere in the darkness, they could hear rats squeaking. There was also a horrible stench of feces and mold.

"This is a really dumb place to hide," Elsa grumbled. "I want to go back up and get dressed for the hunt."

"You . . . can't do that now," Lukas stammered, looking for some excuse. "Father would see us and we would lose the game. We'll have to wait down here for a while, whether we like it or not."

"Well . . . if we absolutely have to, then later on you'll let me use the crossbow. Promise?"

Lukas nodded absentmindedly. They crouched down on the damp straw in the dim light of the torch. After a while they could hear muffled voices up above. Evidently, the strangers had now entered the courtyard, but all they could hear were a few scraps of conversation.

Finally, Lukas couldn't stand it anymore. He had to find out what was going on up there . . . despite his promise to his father.

"Listen," he said to his sister, "I'm going up to look around and see where Father is. Perhaps we can surprise him."

"But I don't want to stay down here alone," Elsa whined. "I'm afraid, and it's cold. You only want to lock me up here, admit it!"

"I'll leave the trapdoor open, all right?" Lukas suggested. "And you'll have the torch. But you have to promise me you'll stay down here, or . . ." He wagged his finger at her. "Later I won't let you use the crossbow, do you understand?"

Hesitantly, Elsa nodded. Then Lukas climbed up the ladder and opened the trapdoor as quietly as possible. He still couldn't make out anything clearly, so he decided to open the door of the keep just a crack.

Through the opening, he could see a few foreign-looking men on horseback. They were wearing black pantaloons, breastplates, and helmets with the tall crest worn by Spanish mercenaries. Lukas knew that the Spaniards were allies of the Kaiser. But who was the haggard, distinguished-looking monk on the freshly groomed black horse? He was wearing a snow-white cowl with a black cape and a silk cap over his thinning blond hair. His nose protruded from his pale face like the beak of a bird of prey. He was talking to Lukas's father, who was standing with arms crossed in front of the prancing horse.

"Evidence against your wife keeps growing," the man was saying. "We will take her to Heidelberg for a thorough questioning."

"No one is going to take my Sophia away," Friedrich von Lohenfels retorted, moving forward a step. "You tried once before to accuse my wife of witchcraft, and I won't let you take her away from me again."

Instinctively, Lukas recoiled. These men were no hostile mercenaries, but they also weren't allies. They'd come to accuse his mother of being a witch, and Lukas knew what they did with witches. They were tortured and finally burned at the stake so that none of their evil flesh would be left on earth.

"You forget that I am a free knight of the empire," his father continued. "The Kaiser and General Tilly both stand behind me. Do you really want to pick a fight with them? You tried once, and failed."

The monk waved dismissively. "The Kaiser is far away, and Tilly has his hands full with the Swedes. Besides, times have changed since our last meeting." With a triumphant smile, he produced a document with a large red seal. "See here. None less than the pope has appointed me grand inquisitor, which means I have permission from the Church to put an end to heretical activities and hunt down witches. So tell me, where is the witch?"

"If by that you mean my wife, she is not here," Friedrich replied defiantly. "She's visiting relatives down on the Rhine."

"Aha! Visiting relatives . . . How kind of her." The monk laughed softly. "Then you'll surely have no objection if we search your castle." He turned to the Spanish mercenaries. "Turn over every stone here."

Horrified, Lukas watched as an especially large soldier approached the keep with his loaded crossbow. He could already hear the steps creaking as the huge man headed up toward the door. He had a long scar across his right cheek.

At that moment, Sophia von Lohenfels stepped out onto the balcony of the castle.

"You can spare yourself the trouble, Waldemar von Schönborn," she declared, her eyes flashing. "Here I am. Take me. I have a clear conscience."

Lukas put his hand to his mouth so he wouldn't cry out. Why had his mother done that? Why hadn't she just hidden as he and Elsa had done? Now all was lost.

The monk smiled grimly, then gave a sign to his henchmen. "Seize the witch!"

"Noooooo!"

It was Friedrich von Lohenfels who had shouted. Brandishing his sword and bellowing furiously, he ran toward the grand inquisitor. At the same moment, the soldier on the stairway to the keep pointed his crossbow at the knight. There was a soft click, and the bolt penetrated Friedrich's chest. He staggered a few paces before collapsing directly in front of the monk's horse.

"You . . . dog," he groaned. "God . . . damn you . . ."

As the knight tried to stagger to his feet again, a second bolt pierced the base of his neck. A slight trembling passed through his muscular body, and then he went limp. Blood mixed with the dirt in the courtyard.

"This is what will happen to all enemies of the true faith!" the inquisitor cried, turning to the servants of the castle who were standing there in the courtyard, paralyzed with fear. "Let that be a lesson to you."

By now the mercenaries had reached the balcony, where Sophia von Lohenfels let herself be led away without resistance. She glanced once up at the keep, as a final farewell to her two children.

Lukas heard a quiet moan nearby and, turning around, saw that Elsa had also climbed the ladder and was now standing directly behind him.

"What . . . is happening?" she asked anxiously. "Where are our parents?"

Lukas could find no words to reply and began to sob silently. Now Elsa, too, began to cry, first softly and then louder and louder. She had seen her lifeless father lying in the courtyard. The growing pool of blood flowing from Friedrich's neck left no doubt that he was dead.

"I want to go to Mother, I want to go to Mother," Elsa kept repeating, like a magical incantation. "I want to—"

"Quiet!" Lukas gasped. "They'll hear us. You must—"

But it was too late. The monk was already gazing up at the keep.

"The children!" he cried. "They're in there. Bring me the girl alive, quickly, but kill the boy."

For a moment, Lukas froze, then started looking around frantically for an escape route. A stone stairway led to the second floor, where there was a larger window they might be able to slip through. He grabbed his crying sister, and together they ran up the steps, while below them they could hear the heavy pounding of the mercenaries' boots.

The window was on the west side and about ten feet above the roof of a shed. Lukas might be able to jump down onto the sloping roof and from there reach the castle wall, but how about Elsa? *Could she?*

"We have to jump, Elsa," he said, pointing to the roof. "Come on, *jump!*"

But Elsa just shook her head, in a state of shock. "That's a stupid game," she wailed. "I . . . don't want to play anymore."

"Damn it, this is no longer a game!" Lukas shouted. "Now hurry up and jump!"

But Elsa just kept shaking her head and crying. Down below, some men had already reached the bottom of the stairs. Lukas recalled what the grand inquisitor had said. For some reason he would be killed now, but not Elsa. *Why?* What did this monster intend to do with Elsa? He had no time to think it over; he had to make a decision. If he stayed here, they would kill him like a dog, and if he ran away, he would be a coward. But he wouldn't be of any use to anyone if he was dead. And Elsa needed him, whatever the inquisitor's plan was for her.

Lukas gave his sister a parting kiss on her tear-streaked cheek. "I'll come back, Elsa," he whispered. "I won't leave you alone, I promise."

When he looked down at the courtyard, he saw that his mother had torn herself away from her guards and was running toward the keep.

"Run, children, run!" she shouted. "You must never—" But then the two guards caught up with her and threw her down on the ground.

"I'll never abandon you, Elsa," he whispered one last time. "I swear, by my life." Then he jumped down onto the roof of the shed.

He slipped on one of the loose shingles and started tumbling down the sloping roof, but before he reached the edge, he caught himself and got to his feet again. Gasping, he ran across the roof while arrows whizzed past. Somewhere behind him, he could hear his sister's screams. He ran along the shed toward the castle wall. He knew there was an old, gnarled oak by the wall close enough for him to grab hold and jump down. For that reason, his father had wanted it taken down. Now Lukas thanked God and all the saints that he hadn't done it.

Lukas reached the spot, slid out as far as he dared, and grabbed on to a few thin twigs. He fell almost ten feet through the leaves until he finally got hold of a larger branch.

"Lukas, help me!" Elsa screamed from somewhere behind the wall. "Don't leave me!" But it already sounded far off.

Lukas climbed down to the ground before he noticed there was one Spanish guard standing in front of the castle gate. The man tried to block his way as more bolts whizzed by him like angry hornets. Now, with a grin, the soldier pulled out his sword.

"This is where your trip ends, you little louse," the man growled.

Lukas remembered what his father had told him just the day before in their practice duel.

In a battle, nothing is ever fair . . . It's only about who wins.

Probably, his father had been thinking about situations just like this. Lukas started to dodge left, which led his opponent to lunge in that direction, and at the same moment, Lukas kicked him with full force right between the legs.

"*¡Maleficio!*" the soldier cried. He dropped the sword and fell to his knees, groaning. As he fell, he tried to reach out and grab Lukas, who was already running by him now and gave the man a punch in the neck.

As fast as he could, Lukas ran toward the bushes bordering the forest. One last bolt quivered as it slammed into a tree trunk, then Lukas disappeared among the beeches and oaks in the forest.

"You'll pay for this!" the man shouted after him. "I'll slit you open like a piece of meat."

It was a long time before Lukas stopped running. He finally collapsed, gasping, in a muddy streambed. Shaking and sobbing, he wished he were dead. From one minute to the next, everything had changed.

It seemed like the Lohenfels family no longer existed.

III

For the next few hours, Lukas was in constant fear of being discovered. This, and the horror of losing his family, made it almost impossible for him to think clearly. After wandering about aimlessly at first, he began covering his tracks with branches as his father had once taught him on their excursions together. Again and again, his body shook with fits of sobbing. Almost blinded by his tears, Lukas stomped through muddy streambeds to throw any hunting dogs off his trail and took remote deer paths known only to him, all the while listening for pursuers nearby. But except for the hammering of a woodpecker or the angry calls of a jay, all was silent.

Around noon, his tears finally dried up. His grief gave way to an emptiness that at least made it possible for him to consider where to go next.

Lukas knew of a little cave at the foot of a cliff that he'd occasionally used as a shelter and decided to hide out there until he could figure out what to do. After sunset, it turned cool, and he wrapped himself in an old woolen blanket he'd put in the cave long ago in case of an emergency, along with a dry loaf of bread and a few prunes. He didn't dare light a fire. The danger that the Spanish mercenaries would see it was too great.

Now it turned dark and cold, and somewhere nearby, a large animal broke through the underbrush, presumably a wild boar or a deer, but perhaps a bear.

Lukas trembled, closed his eyes, and tried for a few minutes to forget his fear—in vain. He felt as lonely as if he were the last man on earth. His father was dead, his mother and sister imprisoned, and he himself was a nameless refugee without a home or a future. One thing was clear to him: never again could he return to Lohenfels Castle. The grand inquisitor had pronounced his death sentence. But why had the mercenaries spared Elsa? This one tantalizing question helped him put aside his dark thoughts, at least for a while.

Mother had spoken the name of the inquisitor, a name that Lukas would never forget—Waldemar von Schönborn, the same man who had once tried to accuse his mother of witchcraft. Was there perhaps some secret shared by Schönborn and his parents?

Thoughts of his family once again brought tears to his eyes. He should have stayed down in the dungeon with Elsa. Then maybe his pursuers wouldn't have found him! And what was even worse: Lukas now understood why his mother let herself be led off with so little resistance. She had wanted to spare her children by giving Schönborn no reason to search the castle.

Suddenly, Lukas heard a loud growl, and it took a moment before he realized it wasn't a bear, but his own stomach. He hadn't had a thing to eat all day. He dug up the hard loaf of bread and the prunes, and began eating his meager repast.

As he chewed on his dry provisions, his courage slowly started to return. His father had taught him never to give up. He was the son of a knight! He would continue fighting, if necessary, to the bitter end. And perhaps there was still hope. He absolutely had to find out what happened to his mother and sister, and then he could possibly help them. But to do that, he'd have to wait until the next morning.

◆　◆　◆

After a restless, almost sleepless night, Lukas set out before dawn on his way back to the castle. With a pounding heart, he approached the place that until just recently had been his home. He avoided the open roads, sneaking through the shadowy forest on deer paths until he was very close to the castle. Finally, he made a sharp turn down a steep path to the river.

A small pebble beach not visible from the castle was located there with a deep pool that his father's servants sometimes used to wash clothes. Lukas lay down behind some large rocks and waited, and he was in luck. Before even a half hour had passed, a maid with a basket of laundry in her hands came down the path. Lukas recognized her, and his spirits brightened. It was dear old Agnes, who had worked for the Lohenfels family for many years and long ago had even been his nurse.

As soon as Agnes arrived, Lukas appeared from his hiding place like a ghost. With a muffled cry, Agnes dropped the basket.

"God be praised, my young lord, you are alive!" she gasped. "You must get away as fast as possible. They're still looking for you everywhere, and if they find you—"

"I must know what happened to Mother and Elsa," he quickly interrupted. "What has happened since yesterday?"

"After the death of your father, a few of those Spanish mercenaries took over the castle," she replied, looking around cautiously. "Your mother and Elsa were taken away by the high cleric yesterday morning, to Heidelberg, it is said. There your mother will be put on trial for witchcraft. Oh God, oh God." She rubbed her tear-stained eyes. "It is all so horrible! It is said this Waldemar von Schönborn is a special envoy of the pope and has the power to punish anyone in the Palatinate for witchcraft. Anyone who falls into his clutches is lost!"

Lukas clenched his teeth and tried to think calmly despite his fears. No doubt Schönborn had taken his mother and sister away on horseback. It was more than thirty miles to Heidelberg, so if he wanted to do something for his mother, he'd have to act quickly. His father's horses, however, belonged to the Spaniards now and were in the castle stables, out of his reach. Like it or not, he'd have to go on foot.

"There is something else you should know, young master," Agnes said, lowering her voice again. "These Spaniards have searched the castle, from the cellar right up to the attic. They have rummaged through every single chest—not even the chapel was off-limits for them, even though they are, like us, God-fearing Catholics! Do you have any idea what they might have been looking for?"

Lukas shook his head silently. Had the mercenaries really not come for his mother at all, but were looking for something else? Was her arrest just a pretext?

"Farewell, Agnes," he said softly at last; then he took the hand of the maid who used to sing lullabies for him when he couldn't sleep. The old woman looked with concern at his torn and dirty clothes.

"You can't go looking like this," she muttered. "These accursed Spaniards will recognize you. Here, take these." She reached into her basket and pulled out a few articles of threadbare clothing and a battered felt cap that was much too large for him. "They belong to my grandson and should fit you. Perhaps they are not exactly the perfect things for a young nobleman, but with these at least no one will recognize you." She took Lukas in a warm embrace and gave him a kiss on the forehead. "And now, go with God, young sire. I will tell no one about our meeting."

Lukas turned away and headed up the path from the river. When he turned around, he saw the old maid waving to him one last time. In the morning light, he could see the walls and battlements of Lohenfels Castle, his old home, which he would probably never see again.

He tried to imagine what his father, looking down from heaven, would expect him to do. Lukas was now the man in the family, and it was up to him to save his mother and his sister.

He would not disappoint his father.

After one final glance, he turned and followed a path that would soon take him to the broad, dusty main road. If he followed this road long enough, he knew, it would eventually lead him to Heidelberg. He'd been there before with his parents, though on horseback then, with a half-dozen servants. They had always stopped in an elegant tavern, and a few times he, Elsa, and their mother had even visited Heidelberg Castle with its famous garden. But those times were past.

As Lukas plodded along the heavily rutted road on the bank of the Neckar, he saw more and more carts, wagons, other hikers, and lone riders on horseback heading toward the city. Twice, groups of soldiers marched past to the beat of drums and the sound of flutes, but fortunately, there were no Spanish mercenaries among them. None of the young lads wearing their oversized felt hats took note of him.

It was now after noon, and the hot sun was burning down. Sweat dripped from his forehead, as he had stopped only once, around midday, to rest and eat the remainder of his bread and dried fruit. Toward evening it became clear he would never reach Heidelberg on foot in one day, and as twilight fell, the road became noticeably lonelier. At sundown Lukas started looking around for an abandoned barn for the night, but suddenly, he heard the hoofbeats and whinnying of horses coming from behind. Horror stories of murders and highwaymen went through his mind. At nightfall, surely all sorts of dubious characters were prowling around.

Instinctively, he threw himself down in the muddy ditch alongside the road, and a few moments later, a single rider on horseback appeared. Lukas could only see an outline in the darkness, but as the horseman drew closer, he saw his breastplate and the familiar shape of his helmet and knew at once the rider was a Spanish mercenary. He was coming from the east, where Lohenfels Castle was located.

Lukas crouched down in the mud, held his breath, and could only breathe easier after the sound of the hoofbeats had faded and finally disappeared. Had the man been looking for him? Or was he on some other mission? Perhaps the Spanish mercenaries found what they had been so eagerly seeking at the castle.

Trembling and with a pounding heart, Lukas slipped into a nearby wooded area, where he spent another restless, hungry night.

Around noon the next day, he finally reached Heidelberg. A wide wooden bridge crossed the Neckar at this point, and the towers of the city were clearly visible. The castle was nestled into the side of a hill and could be seen for many miles around. Behind it lay the gloomy Odenwald Mountains with their impenetrable wilderness.

Carts were backed up in front of the gate at the end of the bridge, with towers on either side. On this day, farmers were bringing their produce to market, but Lukas saw many other people—traveling workmen, grim-looking butchers' journeymen, giggling girls, and simple day laborers in tattered clothing. A few well-dressed merchants were whispering about the Swedish king Gustav Adolf, who had allied himself with some Protestant princes and was continuing his march southward.

Lukas took his place in the long line in front of the gate and waited to be admitted. Two bored watchmen waved people through one by one after asking what their business was in town. Despite his exhaustion, Lukas's heart began to pound with anticipation. What should he tell the watchman? Were there men here looking for him?

"You look rather hungry, lad," an old, almost toothless farm woman said to him all of a sudden. She was standing directly behind him and pushing a small handcart containing a few wheels of yellow cheese, some tantalizingly aromatic sausages, a basket of apples, and a fresh loaf of bread.

Lukas had noticed the little cart some time ago and had been considering stealing a sausage . . . just a little one to satisfy the worst of his hunger. His mouth watered at the sight of all these delicacies. The farm woman seemed to be reading his thoughts and handed him an apple.

"Here, please take this," she said with a smile. "You're a war orphan, aren't you? What happened to your parents?"

Lukas thanked her and accepted the apple. "My father . . . is dead. My mother and sister were taken away by mercenaries," he answered between bites, without saying exactly what had happened to them.

The woman looked at him sympathetically and handed him another apple. Lukas had already finished the first, including the core.

"Yes, many children face the same fate nowadays," she said. "It seems like this war is never going to stop, as if some dark power is at work. Well, at least we've caught that witch from the Odenwald. It is said she eats young boys alive—handsome lads just like yourself."

Lukas nearly choked on his apple. "What kind of witch is she?" he struggled to say.

"Haven't you heard?" The farm woman lowered her voice. With her crooked nose and only two remaining teeth, she suddenly looked almost like an evil witch herself. "The Countess von Lohenfels is a witch! The papal inquisitor in person has been questioning her since yesterday here in Heidelberg. It is said she already confessed to everything, even the dreadful hailstorm last year. Well, tomorrow she will burn at the stake in the market square!" She pointed at the long line of people waiting behind them. "That's the reason so many people are coming to Heidelberg. They all want to see her burn. Who knows, once she has been sent back to hell, perhaps everything will be better again. The crops will be good and the devil will come and take the Swedes."

Lukas became as pale as a sheet. "She will be burned tomorrow?" he whispered.

The woman nodded. "Yes, the witch no doubt wanted to spare herself all the torturing. They say the grand inquisitor was bent on squeezing more information out of her—who the other witches were who danced around with her at night when the moon was full, what promises the devil made . . ."

"Was her daughter also charged?" Lukas gasped.

"Daughter? Which daughter? No, not that I know of." The old woman looked at him suspiciously. "Do you know this witch, perhaps?"

Lukas quickly shook his head. "Oh no, I'd just heard something about it."

In the meantime they'd reached the gate at the end of the bridge, and when the watchman saw the farm woman with Lukas, he waved them both through without any questions. Evidently, he took Lukas to be her grandson.

In the narrow lane just beyond the gate, two carts had collided and were blocking the way. The coachmen were cursing loudly, and neither wanted to back up. In the general confusion, Lukas grabbed two of the tempting sausages from the farm woman's cart along with a large piece of cheese and ran off.

"Hey, stop!" the old woman cried. "That's what you get when you try to help this riffraff. Stop that thief—get him! He knows the witch!"

But Lukas had already scurried off into a side street. The guilt he felt for his theft quickly dissipated. The stupid hag had called his mother a witch, so it served her right to be robbed.

While he was still running, Lukas finished off the sausage and the cheese and began to think it all through. At least it seemed that Elsa hadn't been suspected of witchcraft, or in any case, the farm woman had known nothing about her. Feverishly, he tried to think how he could help his mother. First, he'd have to find the location of the dungeon where she was confined. He began wandering through the alleys, trying to get his bearings from the larger buildings.

Heidelberg's most magnificent structure was the castle, which rose above the city, visible from far off, and was bordered by the huge castle gardens. His mother once told him this garden was famous in the entire Reich and was considered the eighth wonder of the world. Now, in the distance, it looked abandoned; some of the walls had collapsed, and the fountains and squares were deserted. The war had left its traces even in this paradise.

It took a while before Lukas finally found the city dungeon. A grumpy butcher selling his bloody wares at a stand showed him the way to one of the defensive towers in the southern part of the city. The dungeon was a huge multistoried building with barred windows guarded by a half-dozen stony-faced soldiers holding halberds. On seeing them, Lukas's courage faded. He'd never be able to get past the guards. For better or worse, he'd have to wait until his mother was brought to the market square the next day. Then he'd have to see what he could do to save her.

Lukas decided to head back to the marketplace, which was adjacent to a church and the city hall. A bedraggled fellow about sixteen years old was chained to a pillory there, surrounded by a crowd of children throwing stones and rotten fruit and vegetables at him. Lukas shuddered. Would he end up like that, as a common thief and vagabond, without a home or family?

He was about to turn away when he noticed some men in black cowls dragging boards and wooden beams into the square. Laughing and jeering, they began to nail together a platform with a post in the middle alongside the pillory. Around it they piled twigs, bundles of straw, and large branches. Evidently, they were the executioner and his journeymen preparing for a public execution.

The pyre for the Lohenfels witch.

I can't believe this, Lukas thought. *Good Lord, make this just a bad dream.*

Lukas stood frozen at the edge of the square, watching as his mother's execution pyre grew and grew. People kept coming to view the preparations, looking forward to the spectacle. By evening, the men had completed their work. The guards came and drove Lukas and everyone else out of the market square.

"Come back tomorrow!" they called after them, laughing. "If you get here before dawn, you'll no doubt get a good spot to watch. But the witch has the best view of all!" they howled as they left.

Lukas hurried into a dirty alley to find a place to sleep for the night. Mud and feces covered the ground, and a few dead rats lay on a stinking pile of manure. In a dark corner, he found an old barrel that had toppled over, which he lined with a little straw, and rolled up inside like a puppy.

When Lukas looked up at the light coming from the windows above him, he realized that his barrel was lying directly behind the same elegant inn where his family used to spend the night. Through the open windows, he could hear talking, music, and laughter that seemed to come from another world. A world that lay just two days in the past.

How he wished he could have asked his father for advice. Certainly, his father would have found some way to help Mother and his sister. Lukas could see it all clearly in his mind's eye: his father would have wrestled down the guards in front of the dungeon and broken open the door, and together they all would have ridden back home. But Father was dead and Lukas was just a thirteen-year-old boy without friends and completely on his own.

Infinitely sad, confused, and exhausted, he finally closed his eyes and fell asleep.

IV

The next morning Lukas awoke inside the barrel to the muffled sound of drums. He had dreamed of his mother and how she'd placed her hand lovingly and protectively on his forehead. The dream felt so real to him that for a moment, everything seemed all right again, but with the roll of drums, merciless reality once more intruded. This was the day on which his mother would die.

He crawled out of the barrel and made his way to the market square, where a large crowd had assembled. Peering around the heads in front of him, he could see the platform covered with bundles of straw. Expectantly, everyone looked down the wide main road where the drumming was coming from. Finally, a whisper passed through the crowd as a mud-splattered executioner's cart rumbled over the bumpy cobblestone pavement. Lukas craned his neck, and for a brief moment, he could see a slender figure standing in the cart. A heavy lump suddenly formed in his throat, and he began to tremble.

It was his mother.

Lukas had to struggle to keep from shouting her name. The simple linen dress she'd worn on the morning she was taken captive was now torn and stained. She had a few bloody welts across her face, and her right arm seemed strangely twisted, like that of a broken doll. Her hands were bound and tied by a rope to the coachman's seat in front, where the hangman and his journeymen were sitting. Nevertheless, she held her head high, her gaze proud though a bit dreamy, as if she was already in another world.

"She probably thinks she's still a countess," shouted a fat, unshaven fellow nearby. "Hey, Countess, where's your fancy dress?"

"Use your magic and make it appear," another man called, "and it better have wings so you can fly away!"

People laughed, and Lukas felt a stabbing pain in his chest. He was about to jump up and grab one of these tramps by the throat. How could they talk that way about his mother! Didn't they know she had never dressed in silk and velvet, and that she'd always helped people like them?

"By God, if Countess von Lohenfels is really a witch, then she certainly is a good one, not a bad one," someone muttered behind him.

Lukas turned around in astonishment and noticed an old farmer leaning on a cane. When the man saw Lukas looking at him, he cast his eyes down anxiously.

"Keep speaking," Lukas said. "You have nothing to fear from me. I . . . also was somewhat acquainted with the countess."

"Well, then you know she was a healer," the old man replied. "My little grandson came into the world a cripple, and she cured him. She put her hand on his forehead, murmured some words, and the boy was able to walk again. If that was magic, it's all right with me." He nodded approvingly. "And back then, when the well ran dry in Neckarsteinach, she found new water with a divining rod. She is one of the white witches, one of the last of them, and people are burning her as if she were in league with the devil."

"One of the . . . white ones?" asked Lukas, perplexed. "What do you mean by that?"

But there was no time left for an answer. The executioner's cart rolled into the middle of the square, the crowd grumbled as it was pushed back, and Lukas was separated from the old man. He was able to squeeze his way between a few spectators until he was standing right in front of the wagon. It was his mother up there! Despite her torn dress and bloody welts, she appeared to Lukas just as she always had since his earliest memory—loving, gentle, yet in a strange way as wise as a very old woman. If he stretched out his hands, he could touch her dress. She was very close yet infinitely far away. Tears welled up in his eyes.

"Mother!" At first he just whispered it; then he cried louder when he noticed that his voice was lost in the general hooting and jeering. "Mother, here I am . . . *Here!*"

But the other voices were too loud, and Lukas didn't dare call out again for fear of being discovered.

But suddenly, she seemed to notice he was there. Sophia von Lohenfels looked down, her expression a mixture of joy and horror.

"Lukas," she said softly. "My God! He mustn't find you here, or you are lost."

"But . . . but . . ." Lukas's voice failed him. "I've got to help you . . . I've . . ."

"Listen to me, you don't need to help me." His mother smiled kindly, as she used to when he had a skinned knee or a broken toy. "I am already in God's hands. Whatever happens, I am always with you, Lukas, even if you don't see me." Then her face turned deadly serious. "But now run away, do you hear, Lukas? It's important that he never finds you."

"Where is Elsa?" Lukas asked. "What did they do with her?"

People in the crowd began to stare at him suspiciously, and now his mother bent down to him again. "She is—"

At that moment, the hangman yanked the rope to which his mother's hands were bound. She stumbled and fell into the dirty straw in the cart.

"Hey, no talking here!" the executioner shouted. "What magic spells are you mumbling now, witch? The only one you can talk to now is the priest, do you understand?"

Terrified for his mother, Lukas stepped back. His mother got up again, looked at him sternly, and her lips silently formed the words,

Please . . . run . . . away . . .

A monk wearing a black robe and a chain around his neck with a wooden cross stepped out from behind the cart. With an earnest expression, he walked toward Sophia, holding the cross like a shield before him and murmuring a Latin prayer. Again his mother mouthed the words, but this time Lukas was amazed he could hear as well as read them from her lips, or rather, this time her voice came clearly from deep within him.

All will be well, my son. I will always be there for you. And now go!

Lukas was so astonished he fell back a few steps into the dirt. His mother had spoken to him—directly inside his head! How was that possible?

"Hey, I think this lad knows the witch," a farmer next to him cried out. "She mumbled something to him, I saw it. Perhaps he is a witch as well."

Lukas was still dazed. Dirty fingers were reaching out for him, pulling on his hair, but at the last minute, he pulled himself free and pushed his way through the crowd to the edge of the square, his head spinning. Had he just imagined hearing the voice of his mother? *That had to be it. Anything else would be . . .* He hesitated.

Magic?

Lukas looked around and discovered an ivy-covered wall about six feet high. Other children had climbed up onto it to get a better view of the spectacle. He boosted himself up, squeezed between the children, and watched as the monk addressed his mother in a few pious words and made the sign of the cross. Then the executioner and his journeymen dragged his mother up onto the platform. After they'd tied her to the post, they started piling bales of straw around her. Again Lukas felt the urge to simply charge toward the executioner and his henchmen, punch them in the face, and free his mother.

But he knew this was impossible. That would only mean he'd be put to the stake alongside his mother, and then there would be no one left to care for Elsa.

Now the guards pushed the jeering crowd back from the platform. Nearby, under a canopy, a few chairs were set up. A fanfare sounded as a procession of nobles descended the steps of the city hall and took these seats. With a trembling heart, Lukas saw that among the guests was the grand inquisitor Waldemar von Schönborn. He was dressed all in black except for his hood, which shone crimson, like blood. The beating of drums began, and the crowd fell silent.

"Citizens of Heidelberg!" The voice of the inquisitor resounded over the plaza as he pointed with outstretched arms toward the execution site. "This woman is a witch. She admitted it herself, but she kept stubbornly silent on whatever else she knew. She neither gave us the names of other witches nor"—he made a grim pause—"nor did she reveal to us how she acquired her magic powers. Therefore she forfeits the mercy of a beheading ordinarily granted to the nobility and is to be burned alive. Executioner, do your duty."

Waldemar von Schönborn took a seat on his velvet-covered chair while the executioner lit the bundles of straw with a torch. At once, little flames appeared, the fire quickly spread, and the crowd shouted expectantly. Lukas shouted as well, but his voice was drowned out by the cheers of all those standing around. He felt paralyzed; it all seemed like a nightmare to him from which there was no escape and no awakening.

When the executioner climbed down from the platform, the smoke was already so thick it was almost impossible to see his mother anymore. Still, Lukas thought he could see her outline. The heat on the platform must have been horrible, but not a single sound came from there.

At that moment, something very strange happened.

A shining blue cloud suddenly appeared above the smoke and began rising heavenward. Small stars appeared around the cloud, glittering and fluttering like tiny birds.

Lukas shouted again, but when he turned around, he realized the other spectators had not seen the strange cloud. The children at his side also didn't seem to notice.

"Why isn't the witch screaming?" asked a little girl, looking up at her brother.

He just shrugged. "That's surely some kind of magic again. The devil came to help her on her final trip."

Nobody said anything about the blue cloud, which, in the meantime, had become just a pale shimmer until it finally disappeared. But then Lukas felt a soft touch on his cheek, as if by an invisible hand, and once again heard the voice of his mother in his head.

Have no fear, my son. I will always be with you. Take care of your sister.

The flames rose higher and higher as Lukas sat there, stunned, atop the wall. The jeering and laughter all around him seemed miles away. Even after the fire had burned itself out at last and the journeymen were sweeping up the ashes, Lukas sat there unmoved. His mother had touched him and spoken to him. And then this cloud . . . Was it magic, too? Was his mother really a witch? And what did the old man mean before when he spoke of the "white" witch?

Anger unlike anything he had ever felt before rose in him when he thought of Waldemar von Schönborn. This man was responsible for everything that had happened to his family, and he would pay for it!

The hours passed without Lukas even noticing. He was still staring at the execution site, where, from time to time, the wind whipped white and gray ashes up into the sky. The market square had emptied out, and only a few small children were dancing around the remaining embers. Finally, very slowly, Lukas climbed down from the wall and made his way through the streets, through the city gate, and over the bridge with the Neckar murmuring beneath him like an anxious old woman.

His legs carried him, but he himself seemed to still be sitting on the wall. From now on he would be on his own, yet in a sense, not completely alone. His mother had promised to be there for him always, and her words gave him consolation and support.

And soon, he swore to himself, he would find out what had happened to his sister.

V

Some Weeks Later, Somewhere in the Wild Odenwald Mountains

Lukas looked up at the clouds and watched as snowflakes spiraled down like dandelions, melting as they landed on his face. Winter didn't usually arrive that early, in the middle of November. The farmers, too, complained that many of them had lost crops and were starving because the first frost that year had arrived in October.

Shaking with the cold, Lukas wrapped himself in the coat he'd stolen from a scarecrow, which was much too large for him, and continued his wanderings through the forest. He was grateful for the unshapely felt hat that the old maid Agnes had given him, which protected him from the worst of the cold and concealed his soiled face that in recent weeks had grown gaunt and careworn. When Lukas saw his reflection in a fountain, it was a far older boy staring back at him whose face he didn't recognize. Occasionally, when he was out stealing from the barns and stables, he met other villagers, but he had such a grim appearance that they went out of their way to avoid him. If there was a dispute, a short fight with a stick he'd whittled from the branch of a larch tree usually settled the issue. Once again Lukas was aware how much he'd learned from his father. Usually, his opponents were larger than he was, but all it took were a few quick feints, thrusts, or blows to send them packing. He'd also driven off a few hungry wolves that way.

Almost two months had passed since his dreadful experiences in Heidelberg, but to Lukas it seemed like two years. There were days when he wished he'd simply fall asleep and never wake up, but then he remembered he was the son of a Palatine knight, the son of Friedrich von Lohenfels. He would never give up; he would fight and avenge his family. And he had to find Elsa again, as he had promised.

It wasn't yet clear to him exactly how he'd carry out his plan, but for now he thought it was best to lie low. Since his mother had warned him about Schönborn, he'd headed northeast into the Odenwald Mountains, an inhospitable wilderness of widely scattered small towns, where he felt safe from the grand inquisitor's henchmen.

The first few weeks had been somewhat tolerable. He survived on apples, pears, and plums, which grew on the trees in large numbers in October. Occasionally, he'd been able to snare a rabbit or steal a chicken from a remote farmyard, always trying to make sure that as few people as possible noticed him. Since the outbreak of the war, many former mercenaries had come together to form bands of highwaymen who robbed or even murdered travelers.

Recently, the weather had gotten nastier, and the first snowflakes heralded the winter to come. Lukas knew that if he didn't soon find a place to stay, he would probably freeze to death. But what should he do? Perhaps ask a poor family of farmers if he could take shelter with them? People in this region were happy if they could provide for their own children. There was nothing useful he knew how to do on a farm, and one thing they certainly didn't need was another useless mouth to feed. As a nobleman's son he could ride a horse, hunt, and fight, but he knew nothing about sowing and harvesting, how to repair a rake, help in the birth of a calf, or even milk a cow. Of what use could he be to anyone?

Lukas was so lost in his gloomy thoughts that he didn't hear the sound—a faint, ominous crackling in the branches behind him—until it was too late. Before he could turn around, a fist-sized stone hit him directly on the temple. He staggered, fell, and blacked out before he touched the ground. Dazed, he heard footsteps and whispered voices.

Voices of children.

"Quick, quick, look in his purse to see if he has something to eat," someone whispered.

"Look, he's just as poor and skinny as we are," another child said. "Just leave him lying there, or kill him, for all I care. He'll just get in our way."

"First let's grab his purse."

With a trembling hand, Lukas clenched his battered little bag containing a few shriveled apples and some moldy crusts of bread—the last of his provisions—but small, nimble fingers tore the purse from his grip.

"Like I told you," someone said after a while in a disappointed tone, "he has almost nothing. We'd better just smash his head in with a stone before he starts screaming and attracts attention. And then let's move along."

"No . . . ," Lukas gasped.

He shook off his fainting spell, but all he could see around him were vague outlines. He struggled to reach out for the invisible opponent with his right hand, and finally grabbed hold of a foot. He yanked on it, there was a shout, and then the sound of something hitting the ground.

As fast as he could, Lukas got up, squinted several times, and wiped the blood from his forehead until he could see more clearly. He staggered like a drunk, but at least he didn't fall over again.

A small group of boys and girls surrounded him. They were dressed in shabby clothing and had tied rags around their feet. With their lice-ridden hair and dirty faces gaunt from hunger, they reminded Lukas of a pack of wolves. They stared at him defiantly, as if waiting to see what he'd do next. Between the other children and Lukas, a boy of around eight was writhing around on the ground, clutching his foot.

"Damn, the swine isn't unconscious at all," the boy snarled. "He was just pretending. Come on, let's finish him off."

The boy stood up and hobbled a few steps backward. Now the children formed a circle around Lukas and started closing in on him, step by step. In their hands they all held sticks and jagged rocks.

Lukas studied their faces, one by one. He'd often fought more than one opponent and usually won. At the very start, it was important to do something to impress the others, then usually, they'd retreat. This time, though, he was clearly outnumbered. There were over a dozen of them, most of them as old as he was, a few younger ones, and a big, strong boy who looked to be at least fifteen or sixteen. He was the one giving the signal to attack.

"What are you waiting for, you chickens?" he shouted. "Get him!"

Three children came charging at Lukas. He dodged the first, a skinny girl with a rock in her hand; the second, a boy who was just as skinny, he kicked in the stomach, sending him flying onto the ground, where he lay gasping and whimpering. The third boy was the strongest of the three. He was holding a big stick and took a swing at Lukas, but at the last moment, Lukas dodged and stepped back. His own stick was lying in the dirt a few steps away from him, just out of his reach, so for better or worse he'd have to use his fists.

And a trick.

As the boy charged at him with his upraised stick, Lukas did something unexpected. He didn't retreat, but charged straight ahead. The stick whizzed past his head, barely missing him, as Lukas rammed the boy with his shoulder. The boy staggered, and Lukas flattened him with two well-placed punches.

At the same moment, he sensed something moving behind him, and when he turned, he saw that the other boy had gotten up again and was preparing to throw a rock at his head. Lukas blocked the throw with his arm and gave his opponent a punch in the pit of the stomach that sent him flying into the dirt again.

Now three other children approached him, armed with stones, sticks, and clubs.

Lukas gasped. He'd never be able to hold out against the whole group; they'd kill him like a rabid mongrel, but at least he would defend himself to his last breath. Holding up his fists, he awaited the attack, when suddenly he heard a loud voice.

"Just cut it out before he whips the rest of you. The fight's over."

Again it was the older boy who had spoken. His words had an effect. The children stopped and lowered their weapons. Suspiciously, they looked at Lukas, then at their leader.

"Just look what he did to Mathis!" The older boy laughed, pointing at the kid who was still lying on the ground, only half conscious. "This guy is worth more than three of you weenies. We ought to welcome anyone who can fight like that."

Grinning, the older boy approached Lukas. "My name is Marek," he said in a loud voice accustomed to giving orders. "I'm the leader of this pathetic band. It looks like you can take a lot of punishment. Hans!" He summoned a smaller boy, who sullenly approached and handed him a sack. Marek took out a roasted chicken leg and handed it to Lukas with a patronizing gesture. "Here, this is for you. It's the last we have. Consider it a welcoming gift."

Lukas hesitated, but then he reached out and hungrily took a bite of the food. As Lukas devoured the chicken, Marek continued talking, his arms crossed, looking him up and down.

"We are all orphans or homeless outcasts, no better than a pack of wolves, but we still have our honor. Actually, we'd decided not to take anyone else into our group, which would mean one more mouth to feed, but for you we'll make an exception. Who taught you how to fight like that?"

Lukas looked up briefly from his food. "My father."

Marek nodded. "Your father, I see. Then he was somebody better than us, I suspect. Your moves looked a lot like sword fighting, and only nobles are allowed to carry swords."

When Lukas didn't reply, Marek continued. "It doesn't matter, I'll find out sooner or later. By the way, we're all equals here, whether we were squires or beggars before. We have a camp deep in the forest where the farmers and the soldiers can't find us. We have a campfire there, a few warm blankets, and whenever we get back from a raid, something to eat as well." He winked at Lukas and reached out his hand. "So, are you with us?"

The snowfall had gotten heavier, and Lukas could feel himself shivering. It wasn't just because of the cold. Just a few minutes ago, these children had tried to kill him, and now he was invited to join the group. But did he really have a choice? He'd never make it through the winter by himself.

After a while he took Marek's outstretched hand.

"Welcome to the Blood Wolves," Marek said with another grin. "That's what we call ourselves. And now come, we'll show you our camp. It's no palace, but it's ours."

The Blood Wolves' camp was an old bear's den in the middle of the forest, with a hole in the ceiling serving as a natural chimney. Fallen birch trees covered with moss and partially frozen bogs made it almost impossible to reach unless you knew the exact route to follow. The children had spread out fragrant reeds and rabbit skins on the floor of the cave, and every evening made a little fire where they roasted rabbits or partridges caught during the day. Now and then a newborn litter of dormice, an emaciated weasel, or a blackbird would be added to the thin meat stew.

For the next few days, Lukas was busy getting to know his new comrades. They all had their own sad story of how they had ended up here. Mathis was the son of a blacksmith whom the mercenaries had seized and hung upside down by the heels before Mathis's very eyes, after first pouring liquid cow manure down his throat because he wouldn't tell them where he'd hidden his money. Little Martha, who was just eight years old, was the only one in her family to survive the Great Plague and had wandered through the forests alone for weeks until she finally came across the Blood Wolves. Marek, the leader, had marched as drummer boy with Tilly's army until his entire company had been wiped out in a skirmish with the Danes. He was one of the few who survived the slaughter and, since then, had been on the run. None of the gang had any idea what the future had in store for them. And they all had just one goal.

To survive.

Often during the cold, sleepless nights, Lukas thought of his mother, and sometimes she even appeared to him in a dream, smiling. Her final consoling words helped him endure his darkest hours.

I will always be with you . . .

Had she really been a witch? Had he only imagined the strange blue cloud and the sound of her voice? But for the most part, Lukas was too busy just surviving another day to be able to think any more about it.

After a while, the other members of the gang accepted Lukas, mainly because he taught them some of the things he'd learned about stick fighting. He never disclosed to anyone that he came from a noble family, but only said he'd lost both his parents in the war and after that had been a drummer boy just like Marek. Whenever Marek tried to learn more, Lukas fell silent, which made the leader more and more suspicious.

"He's keeping something from us," Lukas overhead him hiss to the others more than once. "The fellow has something to hide, and by God, I'll find out what it is."

Finally, at the beginning of December, the snow fell so hard they had trouble even leaving their camp. There were knee-high snowdrifts everywhere, and two of the children had bad cases of whooping cough. In addition, they had little to eat.

"If we don't want to starve and freeze to death, it's time we went out on a raid," Marek said one especially cold morning as they sat around the fire. "And I know where."

The others looked at him curiously.

"There's a mill not far from here, deep in the forest," he continued in a low voice. "It's well protected behind a wall. Up to now it's always seemed too tricky, because the miller is also a bear of a man. But I recently heard that the miller has spotted fever. He's bedridden and can no longer move. Aside from him there's only his wife, a young apprentice, and two or three little children. We can take care of them."

"You intend to rob the family of a sick man who can't defend himself?" Lukas looked at him skeptically. "Suppose the apprentice sees us and stands in the way?"

"Damn! He won't do that, because we'll attack at night," Marek declared. "And if he does, it's just his bad luck. We'll steal whatever we can get our hands on. Then we'll take off—or do you prefer to stay here and die of hunger, eh?"

When Lukas didn't answer, Marek got up from the fire and knocked the sooty brushwood from his trousers. "So this is what we're going to do. We head out tonight"—he grinned—"and tomorrow, by God, we stuff our bellies with roasted chicken."

VI

At dusk the children headed out on their way to the mill. Only the two sick ones remained behind, while the others armed themselves with sticks or collected stones to use in their slingshots. Marek was the only one carrying a long knife. He also carried a torch wrapped in oilcloth to help them find their way through the approaching darkness. Their march led them through waist-deep snow, and sometimes they had to stop to help the younger ones over the drifts. A brisk wind arose, tugging on the torch and nearly extinguishing the flame.

Lukas clenched his teeth and tried not to lose touch with the group. He was still torn about the robbery. They needed food—without doubt. Above all, the two sick children, one of whom was little Martha, were extremely weak. But did that justify robbing a defenseless miller suffering from spotted fever, along with his family? Lukas decided to make sure they stole only what they really needed. He knew, of course, that Marek had other plans.

After two hours, they came to a clearing covered with snow and glimmering in the pale light of the moon. A wall about six feet high built of loose, rough-hewn stone surrounded a large area with a wooden house and a mill wheel at the center.

"There's no way to get in from this side," Marek whispered, pointing to the right. "But over there the mill stream passes beneath the wall."

"Do you mean for us to swim when it's this cold?" Mathis asked anxiously.

"You idiot! The brook is frozen, of course. We just have to crawl underneath the wall. It's a cinch."

Marek led the group around the wall until they came to a wide opening just a few feet high. Drifts of snow lay over the gleaming black icy surface of the brook.

"But suppose the ice won't support us?" Hans asked.

"It will, you sissy," Marek responded. "I tried it out just yesterday, so I know there's a watchdog over there." Grinning, as usual, he pulled out a roasted pheasant leg, and in the other hand, he held his knife. "I'll take care of the mutt myself. When you hear me whistle, come on through."

With the knife between his teeth, he disappeared through the opening. A short while later, they heard growling on the other side of the wall that soon turned into a painful howl. Then they heard Marek whistling.

Lukas was the first to venture out onto the ice in the mill brook. It creaked and groaned beneath him, but actually appeared to support him. Ducking his head, he scrambled beneath the wall in the darkness. A few moments later, he could see moonlight above him once more, and he knew he'd made it to the other side.

As the other children followed, Lukas wiped the snow and dirt from his face and looked around. The mill was directly in front of him, and next to it a house. Beyond that there was a shed and a stable, from which a soft mooing could be heard. The only person visible in the courtyard was Marek, who stood a bit to one side wiping the bloody knife on his trousers. At his feet lay a large, lifeless dog, its tongue hanging out of its mouth. Marek had planted the burning torch in the snow.

"At least the old cur had one last good meal," Marek said as he put his knife away. Then he started whispering orders.

"Hans and Mathis, look around in the mill and see if you can find any flour. The rest of you will go to the barn and grab the chickens while Lukas and I go over to the shed with the torch to see what we can find there."

Lukas stared at him in surprise, and Marek whispered, "I want to keep an eye on you to make sure you don't get any dumb ideas. Now, let's go!"

While the other children fanned out with soiled linen sacks, Marek and Lukas ran over to the shed. They were relieved to find out that the door was bound only with a simple lock. Evidently, the miller felt secure enough behind his own walls.

Quietly, Marek opened the bolt with his knife, then the two boys entered. Inside, it was pitch-black except for a pale beam of moonlight that fell through a slit in the door. Marek held up the torch to light their way.

"Look around for anything we can use," he whispered. "Axes, nails, blankets, furs . . . Perhaps we'll even find a little money— millers are rich."

Hesitantly, Lukas started looking around. By the light of the torch, he could see the vague outlines of crates and chests. He opened one of them and found a few moldy wolf pelts and a bearskin coat.

Marek took the coat and put it on. "As I told you, there are things we can use here," he said with a giggle. "Be quick now, before someone wakes up."

They opened another chest containing tools and nails and filled their sacks with them. Just as Lukas was about to hurry out the door with his loot, he stumbled over a bump in the floor, a trapdoor handle that had been concealed beneath one of the many chests. Marek saw it too.

"I'll bet there's something valuable under there," he muttered. "Come and help me pull up the lid."

They both pulled on the trapdoor and found a small, moldy-smelling recess underneath. Marek shined the torchlight inside and whistled softly. "Well, look at this. It seems our miller has a little secret."

Lukas bent down, and his heart started beating faster. In the recess, bound in leather, was a gleaming sword with an elaborate hilt, together with its belt. Alongside it rested a dagger the length of a man's forearm, a pistol with a pouch for carrying gunpowder, and a musket.

"It appears the miller fought in the war and put this aside for bad times," Marek whispered. "These weapons are worth a heap of money. Just look." There was a jingling sound of metal coins as he pulled out a small leather bag from beneath the sword. "No doubt this is the booty from his raids," he said with a triumphant look. "We've hit the jackpot. Let's—"

He stopped short on hearing a creaking sound behind them. When Lukas turned around, he saw a little girl standing at the wide-open door. She was perhaps seven or eight and clearly not a member of their gang. She was wearing a white nightgown, holding a raggedy doll, and blinking as she looked sleepily at the two boys with her mouth agape. Until now she had not made a sound. Evidently, she had been on the way to the privy and had seen the torchlight through a crack in the door.

"Damn!" Marek growled. "That's surely one of the miller's daughters. Tough luck for her." He turned to Lukas and handed him the knife. "Quick, grab her and shut her up. Now you can prove you're really one of us."

"You mean you want me to—"

"What else? Slit her throat," Marek interrupted. "If she screams, the apprentice and the miller's wife will come running, and then we'll have an even bigger bloodbath. So hurry up!"

Lukas stared at the girl, who was still standing there in the doorway as if petrified. She had tousled blond hair and a few freckles on her nose. The similarity made Lukas's blood freeze.

She looked like Elsa.

"I would never do anything to hurt this little girl," he whispered.

Sighing, Marek grabbed his knife. "Just as I thought. You're a coward. Then I'll have to do it myself." Resolutely, he strode toward the terrified girl.

Lukas didn't hesitate a moment. He dashed forward and knocked Marek to the ground. The torch slipped from Marek's hands and rolled toward the nearest chest as Lukas jumped on the older boy and struggled to hold him down.

"Run!" Lukas shouted at the girl. "Run away, as fast as you can."

"You'll pay for that," Marek gasped. "I'll kill you."

The older boy was still holding the knife in his right hand, and Lukas was struggling to push Marek's hand away, but the leader was stronger. Inch by inch the blade got closer to Lukas's throat. Screaming and running feet could now be heard, as the girl finally overcame her paralyzing fear and scurried away.

"We have you to thank for this," Marek snarled. "I always knew you weren't one of us."

With all his strength, he thrust the blade forward, but Lukas let go and rolled to the side, dodging the knife. The boys rolled back and forth like two rabid animals, until suddenly, Marek was on top of Lukas, holding the knife just a few inches from his throat.

"You filthy . . . ," he started to say, but then his eyes opened wide. Lukas could smell smoke and saw that the torch lying on the ground had set fire to Marek's bearskin coat. A few of the blankets had also caught fire. For a split second, Marek's grip loosened, but that was long enough. With all *his* strength, Lukas pushed Marek's hand aside, the knife flew back . . .

. . . and lodged in Marek's chest.

Groaning, the older boy rolled away and fell to the floor beside Lukas. There was a final quiver, then his eyes became glassy and empty.

Horrified, Lukas put his hand to his mouth. He hadn't meant to do that! Everything had happened so fast that he wasn't really sure *what* had happened. The leader of the Blood Wolves was evil. He would have killed the little girl without batting an eyelash. But now Lukas himself was a murderer!

This was no time to mull things over. The flames had already spread to some of the other trunks, and soon the entire shed would be ablaze. Outside, more and more excited voices could be heard.

Lukas got to his feet and was about to run outside when he heard a furious shout out in the courtyard. Nearby stood little Hans, staring through the doorway into the shed, now fully illuminated by the blaze. He was trembling and pointing at Lukas.

"You . . . killed him!" he screamed. "Murderer!"

Only now did Lukas notice he was holding the bloody knife in his hand, and Marek lay dead at his feet.

"That's not true," Lukas protested. "It was an accident. He—"

But Hans had already turned and fled. With a curse, Lukas threw the knife aside and was about to run after him.

"Hans, listen to me—" But Lukas tripped on one of the wolf pelts and fell. As he scrambled back to his feet his gaze fell again on the open trapdoor. The sword handle was glittering in the flickering light of the flames, and Lukas felt a strange longing. It was almost the same weapon his father had used, the so-called Pappenheim sword with a broad blade and a basket hilt made of intricately wound wires, named after General von Pappenheim. How often Lukas had dreamed of someday being able to wear a sword like that, and now the weapon was here, lying directly in front of him.

Without further hesitation, he reached back down into the recess, pulled out the leather-bound sword along with its belt, and ran off.

Outside in the courtyard, people were running around shouting, and from the corner of his eye, he could see a few of his comrades crawling back under the wall and fleeing. But Mathis just stood there crying, until he was seized by a big, broad-shouldered lad, evidently the miller's apprentice, who slapped the boy over and over. Farther away, the miller's wife was chasing after some chickens that had run away.

In a panic, Lukas looked around. Which way should he go? Certainly not down to the frozen mill brook, where Hans had surely told the others about Lukas's treason and Marek's murder. But the wall was much too high, and icy. He'd never be able to get over it fast enough.

Then Lukas noticed the little girl standing some distance away alongside a wide entryway, her tiny body still dressed only in a nightgown. Nervously, she raised her hand and waved for him to come over. Lukas hesitated, then ran toward her. Silently, she pointed to the sturdy bolt and lock that blocked the way through the gate. She was holding a large key that had been hidden somewhere nearby.

"Thanks," Lukas gasped, reaching for the key.

He opened the lock and pulled on the bolt, which squeaked as it slid to one side. The gate opened a crack, just wide enough for him to wriggle through. One last time he looked back at the girl, who was smiling at him now. She wasn't Elsa, but the resemblance had awakened something within him that he had been suppressing more and more in recent days. He had to find his sister.

"Thank you," Lukas said again, softly.

He disappeared through the gate and hurried out into the bitter-cold darkness with the sword in hand.

VII

Panting and freezing, Lukas wandered for many miles through the darkness of the Oden Forest. The moon lit his way as he stomped down a barely recognizable road covered with drifts of new-fallen snow.

He had left everything behind: his comrades who considered him a murderer and a traitor, his tattered coat that had slipped off his shoulders during his fight with Marek, and even his large hat that had served him so well up to then. He had never felt so lonely, not even in the long, sleepless nights just after the death of his mother.

The only thing he still had was the stolen sword—he had even left the purse full of coins behind in the miller's shed. But neither one would save him from freezing to death. For God knows, that was the fate awaiting him now. Dressed only in a shirt and trousers, he was mercilessly exposed to the cold. In place of his worn-out shoes, he had only rags he'd tied around his feet as he'd seen the other kids do. He could barely feel his toes, the wind pierced the thin linen cloth of his shirt, and his only chance was to find a village. But there was not a glimmer of light visible anywhere.

At some point, Lukas gave up. His steps became slower, he staggered left and right, and finally he fell over a tall snowdrift and just remained lying there on the side of the road. It was still icy cold, but now he could barely feel the cold anymore. He was just infinitely tired. He knew that if he allowed himself to close his eyes, he would fall asleep and freeze to death, but would that be so bad? At least he'd see his father and mother again—and perhaps even little Elsa. Together they would be waiting for him at the gates to heaven. With his frozen fingers, Lukas clenched the handle of the sword with its perfectly wrought blade. *Just close my eyes . . .*

You mustn't go to sleep, Lukas. Remain strong. Elsa needs you. You must find her—don't fall asleep.

Lukas woke up with a start. That was the voice of his mother!

Or was it just voices from the other world where he would soon be going? Already he heard the sound of music, a fiddle, a barrel organ, and a man's raucous voice. It sounded very, very earthly and not heavenly at all.

"What in all the world . . . ," Lukas mumbled.

With his last ounce of strength, he lifted his sword and looked around in the darkness. Now, nearby in the forest, he could see a tiny light he hadn't noticed before. That's where the music was coming from.

He fought his way through the snow toward the gleam of light. Soon he could see it came from a campfire with a number of men and some women standing around it, laughing, dancing, and passing a jug between them. Off to one side were two wagons and a few decrepit horses tied to a tree. Not knowing what to do, Lukas tottered from side to side. If this was no dream, then certainly this group was a band of robbers, and he could imagine what such a gang would do to a lost, half-frozen boy. Certainly they wouldn't give him a hot meal. But then he decided that he didn't really have any other choice.

Better to be slaughtered near a warm fire than freeze to death out here in the lonely darkness, he thought.

Just as he was about to approach the camp with his hands raised, he heard a menacing growl behind him. He turned around and nearly froze with fear.

Standing up on its two hind legs was a huge bear, growling and staring at Lukas with its little black eyes.

Without a moment's hesitation, Lukas drew the sword from its sheath and stooped down with his weapon in position, just as his father had taught him. The steps he had practiced for so many years helped him conquer his exhaustion. The bear weaved back and forth a bit, then fell down onto its front paws and approached its prey, sniffing and grumbling. Lukas was retreating step by step when suddenly he heard a voice nearby.

"Hey, who do we have here? Stop right there, boy!"

Lukas stepped to one side, allowing him to keep an eye on both the bear and the possible new threat. A short, slender man approached from the camping area. When he saw Lukas's sword, he drew his own weapon, a narrow rapier that seemed to glimmer in the moonlight. The man had a feather in his hat, which was pulled down so far that Lukas couldn't see his face.

"Sacré bleu!" With a furious shout, the man charged.

Lukas quickly dodged to one side, but his opponent was quick, too. He stopped, made a quarter turn, and went into attack position again.

"Deuxième," the man murmured. His blade, much lighter than that of the sword, circled to the right. *"Troisième. Et fin."*

The blade shot forward, and only at the last moment was Lukas able to fend off the thrust of the sharp rapier with his broader sword.

Lukas had fought many small skirmishes in recent months, but only with his stick. Once again, however, it became clear that stick fighting was not so different from sword fighting. The moves his father had taught him from early childhood came naturally to him, but he also knew that in his present condition, he couldn't hold out more than a few minutes. He had to work fast.

Feint, attack, parry, riposte, striking around, chasing . . . Lukas jumped back and forth, ignoring the biting cold in all the excitement. But no matter what he tried, his opponent had a suitable response to each of his thrusts. Even if the man's sword dance was a bit affected, he was a true master of the rapier. In addition, the bear was lurking in the forest somewhere behind Lukas. One false step, and the beast would no doubt rip him to pieces.

As his situation got more and more precarious, Lukas tried a bold attack. He feinted to the right, realizing that for a brief moment his left flank would be open to attack, then followed that with a lightning-fast upward thrust, knocking the man's hat off his head. Then Lukas shot forward and pressed his sword against the man's throat.

"Surrender, or . . . ," Lukas gasped, but suddenly he stopped and stared into the unprotected face of his opponent.

It was the face of a boy.

His opponent was no more than one or two years older than himself, with ash-blond hair and an almost angelic beauty. His nose, chin, narrow lips, high shoulders—everything about him—seemed as perfectly formed and noble as that of a prince. If it weren't for the friendly gleam in his eyes and the dimples in his cheeks, he might have appeared quite haughty.

Just as astonished as Lukas, the boy lowered his blade. *"Mon dieu!"* he murmured. "I thought I was fighting a grown master swordsman. Who in the world . . ."

"Hey, Jerome!" came a deep voice from the campfire area. "Why are you taking so much time out there? Did you wet your fancy pants?"

Two other individuals now appeared. One was a tall, dark-haired fellow with a saber at his side. With his broad back, he reminded Lukas of an unhewn block of wood. In a few years he would probably be a giant. At his side walked a much shorter and younger boy, who gazed intently at Lukas and his opponent. He looked a bit like a watchful cat, always ready to pounce. Like Lukas, he was carrying a sword; his was dangling at his side in a plain sheath.

"If my eyes aren't deceiving me, our good Jerome has just been beaten by a puny street urchin," the younger boy said with a smile. In spite of the darkness, his eyes peering from beneath his shoulder-length brown hair seemed to take in the whole scene. "It will cost you five *kreuzers* if you don't want us to tell our master about this disgrace. Well, what do you think of the offer, Jerome?"

His big friend let out a loud laugh. "Perhaps our Frenchie could find a new job as a tightrope dancer. What do you think, hmm, Jerome? Then you wouldn't need to fight anymore. You could still use your rapier to open wine bottles."

"What dolts you are!" snarled Jerome. *"Mon dieu!* I swear this little fellow fought like the devil incarnate. I didn't know—"

"Perhaps we should continue this conversation around the fire before our hungry Balthasar has you for supper," the younger boy interrupted. "He's standing right behind you, and his chain is long enough—if I remember correctly, at least fifteen feet."

"*Sacré bleu!*" Jerome jumped to one side, and Lukas, too, quickly stepped back a pace. For a few minutes, Lukas had completely forgotten the bear, and not until now did he notice that the creature was tied to a chain. From close up, the bear no longer appeared as dangerous, but rather old and mangy.

"I think it's about time you told us who you are and why you're sneaking into our camp armed with a sword," the younger boy said to Lukas in a voice that, despite his childlike stature, sounded clear and precise, like that of a learned man. "And please remove your sword before Paulus rams you into the ground." He pointed at the rough-looking character by his side. "Or do you want to have a fight with all three of us?"

"If I have to, I'll cross swords with every one of you," Lukas replied defiantly, glaring at the three like an animal at bay. He tried to keep his composure, though his fighting spirit had flagged, and once again he felt the cold and the exhaustion. He hoped the other three didn't notice how he was trembling. Cautiously, he lowered his weapon.

"Aha, a real hero!" The boy laughed. "I hope you're capable of giving satisfaction."

"Satis . . . what?" Lukas asked.

The big fellow at his side just snorted. "Don't pay any attention to him. Giovanni is always talking big like that. Thinks he's smarter than anyone."

"I *am* the smartest of us three," Giovanni answered dryly, "which, however, because of the present competition, is no great feat. By the same token, I couldn't contest your title, Paulus, as the strongest, or Jerome's as the handsomest in our group. *Capisce?*"

Paulus groaned. "You're driving me crazy with your endless babble. Just let the fellow tell us what he was doing here in the forest."

Giovanni nodded. "For once, you dunce, you're right." He looked at Lukas hopefully and reached out his hand. "Now just give me the sword, great warrior, and then, if you like, you can come over to our camp and tell your story there. Judging by the way you look, you need a warm blanket and a drink of hot mulled wine." His eyes rested on Lukas's tattered, mud-spattered trousers. "By God, old Balthasar would probably have just spat you out again in disgust."

Over in the camp, music and laughter could still be heard. As they approached, the first person Lukas noticed was a muscular giant in a bearskin coat sitting in the midst of three athletic-looking young men and towering above all the rest. Two women dressed in all sorts of colorful clothing were arguing over a jug of wine while two other men in ragged coats were playing listlessly on a barrel organ and a fiddle. Farther away, another man in shabby leather armor was huddled down and appeared to be sleeping. His head had fallen forward, but in his right hand, he still clung to a wide two-handed sword.

The moment the four boys entered the ring of light around the fire, the music fell silent. Lukas could feel almost a dozen pairs of eyes staring at him.

"Damn, who did you bring us now?" the bearded giant growled as he picked a piece of meat out of his teeth. "Is he perhaps food for Balthasar? There's nothing on him but skin and bones."

"Actually, your bear almost did eat him, Ivan," Giovanni replied with a grin. "But only after he beat Jerome in a swordfight."

"*A mon honneur*, he fought like a Frenchman," Jerome argued. "He can't be just some simple farm boy, or he never would have beaten—"

"Above all, he's hungry and freezing," one of the women cut in. She was a little older, and a few strands of fiery red hair protruded from under her headscarf. She gestured for Lukas to take a seat alongside her by the fire. "Come now, little one, we won't bite. Sit down with us and get warmed up."

"I'm not little, I'm—" Lukas started to protest in a soft voice, but the man with the fiddle interrupted him, as if he hadn't heard a word of what they were saying.

"Hey, who's to tell us he's not some sneaky little robber sent here to spy on our camp? There are probably more like him lurking around out there."

"Oh, come on, Bjarne!" The red-haired woman waved dismissively. "Had there been any around, your music would have driven them away long ago."

"I . . . thought *you* were robbers and cutthroats," Lukas replied uncertainly.

The men and women laughed as Lukas, feeling more or less relieved, sat down beside them at the fire. The younger of the two women, a pretty girl with large, tinkling earrings, handed him a cup of hot mulled wine while stroking his arm gently, which caused Lukas to flinch instinctively. "Oh, we're just a group of traveling artists," the girl said with a smile. "My name, by the way, is Tabea, and I'm the dancer in the group." She pointed at the three husky young men, and Lukas noticed for the first time that they all looked very much alike. "The Jannsen Brothers can walk on thin wires like they were broad beams and tie themselves up in knots like a ship's rope. Red Sara can read your future from a set of playing cards, and Ivan the Strong Man here"—she pointed at the grim-looking hulk wrapped up in his bearskin—"can bend iron and even get his bear, Balthasar, to perform a Bavarian folk dance. And, oh well, you've already heard the caterwauling of our musicians, Bjarne and Thadäus, and then there are our fencing shows."

"Fencing shows?" Lukas asked, puzzled.

"Our group's main attraction," said Paulus, winking at him while bowing slightly and pointing his thumb at Jerome and Giovanni. "The three of us put on fencing performances. You know, deadly duels, one versus two, sudden lunges, much shouting . . . things like that."

Lukas nodded and sipped on his hot diluted wine, which revived his spirits somewhat. Indeed he knew about these so-called "fencing shows." A few years ago at a town fair in Heidelberg, he'd seen such a group dueling with all sorts of weapons in the town square. He had found it exciting, but his father spoke scornfully of it as disorderly behavior and bar-house brawling. In fact, beer and wine had flowed freely, and after the performance, several fights broke out. But it had been a grandiose spectacle.

"You still haven't told us what you were doing here in the forest and who you really are," one of the tightrope walkers insisted. "So . . . ?"

After some hesitation, Lukas started to tell his story, while avoiding any mention of his actual family. As he had told the Blood Wolves earlier, he only said he'd lost his parents in the war and had for a while struggled through life as a drummer boy.

"After our troops were slaughtered, I fled into the forest," he concluded, "and then hunger and the cold led me to you."

"And the Pappenheim sword?" the strong man asked curiously.

"Oh, that? I took it from a dying foot soldier."

Giovanni looked him up and down suspiciously. "That was no doubt the same soldier who taught you how to fight like that with a sword. He must have been a real master in his field."

Lukas blushed and hoped that nobody would notice in the darkness. Why was it he felt immediately that Giovanni had seen through him? He was clearly the cleverest of the three fencing performers, as he had boasted. Lukas would have to watch out for him.

"A few of the mercenaries took me under their wing and taught me a few tricks," he replied in a firm voice.

"A few tricks?" Jerome chuckled. "*Mon dieu*, you fought like an old warhorse, ah, what am I saying, as elegantly as a Frenchman!" He looked around approvingly. "If you ask me, he could join us right away. We can use another young performer, can't we? What do you think?" he asked the group.

"I'd like a chance to put in a word."

The voice had come from the other side of the fire, where the man with the longsword had been crouched down—the man who Lukas had thought was fast asleep. Now he stood up, staggering slightly, and for the first time, Lukas could see his face. The man was by far the oldest one in the group, with gray hair and a beard, and he reminded Lukas of a sly old wolf. His eyes were bloodshot, and his face was full of little red veins and a number of scars. His leather cuirass, smooth from wear and reinforced with bands of metal, squeaked as he approached Lukas threateningly while reaching for his sword.

"You probably thought the old drunk was sleeping, didn't you?" he growled. "Ha! No sooner has the cat left the house than the mice start dancing on the roof!"

"Indeed, we thought you would allow yourself a well-deserved rest, Master Scherendingen," Giovanni replied, with just a touch of sarcasm in his voice. "Who could be more deserving of that than you?"

"Save your fine words for the women, you macaroni kid." The man whom Giovanni had called Master was now standing almost toe-to-toe with Lukas and pointing his sword directly at Lukas's heart.

"Do you know who I am?" he snapped.

Lukas just shook his head, trying not to show his fear.

"I am Dietmar von Scherendingen," the old soldier continued, "sword master of the swordsman's school in Greifenfels, with a certificate in the use of the longsword. I'm the leader of this shabby band, and a little urchin like you is something I eat for breakfast."

A tense silence settled over the camp. Lukas heard the hissing and crackling of the burning log in the fire.

"They say you can fight with the sword," the sword master went on abruptly. "Guards? Feints? Doubling, failers, winding, and riposte? The entire dance?" He bent down, and Lukas could smell the brandy on his stinking breath. "Because there's one thing you must know. Sword fighting is like a dance, and your dancing partner is none other than the Grim Reaper in person."

"I know, Master." Lukas nodded. "That's . . . something my father always said."

Dietmar von Scherendingen suddenly grinned mischievously. "A clever man, your father. So show me you can dance." He pointed at Lukas's sword and stepped back a few paces.

"Prime!" he ordered, clapping loudly.

Lukas remembered this command from the lessons his father had given him. It was the first of the guards of sword fighting, a position in which the small finger of the sword hand pointed upward and the blade extended forward toward the opponent.

"Ox!" said Scherendingen, indicating Lukas should proceed to the next position.

Lukas swung the blade over his head so it looked like the horn of an ox.

"Plow! Fool! Key! Unicorn!" the master continued, reeling off the names of the other guards of the sword.

In a single, sweeping motion, Lukas changed from one position to the next, and he followed it with a few slashes and thrusts while he whirled around in place. Lukas had studied all these moves as often as possible with his father in the woods and in the castle courtyard and could perform the individual attacks, parries, and feints smoothly and gracefully, as if it were a dance. The mulled wine had warmed him inside, and soon, despite the icy cold, sweat was pouring from his forehead.

"Thwart cut, wrath guard! High cut! Rising cut! Crooked cut!"

The commands were coming faster and faster now. Lukas swung the heavy sword just as he had once brandished the stick—quick, precise, without hesitation. The blade whizzed through the air, hissing and humming, and it sounded almost like a soft melody.

The melody of death, thought Lukas, and for a moment the image of Marek with the blade impaled in his heart flashed through his mind.

"Ox and *finis*! Hurry up!"

The sword master's last command brought Lukas back to reality. Breathing heavily, he reverted to his original position. With his head high, he took his place in front of Dietmar, who looked him up and down carefully, then started to sway back and forth. None of the others around the fire said a word.

"Didn't I say so? As elegant as a Frenchman," Jerome finally whispered, "a real master swordsman despite his young years."

Scherendingen stared at Lukas angrily, then broke out into loud laughter.

"A little urchin who dances like a saber-rattling dervish!" he said after a long pause, and shook his head as he continued laughing. "Damn, I don't know who taught you to fight like that, whether a Frenchman, a German, or an Italian, but in any case, he did a good job." He suddenly turned dead serious again. "But you still have a long way to go if you want to become a master swordsman. The thwart and the low cuts were a bit sloppy, and the last ox came too late. But what difference does that make? Everyone begins somewhere." He extended his arm and squeezed Lukas's left hand so hard it seemed he was trying to crush it. "So what is it?"

"What is what?" Lukas asked, confused and still completely out of breath from his sword dance.

Giovanni stood beside him, laughing. "What is it? Well, welcome to our group, and just don't say no, or we'll toss you to Balthasar for a snack."

Lukas smiled wanly. "Very well," he said, "but only under one condition."

"What would that be, you little squirt?" Scherendingen growled.

"First, I'd like to have a place to sleep here by the fire, and then tomorrow you can do with me what you wish."

Completely exhausted, Lukas collapsed onto the furs, his head sank into the lap of the beautiful, dark-haired Tabea, and almost at once, he fell fast asleep.

VIII

The next few weeks were the most difficult and at the same time the most exciting in Lukas's young life. With Scherendingen's group, he traveled eastward, into Frankish territory. At the time, peace still reigned there, but stories of the atrocities committed by Swedish troops attacking the German Reich from the north were already going the rounds. It wouldn't be long before King Gustav Adolf's soldiers would be rioting and burning here in Franconia and Bavaria, as well. People wanted more than anything else to find something to take their minds off their daily suffering and fears, and so the actors and fencing shows were well received in the villages and cities.

Soon, Lukas learned that Dietmar von Scherendingen, though an old drinker, was still a good commander of his troupe. Usually the actors stayed a ways out of town in fallow fields or forest clearings but were allowed to enter the market squares with their carts, where they were usually eyed suspiciously by the inhabitants. First, Red Sara and Tabea performed a scarf dance to the melodies of the two musicians, allowing their scarves to fall suggestively, one at a time, thereby attracting a larger audience, mostly male. Then came the Jannsen Brothers, riding bicycles and performing somersaults, and finally walking across a thin rope running from the roof ridge of a house on the square to one of the actors' wagons. The next item on the program—Ivan the Strong Man and his bear, Balthasar—always caused great excitement in the crowd. The strong man played his fife while the bear danced to the music, growling from time to time and lunging toward its master. By this time, the first cries of horror could be heard coming from the audience, but they quickly changed to loud applause when Ivan finally took an iron bar, bent it, caught the bear with the crook of the bar, and led the beast back to its cage.

The main attraction, however, was the fencing performance at the end, in which Giovanni, Paulus, and Jerome were introduced in ringing tones as young hotspurs banding together against the old warhorse von Scherendingen. As the battle raged back and forth, the combatants lunged, shouted, cursed, and exchanged blows, and sometimes Scherendingen pretended to be close to defeat, only to disarm his young opponents at the last moment.

Secretly, Lukas admired the skill of the three boys. Each had his own unique way of fighting. The large, muscular Paulus preferred a heavy backsword, a cross between saber and sword, and flailed it around wildly, while the handsome Jerome tended more toward the refined French school with his graceful rapier, always aware of appearances and taking care that his clothing was properly cared for. Giovanni fought like Lukas with a somewhat heavier basket-hilted sword, a weapon that could be used to deliver both thrusts and blows. Giovanni's attacks were always well conceived, like the long, complicated sentences with which he introduced them. Often, in his left hand, he also held a parrying dagger to ward off the blows of his opponent. All three boys, despite their youth, were already true masters of the art.

But they were all overshadowed by Dietmar von Scherendingen. In battle, the old sword master used a so-called *bastard* with a medium-sized hilt, permitting him to use it either one- or two-handed. Despite his age, he spun around with it like a madman, and sometimes he appeared almost to be flying.

It took a while for Lukas to understand that all the moves in this show battle had been practiced. For their daily exercises, the four actors did not use their actual weapons, but practice swords that were more elastic and had a dull point so that injuries were rare. After a few weeks, Lukas was also allowed to take part in these exercises. To his great disappointment, Dietmar gave him only a strange wooden sword in the shape of a saber, which, instead of a hilt, had only a finger hole in the back third.

"That's a dusack," the sword master explained when he noticed Lukas's disappointment. "It's the best weapon for practicing the art of swordsmanship. It's easy, has a dull point, and can be wielded like a short sword."

"But I'm already a good fighter!" Lukas protested.

"You don't know a damn thing. The greatest enemy of a good fighter is his own arrogance. You have a lot to learn before you become a master, and the dusack will teach you humility." Scherendingen grinned. "You can really hurt people with this weapon, you see. Watch!"

He seized his own dusack and went into position in front of Lukas, pointing his wooden weapon at Lukas's sword hand.

"You're left-handed, unlike most of us," he said. "In battle, it gives you a distinct advantage, as your opponents are not accustomed to fighting left-handed people. Use this opportunity to strike a few unexpected blows at the very start. Like this, for example."

Scherendingen suddenly stepped forward a pace and brought his weapon down from the top. Lukas managed to parry, but his opponent slid his own wooden blade smoothly along Lukas's blade until it almost touched his face. Lukas pushed back, but Scherendingen unexpectedly stepped aside, and his young opponent took a tumble. Then, with a violent blow, the sword master struck the dusack out of Lukas's hand. He groaned softly, pain pulsing through his bleeding fingers.

"I said you could really hurt someone with it," Scherendingen said, smiling again. "That was the so-called waker cut. I thought we'd begin with that. Like all our exercises, it comes from the fencing book of the legendary sword master Joachim Meyer, and . . ." He hesitated, and a shadow fell over his face as he carefully looked Lukas up and down. "It's strange," Scherendingen mumbled. "You remind me of someone else, another left-handed fighter. If I only knew . . ." He shook his head. Then he pointed brusquely at Lukas's dusack, lying before him in the snow. "Raise it up, then into the boar's guard, with your hand low and the point up toward your opponent. Now do it!"

Lukas assumed the position, and the battle continued.

On many more occasions in the following weeks, Lukas had to pick up his dusack out of the dirty snow, but Scherendingen gave him no pause. Every morning he woke him, usually with a splash of water in the face, before anyone else and, after a quick breakfast, took him behind the camp. He called it the *morning dance*, though for Lukas, it was more a morning torture. Soon he had more black-and-blue marks than he could count. His fingers ached even when he was holding nothing but a spoon, but at least it helped him forget his worries.

Lukas was grateful for anything that took his mind off his dark memories.

"If you really want to be a sword master, you must be able to dance with the sword even in your sleep," Dietmar declared as he drove Lukas back against a wagon with a few well-placed blows. "Wrath cut, steer guard, parry, blind cut, winding cut . . . it must all be part of you—in your blood." The blows rained down heavily on Lukas. "Roaring cut, parry, rose cut, failer, feint, then back to the thwart cut."

There were so many different positions, thrusts, and blows that Lukas's head was starting to spin. His father had taught him some, but most were new to him. To use them in a fight, he had to repeat them dozens and dozens of times, like an endless dance. Often, at the end of the day, he fell into the straw beside Giovanni, Jerome, and Paulus and was asleep even before he could turn over.

Sometimes they practiced together next to the camp with a stump of wood that already looked quite battered. The master had placed a cross on the stump that separated it into four parts corresponding to the various parts of the body. The young fighters used this to practice moves as Scherendingen barked commands that mostly applied to Lukas.

"Damn, how lame you are, lad! An old farmer can strike a better blow than that with his scythe. Just look at Jerome; he's faster than his shadow. And once more—change, bar, slide, and back to the first position."

Scherendingen always made sure Lukas knew he was not yet satisfied with him. Often the others were allowed to go into the village after an hour to enjoy themselves, but for Lukas, practice continued relentlessly.

"On guard!" the master cried. "Are you rooted to the ground, lad? Your feet are like two little warriors fighting their own battles. Begin again, and then—"

"Hey, Master, give the lad a rest. You'll kill him yet with these miserable exercises."

It was Giovanni, who had just returned from the village. Stepping out from behind a cart, he said sarcastically, "If you're looking for an opponent to shout at and beat, take it out on the stump. That wood can take it."

"Indeed. A stump of wood is a better opponent than that kid there." Scherendingen stepped away from Lukas and motioned to him, indicating that the day's instruction was over. "Now take off before I throw your dusack at you, you good-for-nothing."

Breathing hard, Lukas walked away with Giovanni.

"The master is right, I'll never be a good sword fighter," Lukas muttered. He was having trouble suppressing his tears. His fingers ached as if they were all broken. "I'm one big disappointment."

"Oh, come on," Giovanni said. "The old man likes you and believes in you."

"He believes in me?" Lukas just stood there in astonishment. "Why then does he pester me all the time and shout at me as if I were a failure?"

"That's his way of saying he thinks you have a lot of talent." Giovanni grinned. "He just wants to push you, that's all. So you have better control of your anger. He told me himself he soon wants you to take part in the show battles."

"Really?" Lukas's heart beat faster. "Together with you? Then I could finally prove I'm worth something."

"You're already an excellent kitchen boy," Giovanni replied with a laugh. "And Red Sara and Tabea are already crazy about you." He winked at Lukas. "Especially Tabea. Perhaps you should just become a cook and travel with the army."

"Wouldn't that be great," Lukas replied glumly. "Spend all my life washing plates and peeling vegetables. I'd rather throw myself on my sword."

In the meantime, they'd left the camp behind them. For several days, the troupe had been resting just outside a pretty village still unscathed by the war. Spring had already arrived, and the seed was growing in fields still partially covered with snow. In the budding trees, birds were chirping.

"I think you deserve a little diversion," Giovanni said as they approached the small town. "There's a fair in the village where people are celebrating, drinking, and dancing." He paused. "And there are a few pretty girls there, too. So, what do you think?"

Soon they'd arrived at the village tavern, which was full of noise and music. Inside, the furniture had been cleared, people were dancing to the music of a fiddle, drum, and bass, and the air was full of the odor of sweat and roasted mutton. At the tables along the side sat a few maids and journeymen exhausted from dancing, drinking wine out of huge tankards.

"Hey, look at that. Giovanni brought the kid along!" Paulus bellowed. He had taken a seat at one of the tables in the rear and was arm wrestling with a broad-shouldered young farmhand. "I thought the old man would never let the little one out of his clutches." Paulus pushed his opponent's hand down onto the table and swept up a few more coins, with a grin. "A good business I've got going here," he said as another journeyman stepped up to his table. "With three or four more contests like this, I'll be able to set up a fencing school in this town."

"How about a school for brawling, wrestling, and drinking— wouldn't you like that better?" Giovanni laughed. "Where is Jerome?"

"Where else? Naturally, where you can find the best cherries for picking." Paulus pointed to a neighboring table, where handsome Jerome was at that moment reading the palm of a young maid. He was surrounded by a crowd of girls, all looking at him with fluttering eyelashes.

"Oh, I see a great future awaits you as a princess," Jerome was whispering in his inimitable French accent. "A prince is coming to carry you off on his mighty steed."

"And . . . when will this prince be coming?" the maid asked breathlessly.

"Voilà, he's standing right in front of you." Jerome grinned from ear to ear, showing two rows of bright white teeth. "May His Excellency have the honor of the next dance with you?"

The maid giggled and left with Jerome, who winked brazenly at his friends.

Giovanni rolled his eyes. "He may not be the brightest one in our group, but he certainly has a way with girls," he said with a shrug. "A few silly words, and he's already got her wrapped around his finger."

They joined Paulus, who was sitting alone now. Evidently, no other farmhands wanted to challenge him in arm wrestling.

"How did you all get to know each other?" Lukas asked after a while.

"Scherendingen hired us one by one to be his foot soldiers," Paulus replied. "Jerome comes from a French Huguenot family, and his parents were traveling actors. They were murdered by mercenaries. Probably the only thing that kept him alive was his shameless charm and his skill with a rapier." Paulus then pointed to himself. "I myself come from Cologne, where my father was a well-known armorer. One day the mercenaries simply took our weapons without paying. My father resisted, so they strung him up on the nearest church steeple," he continued gloomily while rattling the saber at his side. "This is one of the last weapons my father forged, sharpened on both sides and so heavy I can slice an ox in two with one blow. I've sworn to cherish it for my father's sake."

"And you?" Lukas asked Giovanni. "Where do you come from?"

The skinny lad smiled. "I'm the third son of a lesser nobleman in the Verona area," Giovanni announced. "My parents sent me to a monastery, where I learned to read and write. They wanted me to become an abbot or even a bishop someday, but life as a vagabond was much more to my liking, so I ran away."

"In the monastery, Giovanni read tons of books," said Jerome, who had returned and taken a seat next to them. A few of the girls looked over at him, disappointed. "He simply knows everything. Scherendingen says he's a walking lie berry."

"Library," Giovanni corrected him with a sigh, then turned to Lukas. "And what brings *you* to us? Despite all the weeks we've spent together, we know precious little about you. And don't start in with that story about the lonesome drummer boy! The first time I heard it, I knew it was a lie."

Lukas had always kept quiet about his past, partly because he wanted to forget it and partly because he was afraid the inquisitor Waldemar von Schönborn might still be looking for him. But he felt so lonely and needed a few friends with whom to share his secrets. Ever since he'd joined Scherendingen's troupe of actors, his life appeared to have meaning again.

And so Lukas began telling his story, omitting only the part about his mother's unexplainable voice and the strange blue cloud when she was burned at the stake, fearing the three boys might think he was insane.

The others listened silently.

Finally Paulus shook his head. "That's horrible," he said. "I mean, Jerome and I have also lost our families. But this? Your father murdered, your mother burned as a witch, and your sister missing? I'm sure we all feel sorry for you."

"You said the inquisitor and those Spanish mercenaries were looking for something at your castle," Giovanni interjected. "Have you figured out what it was?"

Lukas shook his head. "Unfortunately not, but it must have been something very valuable, as they turned the whole castle inside out looking for it. And something else was strange. The mercenaries were told to kill me, but the inquisitor wanted Elsa alive."

"So you think she's still alive?" Jerome asked.

Lukas sighed. "If I only knew! In any case, I promised her I would not forsake her, and I must look for her."

"And you really learned all your fighting skills from your father?" said Paulus, changing the subject. "Then he must have been quite a good warrior."

"Indeed he was. He fought for a long time under General Wallenstein as a soldier in an elite unit called the Black Musketeers." Lukas looked around at the others with a questioning gaze. "I don't know if you've ever heard of them."

Paulus broke out in laughter. "You're asking if we ever heard of the Black Musketeers? Well, of course! These troops are legendary and considered the best warriors in the Reich. It is said that only with their help was Wallenstein able to defeat the Danes back then." He grinned. "We also personally know one of their most outstanding men."

"Who is that?" Lukas asked with surprise.

"Why, Dietmar von Scherendingen," Giovanni declared. "He was a very famous teacher at the sword master school in Greifenfels. But then he met an opponent stronger than he was: accursed alcohol. He was expelled, and sometime after that, he joined the Black Musketeers." Giovanni shrugged. "He doesn't say much about the group—just a word now and then when he's drunk. It was a pretty sad chapter in his already very sad life. Just don't talk with him about it if you don't want to risk setting off one of his famous fits of rage."

Lukas froze for a moment. His father and Dietmar von Scherendingen had fought in the same regiment! It felt as if his father had risen from his grave. He couldn't help thinking about what the sword master had said to him just recently.

You remind me of someone else, another left-handed fighter . . .

His father had also been left-handed. Was it possible that Scherendingen was talking about his father? Did the master perhaps also know his mother? Perhaps he knew something about the secret that the inquisitor was looking for.

Lukas would have to ask him about it sometime soon.

"I think we've been brooding long enough about this," said Jerome, wrenching him away from his thoughts. "Let's see if we can find a few girls to dance with." He'd already stood up and was waving to some young girls to come over. "Life is too short to only dwell on the past."

IX

The practice duels with the master continued in the following days and weeks. There were evenings when every muscle and every bone in Lukas's body ached, including some he'd never known about. But he also felt he was getting stronger, more skillful, and ready for battle.

"You eat like a hungry wolf," Red Sara said to him one day as he gulped down the steaming stew even more ravenously than usual. "If you keep on like that, the stew will soon be coming out of your ears."

"Let him be," replied Tabea, who, like the other actors and sword fighters, was sitting around the fire, relaxing. "As you can see, the boy is growing," she said with a smile. "In one more year, an imposing sword fighter will be standing before us. The master says Lukas is the best swordsman he ever trained. He apparently sees promise in the lad."

Lukas was especially fond of Tabea, and she of him, evidently. She was sixteen, not much older than Paulus and Jerome, and sometimes she cast odd glances at Lukas, which embarrassed him. Once or twice, she had run her fingers through his hair playfully or touched him as if by chance. Each time, he was afraid he was going to blush, and Jerome in particular liked to tease him about it. This time, again, he could feel his face flush.

"The . . . other lads are a lot stronger and better," he mumbled, looking down into his pot of stew. "I'll never be as good as they are."

"Don't hide your light under a bushel," Paulus muttered between two spoonfuls. Every evening he had three bowls, and his biceps bulged so much under his thin linen shirt it looked like it could rip at any moment. "You'll never be the strongest one in your group, no, but you're clever and nimble enough for three. And you have the gift of moving quickly and smoothly with your sword. Not many people can do that—you're a real sword dancer."

"That won't be of any use to him if the Swedes wipe us out," replied one of the Jannsen Brothers gloomily. "Haven't you heard? Nördlingen has already fallen, as have Frankfurt and Würzburg. The entire North of the Reich is in the hands of these wild men, and anyone who doesn't surrender and join them will be mercilessly slaughtered."

Ivan stared into the fire. "They fight like wild men, and with their cannons and muskets, they are far superior to any swordsman, no matter how fine his dance."

The two musicians, Bjarne and Thadäus, nodded sadly, picked up their instruments, and started playing a melancholy tune. For a long time, no one said anything. Lukas thought of the dreadful stories he'd heard about the war. Last year in Magdeburg, twenty thousand citizens had been slaughtered by mercenaries, who then completely destroyed the city. Similar things had happened in other parts of the Reich. Whenever the troops passed by, no matter which side they were on, they left behind death, destruction, hunger, and disease. When he was young, Lukas had always imagined war as something heroic. In his dreams, he saw his father with a sword and gleaming armor riding out on exciting adventures in pursuit of the infidels, but for some time now, he had understood that war was not an adventure, but left horror and misery in its wake.

"There is only one man who can stop the Swedes," Giovanni said after a while. "Wallenstein. He's the best general in the entire Reich. The Kaiser had dismissed him because he was getting too powerful to suit the German princes, but I've heard the Kaiser has once again appointed him to lead the troops."

Lukas turned to Dietmar von Scherendingen, who had been sitting there silently, sipping occasionally on his mug of brandy. Lukas cleared his throat.

"You yourself fought under Wallenstein, Master," he said in a soft voice. "What do you think? Will he be able to turn the tide?"

Scherendingen let out a loud belch and laughed bitterly. "Tilly, Wallenstein . . . Why should we care which of the great men invites the devil to dance with us? The Swedes will be here soon, in any case. We need to make sure we get out of here." Suddenly he grinned. "But first we'll put on one last great performance for the people who live here. Augsburg is only thirty miles away. It's a great city, and above all, a very rich one where we can pick up a lot of money," he said, looking Lukas in the eye. "And this time you'll be one of the group."

Giovanni had already indicated that Scherendingen wanted Lukas to take part in the show battles, but now that things seemed to be getting serious, he was stunned.

"What . . . will my task be, Master?" he stammered.

"Well, this time I'm going to change the performance a bit. The four of us"—Scherendingen pointed at the three other boys and himself—"will all fight against you."

"All four against *me*?" Lukas shook his head. "How are we going to do that?"

"Isn't he still a bit too small for that?" Ivan asked. "Perhaps—"

"Nonsense! No excuses now!" Scherendingen interrupted. "A little guy against four bigger and stronger opponents will get us a laugh, and the people desperately need something to laugh about. Besides, it's something different, and the spectators will come in droves." The master rose to his feet and emptied his cup in one long gulp. "We'll begin practice tomorrow. I expect full concentration from every one of you." He looked at the boys sternly. "Go to bed early if you want to feel your fingers tomorrow."

Scherendingen walked away, and soon all the others went to bed as well. Lukas, however, had a hard time falling asleep. What would happen if he bungled his first show? Would the master throw him out? For the first time since the death of his parents, Lukas felt as if he'd found something like a family to which he belonged. Giovanni, Jerome, and Paulus had become very good friends, and he didn't want to lose anyone again. On the other hand, he also knew that someday he'd have to leave the group in order to take out his vengeance on Schönborn.

And continue his search for Elsa.

Finally he drifted off, but he did not sleep well. He felt himself tumbling through a world of dreams shrouded in clouds of fog. On the other side of the fog, something seemed to be lying in wait for him, a black shadow with red eyes that looked like burning coals. Sometimes the fog lifted a bit, and then Lukas saw the outlines of a huge, black wolf. Saliva dripped from its jaws; it sniffed the air and seemed to be searching for something. In the dream, Lukas's heart froze when he realized whose trail the beast was following.

He's looking for me!

The great wolf ran back and forth within the cloud and seemed to be looking for a way out, but couldn't find it. Suddenly it raised its head and looked directly at Lukas, and at the same moment, Lukas heard the voice of his mother.

Run! He mustn't find you. He must never find you.

The wolf prepared to jump . . .

Screaming, Lukas woke up.

Giovanni jumped up from where he was sleeping near the fire and looked at him sleepily. "Have you had a bad dream?" he asked sympathetically.

Lukas nodded. "It . . . was a large wolf, it was looking for me, and then I heard the voice of my mother . . ."

Giovanni yawned. "You miss her, and it's understandable that you dream of her."

"This dream was different. Everything looked so real, as if that wolf was really looking for me, and the voice—" Lukas stopped short, remembering that his mother had said almost the same thing to him long ago. For a moment, he considered telling Giovanni about the ghostly voices and the blue cloud hovering over the execution site. But then he decided to remain silent. He needed to concentrate on the exercises for the following day. His friends should not think of him as too dreamy or weak for this battle.

Giovanni seemed to notice his hesitation. He looked intently at Lukas with his discerning eyes. "If you have something to tell me or the others," Giovanni said softly, in order not to waken the other sleeping boys, "please don't hesitate. We're always here for you, do you understand?" He smiled. "One for all and all for one. I heard those words somewhere before, and they apply to us as well."

Lukas nodded gratefully. "Thanks. Perhaps . . . I'll tell you more some other time." Then he rolled over and closed his eyes.

This time, he fell into a deep sleep.

The wolf had disappeared.

X

Just a week after that, Lukas experienced his first swordfight.

Every day, he had practiced with the others from early morning until after sundown, with only short breaks during which he wolfed down Sara's stews. Dietmar von Scherendingen had decided to add a few features to the show, among them, that the use of the arm not holding the sword was permitted in battle as well. All four boys fought using daggers with wide cross guards that parried and diverted the opponent's blow. Occasionally they also used small buckle shields, ropes, or capes that they threw out like nets to trap their opponent.

In contrast with the exercises of the last few weeks, Lukas could now use his Pappenheim sword again, making it very important that every thrust, every step, every blow was calculated precisely so that no one was badly injured. It all had to look like a mortal battle, though basically it was just a dance with five partners, an artistic drama in which each performer had to play his prescribed role.

They arrived in Augsburg just as the Swedes had begun pillaging and setting fire to cities and towns throughout Swabia and

Bavaria. This powerful imperial city was one of the few places where Catholics and Protestants still lived together peaceably. However, while the Protestants welcomed the Swedes, who were also Protestants, the Catholics felt petrified with fear, and the last remaining soldiers loyal to the Kaiser were preparing their retreat.

The day before the show battle, Bjarne and Thadäus marched through the streets with their barrel organ, fife, and bells, announcing the upcoming performance. In the main square next to the newly built city hall, the other members of the troupe constructed an improvised circus ring consisting of four wooden beams in a square, denoting the area of battle. There were no chairs, and the spectators stood along the side of the battle area. Before the performance, Sara and Tabea passed a hat through the rows of people, and anyone who didn't drop in a few coins was greeted with loud jeers and the mockery of the crowd.

After more than a hundred people had gathered and a number of coins were collected, the spectacle could finally commence. As always, first came the dancers, followed by the artists, and Ivan with his bear. Finally, Dietmar von Scherendingen stepped up to a small, wobbly lectern in his battered leather cuirass, holding the bastard sword in his hand. There was a dramatic pause, and the spectators waited expectantly for the sword master to introduce himself.

"Honored guests!" he thundered. "I direct your attention to a fighter unlike any the world has ever seen. Strong, agile, as clever as five foot soldiers, and a fearsome mercenary who knows every trick in the art of swordsmanship. He was present at the Battle of Magdeburg, where he killed more than three dozen Swedes with his sword. Both Bohemians and Danes screamed and ran when they saw him coming, his reputation is legendary, and now he is here with us . . . the fearrrrsome Luuuukas!"

As he spoke the last words, he pulled Lukas out from behind a small curtain between the two actors' wagons. People roared and laughed when they saw that Fearsome Lukas was just a skinny kid.

"Hey, what happened to him?" jeered an elderly farmer. "Did a battle-ax cut him down to size?"

"It probably made him a head shorter," another person cried.

"Take pity on us!" someone else laughed. "He probably can't even hold a sword yet."

Lukas blushed and had to restrain himself from hitting one of them in the face with his sword handle. Scherendingen had told him the people would make fun of him; that was part of the plan. Nevertheless, Lukas felt hurt. Hadn't he grown in recent months? Hadn't Tabea said he had what it takes to be a great sword fighter? He was trembling with excitement. It was one thing to practice the sword dance in an out-of-the-way field, but something quite different to do it in front of a large, ugly crowd just looking for the smallest error.

Paulus came up from behind and patted Lukas encouragingly on the shoulder. "Don't let the idiots upset you," he whispered. "Just go ahead and fight the way we practiced it. They'll be amazed."

Giovanni and Jerome now also stepped out from behind the curtain, and the battle could begin.

At first, the three boys attacked Lukas one by one, and he withdrew, apparently in fear, but then with a few well-placed thrusts, he beat them and disarmed them. Then, with much shouting, they charged him all together. Paulus played the part of the crude bully, thrashing his sword around wildly at Lukas. Giovanni and Jerome kept trying to outdo him in the dance, but each time, Lukas cleverly evaded them, spun around, and threw his coat and rope at his opponents, who got tangled up in them and fell to the ground again. Lukas concentrated completely on each of his movements, trying to shut out all the noise around him and thinking only of himself and his respective opponent, in order to avoid making any mistakes.

For the first time, there were cheers from some spectators, and the whistles and jeers finally died out. Evidently the people understood that the boy had real talent.

At this moment, Bjarne began a loud drumroll, and Paulus, Giovanni, and Jerome stepped back with a few bows. Now Dietmar von Scherendingen entered the arena. Threateningly, the master swung his longsword around, switching from one position to the next and then making mock attacks on Lukas, like a dancing berserker. A few times, Scherendingen's huge blade whistled past Lukas's face, but he didn't retreat, just as they had agreed earlier.

"Ha! Now the old warhorse will blow out his lights!" the older farmer yelled. "He fights differently than the three boys." He looked around for confirmation, but most spectators were staring transfixed at the two swordsmen who appeared so unequal. Lukas glanced at the crowd. Surely most of the people here knew that this battle was a sham, but they seemed to have forgotten that and were hoping to be surprised.

Just as Lukas was about to turn back to his opponent, he caught sight of a man in the crowd who seemed to be a stranger to the area; his skin was brown and tanned like old cedar, and his clothing, too, looked strange, like that of a mercenary from a foreign land. He was wearing baggy black breeches and a scratched cuirass over a brilliant red quilted gambeson. It took Lukas a moment to understand this was a sort of clothing he had seen once before.

The man looked like one of those Spanish mercenaries who had killed his father and abducted his sister!

He was looking straight at Lukas, and his narrow lips were murmuring something that Lukas couldn't hear, but he couldn't help thinking how one of these men had shot his father with a crossbow. The image of Lukas's dead father suddenly rose up like a ghost in his mind, infusing it like a poison.

"Damn, what's wrong with you?" Scherendingen cursed as he noticed Lukas's hesitation. "Pull yourself together, concentrate, lad!"

Lukas quivered, shook himself, then turned back to the master, who had begun to come at him again with attacks, thrusts, and feints. They had practiced the sequence carefully, and at the last rehearsal, everything had gone well, but now Lukas could sense he'd lost his concentration. He hesitated, moved too slowly, and one of Scherendingen's blows almost struck him on the head.

"Didn't I tell you?" the farmer crowed cheerfully. "The kid is no match for the old warhorse."

Scherendingen's movements also became a little slower, and even though the battle was still raging back and forth as they had practiced it, everything seemed erratic, like poor acting.

"What's the matter, lad?" Scherendingen panted between blows. "Don't disappoint me! I know you have the stuff to become a great show fighter, so come on and fight like a man!"

Suddenly, Dietmar von Scherendingen seemed to grow taller. Lukas wiped the sweat from his eyes, blinked, and realized to his horror that it wasn't the master, but something else. Behind Scherendingen, a ghostly apparition was rising like a bank of fog and slowly beginning to take shape. Lukas tried to scream, but the scream lodged in his throat.

Before him stood the wolf from his dream.

The thought flashed through his mind that this was impossible. *Wake up, this can't be happening!*

But the wolf did not go away. It rose up behind Scherendingen and glared at the boy with its small, evil eyes. No one but Lukas seemed to notice it. He dropped his sword and dagger and looked up at the nameless horror.

"He's giving up," the people shouted. "The boy is giving up!"

Scherendingen shook his head sadly and turned to Lukas.

"I really thought that—"

At this moment, the black phantom pounced on the young fighter. Shouting, Lukas picked up his weapon again. He was no longer conscious of what he was doing; he was completely overcome by naked fear, but his fear bestowed an almost supernatural power on him. Like a Fury, he threw himself at the wolf that was now standing directly between him and Scherendingen. His blade whizzed through the shadowy figure as if through the air, but to the spectators it looked like Lukas had again taken up the fight against his master. The blows rained down on the old warhorse like a torrential downpour.

The old soldier seemed astonished, but then he resumed the battle. Lukas now had two opponents: the wolf and the master, but in his mind they appeared fused together as one. Lukas's blows landed more precisely than ever before in his life. Scherendingen kept retreating until finally he stood with his back against a wooden barrier.

"The lad is fighting like the devil," one of the spectators shouted. Other voices joined in: "Hurrah! Lukas, Lukas, Lukas!"

Fired up by the shouts from the crowd, Lukas swung his sword through the air, sliding from one position to another like a cat. Scherendingen parried the blows, but his strength appeared to be waning.

"Enough, lad," he gasped. "That was more than I expected, much more."

But the wolf's evil eyes bored into Lukas, and he knew the wolf had recognized him.

He found me! Lukas thought. *He has been seeking me, and now he has found me!*

The wolf's lips twisted into one final, malicious grin, and then the phantom suddenly vanished. Only a gray cloud remained, and soon that also vanished. Lukas swung his sword at it, but struck instead Scherendingen's sword hand, sending his weapon flying away into the dirt.

After a moment of stunned silence, a huge cheer went up. People applauded, threw their hats in the air, and slapped each other on the shoulders.

"What a battle!" they shouted. "Three cheers for the young lad. He can take on the Swedes all by himself."

Only Dietmar von Scherendingen seemed uncertain. He was bathed in sweat, staggering slightly, and still struggling to catch his breath.

"Good Lord," he finally said. "That . . . isn't what we agreed on. God knows what could have happened." But then he grinned from ear to ear. "But what difference does it make? It was a great spectacle—especially the terrifying look you gave me! For a moment I thought you really wanted to run me through." He laughed and led Lukas, still quivering, out of the ring and over to one of the actors' wagons. "Damn! This lad knows all the tricks!"

As soon as Lukas entered the wagon, his three friends bombarded him with questions. They could still hear the cheering outside. Scherendingen had returned to the spectators to accept their ovation and collect some more coins.

"Now what was *that* all about?" Giovanni asked, shaking his head. "Were you really trying to kill the master and take his place?"

95

"No, no, I—" Lukas started to say, confused, but Jerome interrupted him at once.

"It was the best performance in a long time!" he said excitedly. "First this hesitation as you almost surrendered, and then this lightning attack, like a snake. *Mon dieu! C'est sensationell!*"

"There are only two possibilities," Paulus grumbled. "Either the master will cut Lukas to pieces, or he'll give him a medal. In any case, no one has ever fought with him like that." He winked at Lukas. "At least no little squirt like you."

"Just stop and listen to me, will you!" Lukas pleaded. "I didn't plan it that way. There was a wolf, it attacked me, and . . . and . . ." He stopped, realizing how crazy it all sounded.

"A wolf?" Paulus asked, frowning. "What kind of wolf?"

Lukas hesitated, but he finally decided to tell his friends the truth; he couldn't remain silent any longer.

"Sometimes I see and hear things," he began quietly, "that nobody else can see and hear. It all began with the execution of my mother."

He told his friends about the blue cloud and the voice of his mother he'd heard again on that cold winter night just before he discovered the actors' camp. Then he told them about his nightmare and the wolf.

"This wolf was really there," he concluded, "in the dream, and today in the battle, like . . . like a ghost! It was standing behind the master; then it attacked me." He shook his head. "And among the spectators there was a strange fellow, perhaps a Spaniard. He was dressed just like those mercenaries who killed my father and abducted my mother, and he was mumbling something. Who knows, perhaps he was summoning this wolf."

Giovanni looked at him skeptically and frowned. "A phantom wolf then, and a mumbling Spaniard. Hmm . . . Maybe the last few days were just too much for you . . . the loss of sleep, the constant practice—"

"You don't believe me!" Lukas stared at his friends in despair. "You think I'm crazy."

"I just think you've gone through a lot in the last half year," Paulus said, trying to calm him. "Perhaps you should simply try to get a good night's sleep."

"But don't you understand?" Lukas said. "This wolf was looking for me, and now it has found me, and it has put the Spaniard on my trail. I don't know what this fellow wants from me, but . . ."

He fell silent as the door to the wagon was flung open and Dietmar von Scherendingen appeared in the entrance.

The master looked surprised and hesitated for a moment before asking, "What's going on here? We took in more money today than ever, and you guys are moping around with faces like three days of rainy weather." Then he grinned. "Is it because you think I'm still angry at the kid for almost beating me in battle? Well, don't worry, it's all forgiven." He winked at Lukas. "But don't rejoice quite yet. I'll pay you back, kid, by tomorrow at the latest. I've decided we're going to stay in Augsburg a little longer. So prepare yourself for a rematch, Lukas. Now be off! The people want to see their hero!" Laughing and jingling his purse of coins, he turned around again to the cheering public.

Lukas groaned and slumped down on a chest in exhaustion, closing his eyes and fearing the huge wolf could appear again, while the spectators outside continued shouting his name.

XI

All that week they gave daily shows, all so well attended that the citizens of Augsburg came hours early looking for the best places to watch. Everyone wanted to see Fearsome Lukas, this little devil who was nonetheless able to hold his own against four experienced swordsmen at the same time. Lukas didn't fight now with the same determination as on that first day, but his fame spread. Parents brought their children along, giggling couples watched together, and as time went on, he mastered the tricks better than ever. The wolf and the Spaniard never returned, and so he was able to concentrate fully on the battle.

Often Lukas wondered if he had only imagined the strange events of the first show in Augsburg. Perhaps it really had been due to the lack of sleep. He no longer had bad dreams and was well rested and able to concentrate. During their morning practice sessions, Scherendingen was no longer so strict with him. Sometimes he even gave Lukas a fatherly pat on the head, and at such times, there was a sparkle in his eye.

An innkeeper and enthusiastic fan of theirs gave the actors a cheap room near Saint Ursula's Convent, so the actors no longer needed to spend the night in their damp, stuffy wagons. Now they had a hot meal three times a day, and the inn's beds were nearly free of fleas and lice. Seldom had they lived so well as here in Augsburg. From his earnings, Jerome bought himself a new hat with a wide brim and rooster feathers, and Paulus bought two heavy parrying daggers almost as long as his forearm from a local blacksmith. Giovanni spent many hours in the library of the neighboring monastery, where the nuns took a great liking to him and allowed him to browse through the books there at any time of day or night.

Lukas, on the other hand, didn't care much for shopping or socializing and usually practiced the individual moves on the tree stump or with Scherendingen until he could perform them even with his eyes closed.

"You really should give yourself a break," Paulus said to him as they were sitting before a pot of stew in the tavern at the end of the week. "If you keep up training like that, the Augsburg bishop will appoint you his personal bodyguard." He licked off his spoon and with gusto helped himself to another portion.

"The only good job you could get with the bishop would be as his taster," Tabea said with a laugh. Then she turned to Lukas and winked. "But you're right, Paulus. The Augsburgers have fallen in love with our little kid just as much as we have."

"You mean *you* have." Sara giggled.

As usual, Lukas turned red and leaned way down over his bowl. He still hated it when they called him a *kid*, but somehow the word sounded different, almost pleasant, when Tabea said it.

"As nice as it is here, we'd better leave soon," one of the Jannsen Brothers interrupted. "They say the Swedes have gotten as far as Friedberg, and that's not even twenty miles from here! The last of the Bavarian duke's foot soldiers withdrew from

Augsburg yesterday, with rolling drums and muskets at the ready." He leaned over and continued speaking softly. "The patricians no doubt plan to surrender without a fight. Just the same, I want to be far away when King Gustav Adolf's swine come marching in."

"Out in the country, things are no better," Ivan grumbled into his beard. "There are mobs of hungry mercenaries wandering about out there. From the city walls you can see the villages burning."

The others nodded in agreement, and soon an anxious conversation started about what to do now. The good mood had evaporated.

"I've asked around," said Scherendingen, who until then had been quietly sitting in a corner, as he did so often, drinking his wine. At once the others fell silent. "In the east there is still a narrow corridor we can use to escape. If we break camp early enough tomorrow morning, we should be able to make our way to Landshut, which is still firmly under the Kaiser's control, and there we'll be safe."

"What do you mean by 'safe'!" Sara complained. "Our troops are not much better. I've heard dreadful stories of people being forced by the mercenaries to swallow liquid manure until they choke to death. *Swedish brew* is what the farmers call it. The imperial soldiers impale screaming infants on their lances, and—"

"Keep your horror stories to yourself, old witch," Scherendingen shot back. "We'll fight our way through to the imperial Bavarian troops tomorrow, and now not another word!" He belched loudly, staggered to his feet, and went to bed.

The others remained behind, silent except for Ivan, who just shook his head and grumbled, "The old man is getting worse and worse. Sooner or later, he'll drink himself to death."

"But before that, he'll fight as drunk as the Lord against the devil," Giovanni said with a laugh. "And now let's be positive. You'll see, everything will be fine. We'll travel like princes with the Kaiser's troops in the imperial baggage train."

Lukas sipped on his warm diluted wine. He admired Giovanni greatly for his intelligence, but this time he was afraid his friend might be mistaken.

Very early the next morning, the actors headed out of the Augsburg city gate in their two wagons. On the eastern horizon, they could see a red glow, as if the sky were burning, and indeed, they soon came across abandoned villages and small towns. In their fear, people had fled pell-mell, leaving behind only a few old people, who followed the actors with tired eyes.

Around noon they finally reached a region that had already been plundered. Many of the farmhouses had been burned down, and the mercenaries had thrown bodies of dead animals in the wells to poison the water. At a road crossing hung the corpses of two farmers. Lukas stared in horror at the bodies swaying gently in the wind.

"No doubt they wouldn't tell the Swedes where they'd hidden their few possessions," Paulus observed darkly.

"But we don't know if it really was the Swedes, or our own men," Scherendingen replied. "Actually, we should now be in imperial territory." He shook his head, trying to think it through.

The master had the wagons stop for a short rest in another little town that had been burned down. There were dead bodies here as well and an overturned oxcart burning in the road.

"I don't like this at all," Scherendingen grumbled. "Let's first look around to see where the enemy is. Otherwise, we could run right into a trap. That's your order, lads. Unhitch the wagons and look around, and be back by sundown, is that clear? In the meantime, the rest of us will stay here."

Lukas helped his three friends unhitch the horses from the shafts, then they quickly saddled up and headed north, where other villages could be seen burning in the distance.

They had been riding along silently for a good hour side by side when they saw a dark line on the horizon quickly approaching. Giovanni gave the sign to stop.

"Damn! That's an army," he whispered, "and a pretty big one, too. But whose army is it?"

"To find out, we'll have to get closer, whether we like it or not." Jerome pointed to the north, where another burned village with a church in the middle was visible. "If we go there and climb the steeple, perhaps we can learn more."

Soon they came to the destroyed town, where bodies were also hanging from the trees and dead cattle lay in the scorched fields. Small fires were burning everywhere, as if the attack on the village had happened just recently. Lukas tried to put the images out of his mind and entered the vandalized church along with the others. All the windows had been smashed, the sacristy plundered, and on the altar was a steaming, stinking pile of human feces with flies buzzing around it. The clock tower, however, seemed intact, even if the wooden stairs were charred and crumbling.

Standing up above between the bells, the friends looked out on a devastated landscape, with fields trampled underfoot, trees felled and taken away as firewood, and columns of smoke above places where towns used to be. There was no life here anymore; not even a bird was chirping.

"This . . . is horrible," Lukas gasped.

"It's war," replied Jerome. "It eats its way through the land like an insatiable beast."

"Can you make out the flags over there?" Giovanni was pointing toward the marching soldiers that could be seen clearly from up here. He squinted, then cursed softly. "They're Swedes, damn it!"

"That means our way to the east is blocked now, as well," Paulus said. "We should have stayed in Augsburg."

"But it's not too late to do that," Giovanni replied. "Let's turn around and warn the others." He started down the stairs, where they had tethered their horses alongside the village church.

"Quickly!" he called to his friends. "It's going to take us much longer to get back to Augsburg with the wagons than if we only had the horses, and if we want to be there before nightfall, we've got to hurry."

Though their horses were already weary, they leaped on them and rode southward at breakneck speed. Still it was a while until they saw before them the destroyed village where they had left their companions.

Lukas felt right away that something wasn't right. A dark foreboding seized him, and he spurred his horse on.

What awaited them exceeded his worst fears.

XII

A new column of smoke curled upward from the same road in the village where the group had set up camp.

As the boys drew closer, they recognized both of the actors' wagons fully ablaze. Lukas saw two of the Jannsen Brothers bending down over a motionless figure in the middle of the road. It seemed to be Yorrick, the youngest of the brothers. Someone was sobbing loudly, and a shrill cry came from one of the wagons.

"My God, we've arrived too late," Paulus gasped. "The Swedes have already been here."

They quickly jumped down from their horses and ran toward the burning wagons. The first thing Lukas saw was the dead bear, Balthasar, riddled with bullets from a musket and bolts from a crossbow. Ivan lay on his side, his hand stretched out as if in a final greeting, and his body covered with wounds. Farther ahead were the musicians Bjarne and Thadäus, who appeared to have been killed by a number of blows from a sword. Tabea was standing alongside the two Janssen Brothers, her face smeared with dirt and blood. When she saw the four friends, she let out a cry of relief.

"Thank God, Lukas, you're alive!" She ran toward the boys and took Lukas in her arms. "I was afraid they'd gotten you, too."

Lukas still couldn't take his eyes off the horribly mangled Ivan and the dead bear. It took a few moments for him to understand what she was saying.

"Gotten me, too?" he asked. "But why—"

"They were looking for you," Tabea interrupted, "God knows why. They . . . kept asking about you, but we were silent, then they took Ivan and the others . . ." She stopped and began crying softly.

"What did the Swedes want from Lukas?" Jerome asked. "They don't even know him."

"But . . . they weren't the Swedes at all." Tabea shook her head in despair. "They were other mercenaries, with dark skin and odd-looking helmets . . ."

"Spaniards!" Lukas cried. "They were Spaniards, just like the man in Augsburg." He turned to his companions. "Didn't I tell you? The man was looking for me."

Paulus groaned. "Are you going to start in again with this tale about the huge wolf?"

"A huge wolf?" Briefly, Tabea looked muddled, then she whispered, "Ivan also spoke about a wolf, just before he died. He was the first to notice the men and tried to block their way with Balthasar. He said a horrible beast attacked them, a . . . huge wolf, but we didn't see anything. His injuries . . ." She paused for a few seconds and pressed her lips together. "They're not just from the muskets."

"How is the master?" Giovanni asked.

Tibia pointed behind one of the burning wagons. "Sara is caring for him. He fought like a wild man, but in the end, there were just too many of them." She paused again. "A few of these mercenaries looked very strange. Their eyes appeared lifeless, and it seemed like nothing . . . no one . . . could stand in their way, even though Scherendingen attacked them again and again. He . . . tried to protect us . . ." She fought back tears. "It's no doubt just a matter of time until the Lord takes him away."

The friends ran around the wagon, which had been smashed to bits, and found Red Sara kneeling next to Dietmar von Scherendingen. His leather armor had been pierced and ripped in several places, as had his shirt and trousers, and the ground was soaked with his blood. Sara looked at Lukas and the others with weary, tear-stained eyes. She had started bandaging Scherendingen's worst wounds, but it was clear to Lukas that any help was too late.

"There's nothing more I can do for him," Sara said, "other than trying to relieve his pain." She smiled sadly at Lukas. "It's good you are here, Lukas. He's asked about you several times."

With trepidation, Lukas bent down to look closer at Scherendingen's chalk-white face. Blood ran out of the old warrior's mouth, and he already looked like a corpse. When he recognized Lukas, however, his gaze became firmer and he seemed relieved.

"So you are alive?" he mumbled. "That's good."

"Master, I'm . . . I'm so sorry," Lukas began, but Scherendingen waved him off.

"Please, no long words. I have little time left, and there are a few things I want you to know." He groaned and sat up a bit. "A few days ago, Giovanni told me about your past."

Lukas looked up at Giovanni, who just shrugged. "You never dared to ask," Giovanni said. "I thought I could help you this way."

"Lukas von Lohenfels," Scherendingen continued, "a good name from a noble, battle-tested family, and indeed, you are worthy of it." He stopped for a moment and coughed up blood. "You know already that I was one of the Black Musketeers, a good fighter, but there was one, damn it, better than I . . ."

"You knew my father, didn't you?" Lukas asked softly.

Scherendingen nodded, his face contorted with pain. "Yes, we were comrades-in-arms. By God, I never saw a braver or more skillful warrior. He danced like the devil. You have the same talent . . . I saw it at once. Fate brought you to me so that . . ." He groaned again, and it was getting harder and harder for him to speak.

"Listen, Lukas, many years later, I saw your father again," he continued. "He told me a secret, one that has to do with your mother, and I'm sure these Spaniards believe you know something about this secret. That's the reason they are looking for you."

"But I don't know about any secret!" Lukas insisted.

Scherendingen smiled briefly. "All the better. Then you have no secret to give away, but they'll keep looking for you nevertheless."

"Who are these men?" asked Giovanni. "What do they want from Lukas?"

"They . . . are in the service of a dark figure, a former monk, who has risen through the ranks to become the grand inquisitor," Scherendingen murmured. "His name is Waldemar von Schönborn."

"Schönborn!" Lukas almost shouted as he heard the name. "That's the man who had my father killed and my mother burned at the stake!"

Scherendingen nodded gravely. "And now he's looking for you, Lukas. You must be very careful of this man. More recently he has risen to the position of father confessor to General Wallenstein. I have no idea how he found you, but if he has done it once, he'll do it again. He has resources you can't even imagine. These Spanish mercenaries . . ."

The old man started wheezing, and another stream of blood came from his mouth.

"Master, please!" Lukas took Dietmar's arm. "You mustn't die!" He looked around for help, but his friends stood aside silently as the master took his last breaths. Suddenly, Scherendingen grabbed Lukas by the hand and pulled him down until his rough lips almost touched Lukas's ear.

"Your mother . . . ," he said in a final gasp. "She was a white one. She had . . ." Then he collapsed. His body trembled one last time, and finally, he lay still.

"Master! Master!" Lukas crouched down before Scherendingen, holding his hand. The old man had become like a second father to him in the last few weeks, and now he was dead, and Lukas was responsible for his death. These Spanish mercenaries had been looking for him, and because of that, his friends had to die. Wherever he went, he brought sorrow and death. Bitter tears ran down his cheeks, mixing with Scherendingen's blood.

At last, Paulus gently pulled him away from the dead master, and Sara took him, like a mother, in her arms.

"He is now in a better place," she consoled him. "Perhaps he's already up there looking down on us, and he is proud of you. You were his best pupil."

It took a long time for Lukas's tears to dry. He sat down with the others alongside one of the burning wagons as the sun set over a devastated land. Tabea had bandaged up Yorrick as best she could, and he lay breathing heavily beside them. Lost in thought, Lukas stared at the burning wood that at one time had been their actors' wagon. Scherendingen's final words kept going through his mind.

Your mother . . . She was a white one . . .

"What is a white one?" he suddenly asked, turning around. "At the end, Dietmar called my mother a white one. What is that?"

Red Sara cleared her throat and looked down. "The final words of dying people are often strange," she began hesitantly. "We mustn't attach too great a significance to them."

Lukas could tell by looking at her that she was lying. "I want to know the truth!" he demanded. "I have a right to that. She was my mother!"

Sara sighed. "Very well. The whites are powerful witches, good witches. It's said there used to be many of them. They helped in the villages, served as midwives, and knew all about herbs and also probably magic. The Inquisition pursued them, tortured them, and burned them. The Church didn't want to believe there could also be good witches. Not many of them are still alive today, and most are hidden deep in the forest or in the mountains."

"And my mother was this kind of good witch?" Lukas asked. "A . . . white one?"

"How can I know that?" Sara shrugged. "I didn't even know her, but I do know that the white witches are still being mercilessly pursued. I myself was nearly sent to the stake once because of my red hair, and indeed my mother, who was a midwife, taught me one thing or another about witches' herbs and talismans."

"Lukas dreamed of a big black wolf," Giovanni added. "He said he actually saw it in Augsburg at the jousting field as one of the Spaniards mumbled something. Ivan, too, spoke of seeing such a wolf. For a long time I didn't think it possible . . ." He paused. "But perhaps this wolf is actually some kind of ancient magic. During my time as a novitiate, I browsed through some books in which witchcraft was condemned. They mentioned certain magical incantations."

"Nonsense," Paulus muttered. "Magic is humbug! I only believe things I can see and fight with my sword."

"It's said there are certain vapors and gases that make people sick and can even cause the plague," Giovanni replied matter-of-factly. "Can you see them, Paulus? No. But still they're there, invisible, all around us. Perhaps there's lots more out there that we simpleminded little men can't even imagine."

"That's too much for me," Jerome complained. "I know only one thing. Lukas must avoid these men, and above all this . . . what's his name, Schönborn?"

"No, I won't do that," Lukas said.

"What?" Paulus stared at him, amazed.

Lukas stuck out his chin defiantly. "I've sworn an oath to my dead mother. I shall look for my sister, Elsa, though I don't even know if she's alive, and the only one who can tell me is Waldemar von Schönborn. He took her with him back then, and I will find him and take my revenge for my dead parents, but first he will tell me where I can find Elsa."

Giovanni laughed. "And how do you think you're going to do that, you hero? You don't even know where this Schönborn is."

"Oh, yes, I do. Scherendingen told me that Waldemar von Schönborn is now the father confessor of General Wallenstein, and his army is marching now against the Swedes."

"Just a moment!" Paulus raised his hand. "So you're simply going to march into Wallenstein's camp, look for his father confessor—who is, incidentally, a mighty inquisitor, the man who's looking for you everywhere—and ask him where your sister is?"

"The last place he'll think to look for me is right where he is," Lukas responded. "Of course I won't be able to question him personally—I know that. But perhaps I'll learn something any-way." He turned to them with a piercing gaze. "This is a promise I made to my mother."

"Your dead mother," Jerome murmured.

"In any case, we won't be there to see it," one of the Jannsen Brothers said with a sigh. He pointed at the injured Yorrick. "Our brother needs help as soon as possible. We'll stay here overnight, and tomorrow we'll consider ourselves lucky if we make it safely back to Augsburg."

Red Sara, standing at his side, nodded. "I, too, will return to Augsburg with Tabea. It's much too dangerous out here for us. But there's one more thing . . ." She took out a pendant that had been well concealed until now, hanging on a leather strap around her neck. It was a silver star with five points, tarnished and blackened with age. "This is a pentagram," she told the oth-ers, "a mighty symbol my mother once gave me that will protect you from evil magic. I wear it as a talisman, but perhaps it's more than that." She handed it to Lukas. "Here, take it. You will need it now more than I do."

"Thanks," Lukas said in a soft voice, and put the talisman around his neck. "It will remind me of you always."

Now Tabea, too, came toward him. She stroked his cheek tenderly, and a warm wave seemed to pass through him. "Are you sure you don't want to come with us?" she asked hopefully. "We could start all over again, you and me . . ." She smiled. "After all, we are both dancers, in our own way."

Lukas shook his head and struggled to hold back his tears. Recently, he had become very fond of Tabea, and there had been moments when he could see them as a couple. Lukas knew that was not possible now, but as their farewell drew nearer, he wanted nothing more than to throw himself in her arms.

But what he said was "I . . . can't . . . Somewhere out there is my sister, and I must find her. I promised her that, and what happens now, only God knows."

Finally he turned to his three friends. "Thank you, as well, for everything you have done for me. I will never forget you, and—"

"Hey, what are you trying to say?" Giovanni interrupted.

"Oh, let him go ahead," Paulus grumbled. "I like these flowery farewell speeches, even if they're out of place."

"What do you mean?" Lukas asked.

"Well, did you really think we'd let you go into this lion's den all by yourself?" Jerome grinned. "We're going with you, of course. Maybe your idea is crazy, but I love crazy ideas—after all, I'm half French. Besides, there's a group in Wallenstein's army that we all admire, and I certainly intend to join them."

"The Black Musketeers," Lukas murmured.

"Jerome's right," Giovanni nodded. "Perhaps the Black Musketeers need a few crazy people in their ranks. We'll be well taken care of there." He smiled. "How does that saying go again? One for all . . ."

"And all for one," Paulus added, laughing. "I only hope there's something good to eat in Wallenstein's army. I've gotten used to eating well again."

Lukas cast a long and grateful look at each of his three friends. "So it's agreed," he said. "We'll join Wallenstein's Black Musketeers." His eyes narrowed. "And this accursed Schönborn will see what it means to pick a fight with a Lohenfels and his friends."

XIII

In the following weeks and months, the four friends wandered through a desolate land. All of Bavaria seemed destroyed, as if an enormous dragon had flown over the once so delightful countryside and had extinguished all life with its fiery breath.

Actually, summer was approaching, but there was little sign of it in the air. In the burned-out villages and cities, Lukas saw only crows and ravens gorging themselves in a gruesome feast. Corpses lay everywhere, as people were no longer able to give their families a decent burial. Those who were not slaughtered by the soldiers succumbed to hunger and disease. In some parts of Bavaria, the plague had returned, one of the worst ever, Lukas learned. There were days when the boys did not meet a single living person. Farmers' fields had become overgrown, and starving dogs growled at the travelers from the charred ruins.

Lukas didn't even want to imagine how difficult it would be now to travel alone through this devastated area. Above all, he was grateful that Giovanni, Paulus, and Jerome hadn't abandoned him. Only half a year ago, he'd been a nobody drifting aimlessly through the world, but now he had friends and knew what he had to do.

He would find his sister and avenge the death of his parents.

The comrades learned from some fleeing farmers that General Tilly had lost a major battle to the Swedes somewhere along the Lech River and had evidently been seriously wounded. A few days later, they learned of his death. Munich, Bavaria's proud royal residence city, had also fallen.

"The only one who can help now is Wallenstein," Paulus declared as they sat freezing around a small campfire in the evening. "The word is going around that he is assembling his troops in Bohemia near Eger and intends to combine forces with the Bavarian duke in order to rout the Swedes. If that's correct, we have a long trip ahead of us."

"The faster we get this horrible place behind us, the better it will be," mumbled Jerome.

As if to underline his words, a pack of hungry wolves not far away began to howl as night descended like a mask over the land.

At least the black wolf in Lukas's dreams did not return. Sometimes when he awoke early in the morning, bathed in sweat, the amulet that Red Sara had given him felt warm, almost hot. Lukas wondered if it really offered him protection from the wolf. It probably was just a piece of worthless metal, but he always wore it around his neck, especially as it reminded him of Sara and the good times with the actors.

They assumed that Wallenstein's army was quartered in the east, and the closer they got, the more Lukas forgot his earlier life. Sometimes he struggled desperately to remember the faces of his mother and father and had to admit to himself that they were fading away. His memory of Elsa was also vanishing like snow in the sun, and soon even Tabea would be nothing but a shadow.

One morning, when Lukas looked into a pool of water, the image looking back at him was an older, unfamiliar face—not that of a skinny thirteen-year-old kid, but a warrior, embittered, sinewy, and muscular, with piercing eyes.

I am no longer a child, Lukas thought.

He used to yearn for the time he would be grown up, but now, suddenly, it no longer seemed so appealing.

After many weeks of marching, they finally encountered more people. The villages were inhabited again, barley was growing knee-high in the fields, and summer had arrived in the country. Traveling journeymen told them of a mighty army of almost a hundred thousand troops gathering near Eger in Bohemia.

"Wallenstein's army," Paulus said, nodding approvingly. "There is no other that large." He broke out in a broad grin as he hastened his steps. "So now, finally, we're entering the lion's den."

Two days later, after passing over a few more hills, the friends came out of the forest and saw on the horizon a black, pulsing spot that looked like a huge, festering sore on the countryside. As they moved closer, details became visible to Lukas—first, colorful tents and the smoke of hundreds of campfires, then not long afterward, the carts and covered wagons rolled by them, full of weapons, baskets, and clattering pots and pans. Sounds came at them from every direction—drums, fiddles, fifes, occasional cannon shots, shouts, and laughter—and the air reeked of beer, liquor, gunpowder, feces, and the smells of thousands of men. Before they knew it, the four friends found themselves in the middle of the largest army encampment they'd ever seen.

"Mon dieu," said Jerome, squinting. "This army seems to go on forever! I wonder if the great Wallenstein is sitting somewhere nearby at one of the many fires, spooning his soup."

Giovanni laughed. "Certainly not. It will be a long time before we get to see the noble gentleman. It's said he travels like a prince, and his menservants even carry around a silver washtub for him. But perhaps we'll soon meet the Black Musketeers."

Lukas felt a strange excitement rising within him on hearing Giovanni's words. They had traveled so far, and now they would finally meet the heroes of his childhood, the legendary regiment in which his father once fought.

"But how are we going to find the Musketeers in this turmoil?" Paulus asked. "Should we just approach the next person to come along and politely ask?"

"Why not? You've got to be a bit pushy to get anywhere." Jerome grinned, and to the great astonishment of his friends, he turned to a group of scantily clothed women just passing by. There was a brief conversation, the girls giggled, wiggled their hips, and glanced seductively at Jerome.

"Do you have any idea who they were?" Giovanni demanded when Jerome rejoined the group. "They were—"

"Prostitutes, I know," Jerome interrupted as he bit into a fragrant sausage that one of the women had handed him. "Wherever there are mercenaries, love is for sale. The prostitutes travel with the army, and they usually know their way around better than anyone else in the camp. It was also like that in the actors' camp where my parents lived. The girls told me where to find the Black Musketeers," he said, "but they warned me, our heroes live in the worst part of the camp, with only murderers, cutthroats, and a lot of rats."

"I don't know about you, but I haven't walked three hundred miles to give up so easily," Paulus snapped back. Then he marched right off in the direction Jerome had shown them.

"Hey, wait!" Giovanni called after him. "We'll come along with you, of course!"

Together, the friends started out on a march that would take them more than an hour through the noisy, bustling army camp. By now, evening had descended. As Lukas hurried past the many campfires where soldiers had gathered to sing, play dice, and drink, he could hear a large number of different dialects and languages. In Wallenstein's army, Bavarians, Swabians, and Bohemians fought side by side, but there were also Croatians, Spaniards, Swiss, and even Frenchmen among them, all wearing the typical garb of the lansquenets, or mercenaries—slit trousers, colorful ribbons on their doublets, and beards that were unruly and untrimmed. More and more wagons had arrived, and the camp followers had settled down in front of them—the women chatting, cooking, and doing laundry while the children played with tops and homemade puppets.

"The mercenaries brought their whole family with them," Lukas remarked.

Jerome nodded. "That's the custom. The men do the killing, and the women care for their injuries. They hoard their plunder and sell it to peddlers. Their camp is like a big city." He winked at Lukas. "Life goes on, even in war."

After a while, the scene changed; Lukas thought the wagons looked dirtier, and the songs sung around the campfires sounded louder and more obscene. Drunks came careening toward them, and brawls or knife fights had broken out here and there. A number of times, Lukas could sense lustful glances that felt like little pinpricks behind his back.

"Oh-ho there! You four little doves," an old lansquenet called out as he hobbled toward them on two crutches. All that remained of his right leg was a rotted wooden stump. He grinned, showing a row of black stumps in place of teeth. "It looks like you're lost. For a *kreutzer*, I'll bring you little turtledoves unscathed to the general's tent."

"For two *kreutzers*, keep your mouth shut and take us to the Black Musketeers," Paulus retorted.

"Oh-ho! You need directions to the Musketeers?" The old man tipped his head to one side. "Such smart young lads. Why do you want to go and see them? I can cut your throat for less."

"Just do what we tell you," Giovanni replied, placing two rusty coins in the man's hand.

"Whatever you say—it's your life." The old man shrugged, then waved for the boys to follow him.

In the meantime, it had gotten dark, and shadowy figures, giggling and groaning, scurried past them; somewhere nearby, there was a shout that was suddenly muted, as if someone's throat had been slashed. The wagons here stood as close together as buildings in a city. In the muddy, feces-smeared lanes between them, other dark figures lurked, seemingly just waiting for Lukas to turn his back on them. Instinctively he placed his hand on his sword.

Abruptly the old man stopped and pointed his cane at several wagons standing in a circular formation off to one side. Behind them, a large bonfire was burning.

"Here you are, the Musketeers," he said. "But don't say I haven't warned you." He hobbled away, leaving the boys to themselves.

Paulus nodded with determination. "Well then, let's go and see if these notorious soldiers can use a few more fighters."

Leaving the wagons behind them, they strode toward the huge fire. Not until then did Lukas realize there were a number of individual campfires, each with a scruffy bunch of men sitting around them. Most of them were dressed completely in black and were wearing hats with feathers in them and bucket-top boots. A few were dancing to the beat of a bass drum while others were cheering and clapping. As the friends approached, the drumbeat stopped and the dancers looked at the uninvited guests with surprise and amusement.

"Well, who do we have here?" an especially wild-looking fellow with a shaggy beard and an eye patch demanded. "Hey, men, sharpen the butcher's knife. There's some tender young lamb chops here."

Lukas bit his lips, but strangely, he felt no fear. These were the men with whom his father and Dietmar von Scherendingen had fought. They might be coarse, but they were heroes.

Or maybe not? Lukas thought. *They don't look like heroes at all . . .*

And only then did he start to tremble a bit. To hide his fear, he turned to one of the men.

"Is this not the camp of the men called the Black Musketeers?" he asked in a firm voice.

"We sure as hell are," replied one of the mercenaries. The large man dressed in black turned to those standing around him with a grin. "And we eat pretty boys like you for breakfast. Right, men?"

"I've heard you're the best in Wallenstein's army," Lukas continued. "But perhaps I'm mistaken. All I see here is a bunch of loud, drunk fellows who are nothing to be afraid of."

"Hear, hear! The kid's getting fresh," hissed the man with the eye patch. He pulled out his sword and advanced threateningly toward Lukas. "Let's see how fresh he is when I slit him open like a little baby deer."

"Behave yourself, Wanja!" a deep voice rumbled somewhere in the crowd. "The boy is right. We're soldiers, not child beaters. So get ahold of yourself before I have to teach you some manners."

The mercenary with the eye patch flinched and finally put his sword back in its sheath. "All right, Zoltan," he mumbled. "I didn't mean it that way."

Another large man at the other end of the circle now rose to his feet. He, too, was dressed completely in black, except for a bright feather on his hat. He was over six feet tall and had broad shoulders and a full, bushy beard and bucket-top boots that reached over his knees. In contrast to his friends, he wore a doublet of precious velvet so dark it seemed it had soaked up every ray of light in the world.

If the devil ever walks among us, this is certainly the way he looks, Lukas thought.

Suddenly the man grinned, showing two rows of white teeth, and gave Lukas a friendly pat on the shoulder.

"I like it when someone shows courage," he growled. "And by God, all four of you show it, just marching in here on us Musketeers. My guards could have skewered you even before you could count to three."

"Then your guards sleep soundly," Giovanni noted dryly, "or have been enjoying some especially strong brandy. We just casually walked in."

The giant, whom the other mercenary had called Zoltan, was apparently their leader. "By God, you're probably right." He laughed. "Tomorrow morning, I'll whip their asses for that. But now I'd like to know who you four boys are."

"We are young men with no place to call home, but with our hearts in the right place and our hands on our swords," replied Giovanni in a proud tone. He bowed slightly. "We know how to use our swords and want to join your group, with your approval."

There was a long silence. Then suddenly, hearty laughter broke out among the men that only stopped when Zoltan raised his hand.

"Are you kidding?" he snapped at the boys. "Do you young pups even know who we are?"

"You are the best," Lukas replied softly, "the Black Musketeers, and for this reason, we want to join you, and no other regiment."

Zoltan shook his head. "You've got a lot of spirit, I'll grant you that, or perhaps it's just stupidity." He looked with contempt at the weapons the four friends were carrying. "You probably think that just because you're carrying a sword, you're all grown-up."

"We can fight!" Jerome answered angrily, taking out his rapier. "Would you like me to prove it, monsieur?"

Zoltan laughed and stepped back a pace. "Help! I'm being attacked by a little Frenchman!" he cried in an anxious falsetto. But then he turned serious. "Listen to me, I'm the commander of this regiment, and I'm telling you again we can't use you. We already have enough porters, so get the hell out before—"

In one quick movement Lukas drew his Pappenheim sword and slashed at the man standing beside Zoltan. There was a rasping sound, a brief gasp, then a large X appeared on the man's doublet.

Lukas had acted rashly, driven by anger and disappointment. Here he stood among the very men his father had fought with, and now the heroes of his childhood revealed themselves as drunken, uncouth characters—no better than robbers and vagabonds. To be ridiculed by them was more than he could take.

"You miserable worm!" the mercenary in the torn doublet shouted, striding toward Lukas. "Just for that—"

But Zoltan held him back. "Wait," he growled. "That was just a lucky blow, nothing more. Now, it's time for you to learn your lesson, all four of you. Karl, Kaspar, Max, Gottfried!" he called out into the darkness. Now four pimply hulks came shuffling over from a neighboring campfire. They were around sixteen years old, all with a dark fuzz around their lips and a rolling, confident gait that promised nothing good. They grinned broadly when they saw the four friends.

"These are our menservants," Zoltan explained. "Steeled in battle, they know all the tricks. They haven't been pampered like you. Kaspar!" He turned to the tallest of the four young men, who was already cracking his knuckles. "Beat these guys up. No sharp weapons, just fists and sticks. I don't want to see any blood, at least not too much. Show these little puppies that the Musketeers are not to be trifled with."

In a few moments, the Black Musketeers had formed a ring around the four boys. The friends had to give up their weapons in exchange for roughly cut willow sticks about six feet long. On the opposite side of the arena stood the four menservants, who were already swinging their own sticks menacingly through the air. Laughter and an occasional hurrah could be heard from the other side of the ring.

"Well, you got us in a fine mess!" Giovanni whispered to Lukas. "We can count ourselves lucky they didn't run us through right away."

"Oh, don't make such a fuss," Paulus argued as he tried out his pole, which was several inches thick. "Lukas defended our honor. We should thank him for that. Besides, we haven't been in a good brawl for a long time."

"Do you have any idea what my waistcoat cost?" Jerome mumbled. "To say nothing of my new fustian shirt. Once this is all over, I'll no doubt have to buy myself a new wardrobe." He grinned impishly. "But who cares? I've never avoided a good fight, and these fellows really deserve one!"

"Very well." Giovanni sighed. "Then let's get it over with." He was carefully sizing up their opponents, and Lukas saw that Giovanni, as usual, already had a plan in mind. He pointed at the heaviest of the four, a sturdy bull-necked fellow called Gottfried. "Paulus, you get the fat guy, I'll take the redhead who's looking over at me so eagerly, and Jerome and Lukas can take the other two. The first one finished will come to help the rest."

As they slowly approached their opponents, Lukas cursed himself again for having irritated Zoltan so much. The four men-servants looked far more dangerous than the usual farm boys he'd always beaten in the past in stick fights. But then Lukas concentrated on what his father and Dietmar had taught him, remembering the words of the old warrior in one of their many practice bouts.

If you hold the stick properly, it can be a sword, a rapier, and a shield, all at the same time, Lukas—a dangerous weapon. Don't underestimate it . . .

Everything happened very fast. Kaspar charged Lukas, shouting and swinging his stick. From the corner of one eye, Lukas saw his friends also face off against their opponents; then came the attack, followed by loud bawling and shouting from outside the arena.

Kaspar lunged, and Lukas stepped aside, then used his willow stick just as his father had taught him years ago. He grabbed it in the middle so that he could attack or defend with either end. First Lukas parried Kaspar's blow from above. His opponent was almost two heads taller than he was, and the blow fell heavily, aimed at Lukas's hands. Lukas delivered a blow from the side. Kaspar shouted with pain when Lukas struck his upper arm, but it only made him angrier, and he attacked with even greater fury. Lukas dodged again, and now used the stick as a stabbing weapon like a rapier. For a brief moment, Kaspar was unprotected, and when Lukas struck him right in the ribs, he staggered and fell backward. Lukas stood over him, gasping, while Kaspar lay on the ground, whimpering.

"I . . . can't breathe," Kaspar panted. "Please help me get up."

Lukas was holding out his hand to help when he was struck straight in the face by a handful of dirt. Kaspar had secretly scooped up some dirt and stones from the ground and tossed them at Lukas! With a sneer, Kaspar scrambled back up onto his feet and rained down a number of painful blows on Lukas. Again, Lukas thought of what his father had told him on his thirteenth birthday.

In a battle, nothing is ever fair . . . It's only about who wins.

Evidently, there were a few things he still had to learn.

Lukas stumbled backward, half blinded, while the blows kept raining down on him. He had already reached the edge of the arena, where the jeering mercenaries awaited him. Blood and dirt were running down his face, and his left arm hurt horribly from Kaspar's blows.

Lukas remembered one of the tricks his father had shown him many years ago in the forest. He quickly fell to the ground, avoiding the blows from above, then swung his stick around in a wide arc. It was a bold move. If Kaspar could ward off this attack, he'd be able to beat his defenseless opponent black-and-blue as he lay on the ground. But Lukas's blow caught the tall, slender boy right in the back of his knee, and with a surprised shout, Kaspar fell to one side. Lukas hit him on his hands, and Kaspar's stick clattered to the ground. Again, Lukas's opponent looked at him with wide, helpless eyes, but this time, Lukas wasn't going to fall for the trick. He raised his stick and—

"Stop! Enough!"

It was Zoltan's voice. For the first time since the battle had started, Lukas raised his head, gasping for breath, and regarded his surroundings. The three other menservants were also lying in the dirt, their sticks broken. Giovanni was bleeding from the forehead but could manage a smile. Jerome and Paulus were gripping their sticks, panting. Then Lukas noticed that a tense silence had settled over the mercenaries.

"You did far better than I expected," Zoltan conceded. "It appears you are really able to fight. So then . . ." He hesitated.

"That means . . . we have been accepted?" Lukas managed to say, panting hard.

Zoltan grinned. "Why not? Our own menservants aren't of much use to us now. They'll be lucky if they can walk again in a few days. Will you take their places in the meantime, as a test, so to speak? And then we'll see who stays, you or the others. Agreed?"

Lukas looked down at his beaten opponent, who, despite his wretched condition, glared back. His earlier helpless gaze had completely vanished.

"Don't think for a minute you can push us out!" Kaspar whispered to him. "I'm going to kill you, kid, the first chance I get."

"Well, if you're going to do that, first you'll have to stand up," Lukas whispered back. He stared at the manservant with contempt, and Kaspar stared back for a while, furious, and then looked away. Lukas couldn't help thinking of the treacherous Marek of the Blood Wolves or the Spanish mercenary in the forest around the castle, and all the farm boys who had enjoyed tormenting him when he was a child. All that was long ago, an eternity, it seemed.

Now he was a warrior.

He raised his head and looked the leader of the Black Musketeers straight in the eye.

"Agreed," he said.

Zoltan pounded Lukas so firmly on his chest that he almost fell backward. The laughter of the huge man thundered across the clearing in the light of the campfire.

"Then welcome to the Musketeers! With us, you'll ride straight to hell and beyond."

XIV

It took only a few days for Lukas to realize that the life of a man-servant was nothing like that of a soldier.

As the youngest in the regiment, the four comrades had to perform the most menial and strenuous jobs. They emptied the stinking latrine pits, took care of the horses, purchased worm-eaten meat and rotten vegetables from the traveling merchants, and every morning, they were the first to get up to stoke the fire and set the heavy cooking pot on the rusty trivet. Any slight delay was punished with extra shifts and more work.

"Damn, this isn't what I thought life would be like as a feared Black Musketeer," Paulus groaned while they dug up another latrine pit near the camp. "Digging holes in the ground for Zoltan's butt! If this continues, I'm going to drown the next mercenary I see in his own excrement."

"You mustn't be so impatient," Giovanni admonished him. "We're still waiting for reinforcements from the Bavarian elector. When they arrive in Eger, we'll attack the Swedes." He grinned. "That will be the end of this cozy camp life."

"Cozy camp life? Don't make me laugh." Jerome wiped the dirt from his forehead and thrust the spade deeper into the ground. "There's not one pretty girl among the Musketeers, only a few old hags, and my shirt smells like a shroud." He sighed. "Zoltan was telling the truth when he welcomed us. This is really how I imagine hell to be."

Lukas, too, had finally reached the end of his rope. He hadn't been able even once to leave the Musketeers' camp in order to look around at other places in the huge army encampment. Where was Wallenstein's headquarters? And those of his officers? Was the inquisitor Waldemar von Schönborn hiding out anywhere nearby? Above all, how could he learn more about his sister's whereabouts? Those were all questions for which Lukas had no answer. But he knew only too well how to dig up a latrine for an entire regiment and groom a dozen mud-covered warhorses in record time.

At least the last few days had given him the chance to learn more about the legendary Black Musketeers—their vulgarity, drinking, and loud boasting had at first put him off, but then he observed them in their mock battles with the longsword, battle-ax, knife, and dagger. Each was a superb fighter. In addition, they knew how to handle the newer muskets—deadly firearms that were nearly six feet long, from which the Musketeers took their name. In battle, most of them fought on foot, man to man, and armed to the teeth. The black clothing made them almost invisible at night, and during the day, they recognized one another from some distance.

I wonder if my father also wore a black doublet like that, Lukas thought. *Did he drink and laugh with these men? Or did he stay more or less in the background, like this silent fellow, Zoltan?*

Since their first meeting, Lukas had spoken only a few words with the regiment commander and had always avoided telling Zoltan anything about his past. He didn't want to be considered a pampered son of nobility, and besides, he couldn't trust anyone. Lukas didn't know if Waldemar von Schönborn was staying at the camp. He had to keep his presence a secret from the inquisitor.

"Turn around carefully," Giovanni suddenly whispered, tearing Lukas from his musings. "I think there's a lot of trouble coming our way."

"Aha!" Paulus grumbled. "The four with the pimply faces. Evidently they're able to get around again after our last little rendezvous."

Lukas looked cautiously to the side and saw the four other menservants approaching. At first, the friends had been able to avoid them, especially since Karl, in particular, and fat Gottfried had barely been able to stand up after the stick fight. In the meantime, they seemed to have recovered. Their eyes flashed with naked hatred.

"Well, just look at this," hissed Kaspar, who still had a shining black-and-blue eye from the blows Lukas gave him. He was pointing at the freshly cleaned latrine pit. "The little pups are shoveling their own grave. So much the better. Then we won't have to do it."

"Watch your mouth if you want to keep your teeth," Paulus replied. He was the only one of the four friends taller than Kaspar. He picked up his shovel and waved it threateningly in his big hands. "We have no quarrel with you, and it also wasn't our wish to fight you—so leave us alone."

"Calm down, brother," said Kaspar, raising his hand. "We just wanted to make you a fair offer. Just listen, it's very simple. We'll forget what happened between us, and in return, pack up your things and leave by morning, or—"

"Or what?" Jerome responded.

"Otherwise, I'd recommend that one of you is always standing guard at night." Kaspar bared his rapacious teeth. "Or it could be that you don't wake up."

"You wouldn't dare!" Giovanni snarled. "Everyone would know you had something to do with it. Zoltan would make short work of any cutthroats in his own regiment."

Kaspar seemed to be considering this. "Is that your final answer? Think it over. That's our last and only offer."

He signaled to his three friends, and with one final smirk, they turned to leave.

"Hey, Kaspar!" Paulus called after them. "Nice black eye you have. Goes very well with your pimples. And, Gottfried, your ass is fatter than the one on Wallenstein's horse!"

When the menservants had disappeared, Lukas looked around anxiously. "Do you think they're serious?

Jerome waved him off. "Oh, they're just talking nonsense. A little brawl? I can imagine that. But murder? They don't dare try that."

Giovanni frowned. "It's possible. In any case, we'd better be careful." With a sigh, he thrust his spade into the ground. "Now let's just finish shoveling this damned hole before Zoltan makes us dig up all the other latrines as a punishment."

A week would go by before they were able to leave, but finally the Bavarian soldiers caught up with them, and the enormous army marched off together toward Franconia to engage the Swedes.

Like a monstrous, fat caterpillar, Wallenstein's army moved through the countryside—tens of thousands of soldiers, hundreds of wagons, neighing horses, women carrying backpacks full of pots, whining children, blacksmiths, cooks, merchants, even a beer brewer and a tavern keeper. This caterpillar was many miles long and consumed everything it came in contact with.

Wherever they went, they found abandoned villages—both people and livestock had fled. Lukas quickly learned that even here in friendly territory, the soldiers were regarded not as friends, but as enemies. Individual units spread out to the nearby towns and villages to steal grain, meat, and wine—contributions, they called it, but for the villagers it was simply theft—and left them to starve.

In the evening, when they sat around the campfire, the soldiers told stories about the war. Some had done nothing but fight all their lives and were proud to be members of the Black Musketeers, a regiment that for hundreds of years produced the best soldiers. They had fought even back in the times of the knights, before muskets were used, always beholden to the sovereign who offered the best pay. Sometimes it seemed to Lukas that Zoltan watched the boys closely on these evenings, as if searching for something in his memory.

Or someone, Lukas thought.

He still didn't dare to ask the commander about his father, since he had no idea if Schönborn might be somewhere nearby. To find out, he'd have to briefly leave the Musketeers regiment, but there was much too much work here for him to do that.

His chance came as a surprise after about two weeks on the march. Zoltan himself ordered Lukas to come to his tent that evening. At first Lukas thought he had done something wrong, but Zoltan got right to the point. He was holding a sealed letter in his hand, which he gave to Lukas.

"This is a report for the commander in chief of the army," he said abruptly. "It must be brought to him as quickly as possible. You will do that for me. Do you know how to ride?"

Lukas nodded silently, hoping that Zoltan didn't notice how he was trembling with excitement.

"Then you can ask Wanja to give you a horse from the stable," said the commander, who had already turned to work on another message and was no longer paying attention to Lukas. "If you leave immediately, you should be back in one hour, or two at most. Wallenstein's barracks are south of the main road, around three miles from here. Did you understand everything?"

"You . . . you mean I should personally hand the letter to the great general?" Lukas replied.

Zoltan looked up and smiled. "Of course not. I hardly believe that Wallenstein has time for a simple servant like you. You will hand over the letter at the entrance to the barracks. And Lukas"— the commander looked at him sternly—"don't do anything stupid. I chose you from the servants because . . ." He hesitated briefly. "Because I trust you. But if this letter doesn't arrive or the seal is broken, I'll skin you alive. Understand?"

It was now the middle of summer, and the evening sun cast its warm light over the surrounding vineyards. For the first time in a long while, Lukas felt lighthearted and happy. His worries seemed only half as bad as he trotted along on his horse. He could scarcely believe how lucky he was. He might soon learn more about Schönborn and Elsa! Even if he didn't meet Wallenstein personally, at least he would be close to him. And surely he'd think of something when he got there.

After about half an hour, Lukas saw on his left the standards of the supreme army command flying atop a little hill—a red lion on a blue background, Wallenstein's coat of arms. Lukas dismounted and led his horse to a circle of small tents where several guards armed with halberds were on patrol.

"What do you want?" growled one of the soldiers.

Lukas replied briefly and produced the sealed letter.

"I'll deliver the message for you," the soldier replied gruffly. "Hand it over."

"I am instructed to deliver it personally to the general," Lukas stressed, and tried to look desperate. "If I don't, the commander will rip my head off, as sure as I am standing here."

The guard sighed. "All right then, boy. Leave your horse here and come along."

With relief, Lukas tied the horse alongside some others and followed the soldier. He had achieved what he wanted! Within the ring of tents stood a massive, rough-hewn barracks. Lukas stopped in amazement. It appeared that Wallenstein's soldiers built a new house for their general every evening. But then Lukas noticed that four wheels were attached to the building's wooden foundation. Evidently, it was some sort of wagon that could be turned into a house very quickly. Here, too, guards were on patrol.

"You're in the right place," said his guide, pointing to the standard flying next to the barracks. "So don't worry, you've carried out your order."

He took the letter from Lukas and went to the front of the building, where he knocked gently. Someone replied, and he entered.

That was the moment Lukas had been waiting for. He looked around carefully, then, trying to look as inconspicuous as possible, strolled around to the back of the barracks, where no guards were posted. Some tiny windows, not any larger than loopholes, were set in the back wall. It had become so dark that Lukas would be hard to see by any soldier walking by.

After one last glance in both directions, he sneaked up to one of the windows and peered inside. In the flickering light of a lantern, a few men were sitting around a large round table covered with maps. The guard was just delivering the letter and took his leave with a final, deep bow. Judging from their dress, the other men were all high-ranking officers. One of them was older and extremely gaunt. With his thin goatee, a face that shone almost yellow in the lantern light, and eyes that flashed impatiently, he radiated an aura of overbearing severity.

"If the Swedish king thinks he can sneak away and hide like a rat in his hole, then we'll have to catch him beforehand," the older man said in a rasping voice. He unfolded the letter and briefly examined its contents. "Now listen to this. Our dear Zoltan has sent us this report," he murmured. "His agents also report that King Gustav Adolf is heading for the free city of Nürnberg to await reinforcements there. We must therefore get ready to leave as quickly as possible and go there ourselves first thing in the morning, gentlemen! Deliver this message to your regiments."

Lukas was stunned. The man who had just spoken was clearly Wallenstein himself. But Lukas could not recognize the familiar face of the grand inquisitor Waldemar von Schönborn among the other attendees. That was probably too much to hope. Dietmar von Scherendingen had told him that Schönborn was Wallenstein's father confessor. Where would such a high-ranking cleric be staying in the army encampment?

Or was the old sword master perhaps mistaken? Lukas wondered. *What if—*

"Oh-ho, who do we have here? It seems I've got my hands on the newest Swedish spy."

Lukas's blood froze as someone grabbed him by the collar and roughly pulled him away from the window. Scared to death, he found himself looking into the face of a young man with a stylishly twirled goatee. He wore the cape of a nobleman and beneath that a robe that appeared clerical. Lukas considered kicking the man in the shins and trying to escape, but then he changed his mind. Guards were on patrol all around him. It was very likely he'd get caught, and then something much worse, probably put to death.

"Ex . . . excuse me, sir," he managed to say, trying to sound as innocent as possible. "I just wanted to see the great General Wallenstein for once with my own eyes. My friends say he wears a doublet of gold."

The man grinned and loosened his grip a bit on Lukas's collar. "And does he wear a golden doublet?"

Lukas shook his head. "No, sir, but he looks like a very powerful man."

"Above all, a very, very strict man," the other replied. "Don't you think so? What do you think he'd do with a young lad eavesdropping on one of his secret conferences?"

"Please, my lord!" Lukas shed a few tears, which was not especially difficult for him in view of how terrified he was. "Don't turn me in! I really meant no harm."

"Hmm . . ." The man twirled his waxed beard and stared at Lukas for a long time. He was about thirty years old, but his confident appearance made him look a few years older. The most threatening thing about him was his penetrating black eyes that seemed to bore right into Lukas's soul. "There is something strange about you, I can feel it," he finally said. "But still your deepest soul remains hidden from me. Extremely interesting. What's your name?"

"Lukas," he replied, trembling, still feeling the man's gaze under his skin, like probing fingers. "I'm . . . a servant in the Black Musketeers regiment sent here to deliver a message."

"Aha." The man nodded. "From the Musketeers, you say? I had no idea that these swordsmen have children like you in their ranks."

"As I said, I'm only a servant there," Lukas replied, breaking out in a cold sweat. "I dig holes for the latrines, comb the horses, things like that . . . In wartime, I beat the drums."

"And you're the first to die in the front line." The man sighed. "Children shouldn't be allowed in battle. It's dreadful for each of you lads."

In any case, he seemed to have accepted Lukas's explanation and released his grip while continuing to look him over.

"What sign were you born under?" he asked suddenly.

Lukas looked at him. "Eh . . . sign? I . . . don't understand—"

"I'd guess Leo," the man interrupted. "Leo or Sagittarius. With Gemini ascendant, or Virgo . . . That would explain some of the mystery. Or . . ." When he saw Lukas's confused expression, he laughed. "Excuse me, that's a hobby of mine. My name is Giovanni Battista Senno. I am Wallenstein's astrologer and read the stars for him."

"Are you some kind of magician?" Lukas said without thinking.

Senno shook his head with amusement. "Oh God, no! Though there are men who might in fact look at me as a magician. There is much that I know that will always be hidden from ordinary mortals, and among that are surely things you would consider magic."

"Such as white magic?" Lukas asked. He bit his tongue, as the words had slipped out before he'd given it any thought.

"White magic?" Senno now looked at him with great interest. "Are you talking about white witches? What do you know about that?"

"Oh, nothing. I heard about it once, that's all."

"Then it's best to keep your knowledge to yourself," the astrologer replied darkly. "There are people who would torture and burn you just for saying those words."

Lukas decided to put all his bets on one card. "You mean people like Waldemar von Schönborn, Wallenstein's father confessor? You . . . are not going to turn me over to him, are you?"

"Should I?" Senno looked at him for a long while, thinking. "And how do you know Schönborn?"

"Well, uh . . . lots of stories go around in the camp. Schönborn is said to make short shrift of heretics and Protestants, a true supporter of the faith—"

"If you continue like that, lad, you're risking your neck," Senno interrupted in a threatening voice. "First there was your nonsense about white witches, and now you're even gossiping about the grand inquisitor of the pope. It's lucky for you that Waldemar von Schönborn hasn't arrived at the camp yet. He has his eyes and ears everywhere." He gave Lukas a bump on the nose. "And now leave quickly before I change my mind."

Lukas hurried away, but even while he was running, he thought he could feel the astrologer's gaze like prickling needles in his back. From now on he'd better be on guard. But he'd learned that Schönborn was, in fact, Wallenstein's father confessor and that he hadn't arrived in the camp yet.

Lukas could feel, however, that the day was not far off when they would meet.

Deep in thought, he mounted his horse again and rode back to the camp of the Black Musketeers.

XV

In the following days, they rushed toward Nürnberg at a brisk pace, covering up to thirty miles a day. It seemed as if the weather had conspired against them. Now, of all times, the sun burned down mercilessly, and the brooks at the side of the road had dried up or were polluted. Lukas's tongue dried out from thirst until it felt like a piece of leather. But Zoltan showed them no mercy, either. No one in the regiment received more than a pouch of foul-tasting water a day, not even the commander.

On the night after his mission to Wallenstein's camp, Lukas told his friends of his conversation with Senno, and also that he had listened in on Wallenstein and his officers. Jerome, especially, was horrified to hear that.

"*Mon dieu*, spying on the supreme commander could have cost you your life, do you realize that?" he said, shaking his head. "And then this conversation with Senno! Can you be sure he's not going to tell Waldemar von Schönborn about you?"

"You idiot," Giovanni replied. "Thanks to Lukas, we know that Schönborn isn't even in the camp. And even if he were . . ."

Senno only knows Lukas's first name. For him, Lukas was probably nothing more than a curious servant boy."

"I wouldn't trust one bit this would-be magician and astrologer," Paulus said, furrowing his brow. "A few of the men here have told me about him, and it wasn't good. He's looking only for his own advantage, and takes every opportunity to endear himself to Wallenstein. Lukas should be more careful in the future."

Hour after hour, every day, the four friends struggled along the dusty road with the army, hemmed in on all sides by wagons, marching soldiers, and horses.

After a forced march of almost a week, they were crushed to learn that all their efforts had been in vain. Before them lay the proud city of Nürnberg, one of the greatest cities in the Reich, but even from a distance, it was evident that the Swedes had arrived some time ago and had set up mighty fortifications around it. High mud walls surrounded the city in a zigzag pattern, as well as moats, freshly built trenches, and palisades armed with spikes. Behind the city battlements, the helmets of the defenders sparkled in the hot light of the midday sun.

"Damn!" Giovanni cursed. "Now we're facing a long siege, and with this heat! We'll wither up like fish on dry land."

But Wallenstein had no pity for his soldiers. On the contrary, he drove them even harder. The very day of their arrival, his besieging forces set up camp a few miles away. Only a few of the soldiers had picks and shovels, and others had to make do with shards of pottery and their bare hands. In front of the trenches the Swedes had built more than ten miles of fences and walls of brushwood. Lukas had never seen such extensive fortifications, built in just a few days by hand.

During their hot, arduous work, the four friends kept bumping into Kaspar and the other servants, who stared at them angrily and cursed under their breath as they passed by, but Jerome was probably right—they were too cowardly to stage a nighttime attack.

"I knew those guys just had loud mouths," said Paulus as they excavated a new trench with six-foot-high walls. But Lukas was not so sure of that.

Zoltan had decided to continue using Lukas as a messenger in the far-flung encampment, but this time on foot, as the horses were needed elsewhere. None of the errands were to Wallenstein's headquarters, however, which lay far to the south, and so Lukas made no progress at all in his search for Schönborn.

In the second week, Lukas again encountered the court astrologer Senno, who was trotting along the freshly dug fortifications on his handsome white horse. When the astrologer noticed Lukas amid all the commotion, he raised his hand in a friendly gesture and beckoned for him to come closer.

"Ah, the lad who's the servant to the Musketeers," he exclaimed cheerfully. "The stars told me we would meet a second time. It appears you have been allowed to leave your regiment again." He smiled. "Or did I catch you spying once more?"

Lukas shook his head. "No, no, sir! I only deliver messages—that's all."

"Very well, then I want you to take a message for me. Come on, that's an order!"

He directed Lukas to mount his horse behind him, and they rode a short way until they were close to the highest hill in the camp. Before them was a single round tent that stood out from the others, looking like a temple from the Orient with its shimmering blue and black colors.

"My home," Senno said, jumping down from the horse. "Come in, it will be easier for us to talk there."

Lukas followed, hesitantly. When Senno pushed aside the tent flap, Lukas stepped in, and what he saw took his breath away. On the walls hung silken flags covered with strange characters, patterns, and animal symbols. Spheres of many sizes hanging on thin, almost invisible threads circled the room near the ceiling, and a table in the middle of the tent was covered with scrolls and colorfully executed documents with zodiacal signs and endless columns of numbers. Among all of these were odd-looking measuring instruments of copper and silver.

Senno noticed Lukas's astonishment and smiled. "It may sound strange to you, almost like magic, but I need all of that for my astrological predictions. This is the only way I'm able to produce the horoscopes the way Wallenstein needs them. Please take a seat."

He pointed to a stool in front of the table, and he himself took a seat on the other side. Only now did Lukas notice a half-empty bowl of meat and bread, which exuded an irresistible aroma.

"Help yourself," said Senno. "You must be hungry."

In fact, for the last three days, Lukas had received only a tiny daily ration of bread and a few wormy apples. He'd hardly been able to sleep due to the gnawing hunger. He pounced on the offering, and silence fell over the room for the next few minutes.

When Lukas had finally finished, Senno pushed the dish to the side with an impatient gesture in order to have a closer look at his guest, examining him with his deep, black eyes.

"What is the message you want me to deliver?" Lukas asked nervously after a while.

Senno waved him off. "Never mind. I only wanted to have a quiet conversation with you—above all, about this here." He pointed at Lukas's talisman still hanging on a cord around his neck. Lukas had completely forgotten the pentagram.

Sometimes it had a hot feel to it, but he attributed that to the summer heat. His dreams of the big black wolf had not recurred, and the more they receded into the past, the more unreal they seemed to Lukas.

"I noticed this amulet of yours the last time," Senno persisted. "Where did you get it?"

"A friend of my deceased mother gave it to me a long time ago," Lukas lied. "It's supposed to protect me from evil. I know that's nonsense, but I just thought it looked nice, so I kept it."

"May I have a look at it?"

Lukas handed the talisman to Senno, who examined it closely, and finally gave it back.

"There's a lot of nonsense going around regarding magic," Senno said. "Every charlatan nowadays makes amulets, but this pentagram, in fact, shows all the signs of having genuine magic powers." He studied Lukas suspiciously, and again Lukas thought he could feel the magician's fingers reaching into his inmost self. "Would you like to tell me more?" the astrologer continued. "At our first meeting you spoke of white magic . . . and now this talisman around your neck . . ."

"Perhaps you could first tell me more about who these white magicians are," Lukas suggested.

"Ah, then a deal." Senno sighed. "Very well." After a short pause, he began. "When you asked me if I was a magician, I . . . well, let's say I fibbed a bit. I know some things about magic—that's part of my job—and I have learned a few things, as well. But it's nothing compared to what the white magicians can do."

"Who are these white magicians?" Lukas asked excitedly. He felt he was finally on the trail of his mother's secret. "Do they really exist?"

"Once, long ago, even before the Romans conquered these lands, there were some people who possessed knowledge that reached far back to the dawn of civilization," Senno said in a soft voice. "These people were called druids, and they had knowledge of what we would today call magic." He smiled slightly. "You shouldn't think of that as blazing balls of fire or magic spells that change kings into toads. They were actually small things. The druids knew how to make dried-up wells flow again, to cure diseases that were otherwise incurable, and to speak with one another in a way that others could not hear."

Lukas was startled. Those were all abilities people attributed to his mother, or ones he had observed himself.

"When the Romans conquered these lands, they pursued the druids mercilessly and killed them wherever they found them," Senno continued. "They knew that with the disappearance of the druids, the power of the native, indigenous peoples would die. Only a few druids survived. They hid in remote mountain valleys and impenetrable forests, and there were some among them who swore eternal vengeance. Others continued to believe in the good and refused to let themselves be torn apart by hatred. Because of this dispute, they finally went their separate ways, and since then, their beliefs and practices have been called black magic and . . ."

"White." Lukas nodded. "I understand. And this talisman is imbued with white magic?"

"So it is. A mighty protective sign." Senno leaned toward him and lowered his voice. "I am open to these matters, but unfortunately the Church sees things differently, so you must be careful."

"Do you mean I must beware of Schönborn?" Lukas asked.

Senno looked at him with piercing eyes. "So it is, even though for reasons other than you perhaps suspect."

The astrologer's last words were enigmatic, but Lukas had no chance to ask, as now Senno approached him so closely that their faces nearly touched. Lukas smelled some sweet, exotic perfume that made him somewhat dizzy.

"I sense you are hiding a deep secret inside you, Lukas," Senno murmured. "It is there, clearly, before me, but I can't grasp it. Don't you really want to tell me more, lad? Perhaps I can help you."

Lukas hesitated. Could he trust Senno? Many considered the astrologer a dubious character who would leave nothing untried that might work to his advantage. And how did he know Senno didn't work for Schönborn? Lukas thought about it for a while and decided to respond with a question.

"If what I'm holding here is white magic," he said, stroking the amulet, "then what is black magic?"

Clearly disappointed, Senno fell back in his chair. "There are many types," the astrologer replied. "Black magic can be used to conjure up illnesses, to make a woman sterile, or to set fire to a house many miles away. With other spells you can make silver bullets that never miss, or make yourself invulnerable."

"Invulnerable?" Lukas echoed. "In other words, you could not die in battle?"

Senno shrugged. "Probably just a legend, but there's a story circulating among the troops now about a potion that offers protection from bullets and sword blows. *Frozen* is what men call it. A frozen man has sold his soul to the devil, so he cannot be killed."

Lukas shivered. "A horrible idea," he said. "Then I'd rather be dead."

Senno laughed. "Don't say that. Most people would give anything to save their wretched life. But each of us is just a tiny dot in the universe," he said as he rose. "Well, it's a shame you won't stick to our deal and tell me more, but unlike an inquisitor, I don't have the rack at my disposal." He winked. "Not that I would use it with you." He motioned toward the door. "Perhaps you'll think it over. My tent is always open to you. But for now I must continue my work on the horoscope for the upcoming battle, because you can be sure of this, Lukas, this battle will come, and woe to those who stand on the side of the loser."

XVI

Two weeks would pass before Lukas saw his first great battle.

The Swedes remained holed up in their fortifications for the time being, but Wallenstein's spies sent reports of terrible conditions in the city. Weakened by hunger and disease, Nürnberg's beleaguered residents were dying by the thousands, and often the many dead had to be stacked up like firewood because there was no room left for the graves.

At the end of August, the Swedes finally tried to break out. For an entire day, they attacked Wallenstein's position in the west, but were soon repelled. Lukas knew that the real battle was yet to come. Until then, he had only been hauling munitions with the other servants, and caring for the horses, but the time was coming when he would have to fight and kill to save his own life.

The horror began early on the morning of September 3.

Wallenstein expected the main attack once again on the flat west side of the fortification, where the bulk of his own troops were already in position. The regiment of the Black Musketeers stood guard at the remote northern section. Here, a long, partially deforested ridge led up to the top, where a ruin of an ancient fortified tower stood. Morning fog still lay peacefully over the valley, and no one expected a major attack here, at the steepest part of the encampment.

"I'll tell you this—as soon as the battle begins, I'll throw away this battered dice box and charge into the fray," vowed Paulus, who was standing with his other friends at the top of the leading wall, his arms propped on his drum. Zoltan had ordered the servants to beat the drums furiously to provide the necessary atmosphere—a job that Paulus did grudgingly. "I'm born to be a fighter and not a musician," he grumbled.

"A truer word was never spoken," Jerome replied. "Your drumming is so off beat that it gives me hiccups every time. If you keep drumming like that when we're in battle, you'll make our whole company fall flat on our asses."

It was supposed to be a joke, but none of the boys laughed. The situation was too tense, and the fear of dying in the coming battle or being crippled by gunfire was too great. Lukas could feel his heart pounding. This was no longer a nice exhibition fight or fake skirmish in a marketplace; this was war, and none of them could say whether he'd live to see the evening.

"Look over at the next trench," said Giovanni, nodding slightly to the west where further fortifications were concealed in the forest. "Kaspar and his friends are beating the drums. I don't know, from the way they're staring at us, who our greatest enemy is—the Swedes over there or the soldiers in our own camp."

Lukas bit his lip.

Perhaps the situation would remain relatively calm in their section, but if the turmoil of the upcoming battle got out of hand, would Kaspar really dare to exploit the situation in order to get rid of them?

Early that morning, they'd all made their confession to a priest for what might be the last time. Many of the common soldiers also made the sign of the cross or spoke a brief prayer. Others murmured as they rubbed talismans that hung around their necks or on their wide-brimmed hats. Lukas, too, reached for the amulet that Red Sara had given him. He wondered if Senno had been telling the truth about the power of the pentagram. Lukas hadn't told his friends much about his last conversation with the astrologer. All the stories he'd heard about so-called white witches, good magic, and evil magic seemed bizarre in retrospect. He was afraid of looking foolish in front of the others.

A thundering cannon shot made him jump. He could see that on the other side of the hill, long rows of Swedish musketeers and pikemen were moving toward them. They'd been concealed in the morning fog until then, but now they stormed up the mountain. There were so many that the end of the line was out of sight—a black, surging crowd moving toward the first fortifications.

This is the main army! Lukas realized. *We are being attacked by the main army!*

"These crazy dogs are really attacking up the mountain!" roared Zoltan from the front line. "Send a message to Wallenstein, and then receive them the way they deserve!"

The imperial soldiers shouted their response, but whether it was one of anger or fear, Lukas couldn't say. The ones in the front line started loading their muskets, while others rolled the cannons onto their bases as the Swedes moved closer and closer. The hair on the back of Lukas's neck stood on end.

The battle had begun.

Along with a few other companies, the Black Musketeers were stationed at the outer wall, which fell off steeply into the valley. A trench lined with pointed stakes had been dug in front of them. The Musketeers' well-known banner served as point of reference—a black dragon with flames spewing from its wide-open mouth. This flag was as large as a ship's sail and fluttered in the morning breeze.

What thoughts were going through my father's head just before a battle like this? Lukas wondered as shivers ran through his body. *Was he afraid, too?*

"All together against death and the devil!" Zoltan roared suddenly, raising his sword.

The Musketeers loudly returned their eternal battle cry: "To hell and beyond!" Lukas, Giovanni, Jerome, and Paulus all joined in the response, making Lukas feel not quite so lonely and wretched.

What followed next was an earsplitting thunder as the cannons before and behind Lukas were fired. The noise was so loud that after a few moments he was sure he'd gone deaf. Then he heard a strange, high-pitched whistling in the air.

"Take cover!" shouted Paulus alongside him. "Incoming cannon fire!"

Instinctively, Lukas threw himself against the muddy base of the wall, and just moments later a twenty-pound cannonball flew by overhead. It landed somewhere behind them, followed by piercing screams. When Lukas turned briefly, all he saw was red chaos, clumps of earth, and severed limbs. The cannonball had made a breach in their lines like a reaper through a wheat field. He threw up.

"Return to your positions!" Zoltan commanded.

Lukas was still lying at the bottom of the trench, trembling. He couldn't believe what he'd just heard. Zoltan was in all seriousness commanding him to get up, even though the cannonballs were still whizzing over them! When he looked into the stern, almost furious face of the commander, he knew as always there would be no mercy. Giovanni, Jerome, and Paulus had already gotten back on their feet.

"Damn it, you cowards, start beating the drums!" Zoltan was screaming. "Move your ass, Lukas, or I'll personally toss you to the Swedes as cannon fodder. Do you understand? This is war, not a kids' game."

Lukas nodded and tried to hide how he was trembling. He banged the drum, and at once he realized what Zoltan intended. The muffled, monotonous rumble had an almost hypnotic effect, helping the soldiers retain the necessary calm in the chaos of battle.

In the meantime, the Swedes had advanced to within a hundred paces of the fortifications. Lukas could now make out individual faces, among them anxious young men, but also cold-blooded veterans who ran toward the wall, screaming and waving their swords.

"Musketeers, load and aim!" Zoltan's next command rang out.

Everywhere along the walls, the men now rose with their muskets. Fuses were lit and held to the priming pan; then there was an explosion and all around Lukas the flash of a hundred muzzles. At the same moment, there was a piercing scream, and it took a while before Lukas realized it came from the throats of thousands of soldiers.

The Swedes were storming the walls.

What followed now was a single, horrible slaughter. The Swedish soldiers tried to scale the earthen walls, more than six feet high, and were pushed back again and again by the men atop the walls with pikes, swords, and daggers. Cannonballs were still flying overhead, and the explosions of the muskets merged with the shouts, the drums, and the clatter of sword blades into one deafening din.

By now, Lukas had cast aside the drum and was fighting for his very life. Paulus had just driven a Finnish soldier clothed in furs back into the ditch full of sharp-pointed stakes. Giovanni and Jerome were now fighting a handful of Scotsmen, who looked strange and frightening in their kilts and wearing blue war paint on their faces. Lukas himself had to fight off a tall Swede who had gotten as far as the wall. With a broad smile, the man swung his sword, barely missing Lukas, who ducked beneath the blow and then lunged forward. He caught the Swede beneath the elbow, sending him screaming and waving his hands through the air back into the ditch.

But now the next Swedish soldier approached from the side. Lukas felt a dull pain as a sword handle struck him on the temple; then, stumbling backward, he saw out of the corner of his eye his opponent raising his arm to strike the coup de grâce.

Now it's over, he thought. *The amulet wasn't able to save me after all, but at least now I'll see my mother and father . . .*

Suddenly, Jerome appeared in front of him, his rapier flashed forward like a snake, and the Swede vanished from sight with one last piercing scream. Stunned, Lukas rose to his feet.

"Thank you," he gasped.

Jerome nodded grimly. "The next time it's your turn to save *my* life," he replied tersely before turning to fend off the next attack.

Still only half conscious from the blow to his head, Lukas fought off attacks from all sides. To his right and to his left, his friends fought, sometimes back-to-back, and together they resisted the waves of Swedish soldiers. The battle seemed endless, and soon Lukas didn't know if it had been hours or days.

Not far from them stood Zoltan, like a huge boulder in the surf, holding the smoke-stained banner of the Black Musketeers rammed into the mound of earth. He was carrying a two-handed sword and swinging it in every direction to protect the banner from all comers.

"All together against death and the devil!" he roared again.

"To hell and beyond!" the Black Musketeers responded.

The sense of community gave Lukas additional strength. His shirt was torn, his trousers smeared with mud, and bloody welts covered his skin, but even though the Musketeers fought like devils, the number of Swedes did not lessen, but grew more and more. They were no longer just fighting at the walls, but behind it, behind bushes and trees, in forest clearings and ditches. Everywhere there was a thundering and flashing of weapons, the forest was in flames, and the whole mountain seemed to spit out fire—and above it all stood, like a watchful eagle, the old fortified tower. Lukas knew that if the enemy succeeded in taking the tower, they could bombard the entire encampment below, and the battle would be lost.

But was it already lost? The Swedes came storming from all directions toward the mountain, and some of the forward fortifications were already in enemy hands.

At that moment Lukas saw a single Swedish soldier ducking under Zoltan's deadly blows as he swung his sword around. The man was armed only with a dagger, but quickly circled directly behind the commander, who had not noticed him, apparently because of the noise.

"Watch out!" Lukas cried out.

Without another thought, he lunged toward the surprised soldier and threw him to the ground. The soldier let out a Swedish curse and tried to stab Lukas, but when the tip of the dagger had almost reached Lukas's throat, the man suddenly winced, blood flowed out of the corner of his mouth, and he rolled limply to one side.

"One for all and all for one," Giovanni declared. He stood over Lukas, his sword raised and smeared with blood. "Do you remember our motto?"

Behind Giovanni, Paulus and Jerome now appeared, gasping for air, as well as Zoltan, the black velvet of his doublet ripped and his beard disheveled. A deep wound ran across his forehead. Together they had defended their outpost for the time being, but the next attack would be coming soon.

"It looks like I was wrong about you boys," Zoltan grumbled, wiping the blood from his forehead. "I can hardly believe that a bunch of puny kids saved my life. Just the same, I have a job for you."

Another cannonball flew over them, and Zoltan spoke louder so they could hear him over the noise of battle. "You can see for yourselves that the enemy has breached our lines and will overrun the entire camp if we don't get reinforcements soon. Wallenstein must be warned immediately, and all of my messengers are dead or severely wounded. Even if I wished it wasn't so, we really need you now." He pointed at the top of the mountain where the old defensive tower stood, encircled by swirling clouds of gunpowder. "The general commands the troops from the old castle. All four of you will go as a group so that at least one of you gets through, and you better watch out that—"

Right next to them, another cannonball landed, breaching part of the wall. Clumps of earth as large as a child's head came raining down on the boys. Lukas dived into the ditch, and for a moment he was buried by the falling soil. Then he shoveled himself out with his hands and took a deep breath of the air polluted by the clouds of gun smoke. Alongside him, Paulus, Jerome, and Giovanni were coughing up dirt and dust.

"Where . . . is Zoltan?" Lukas gasped.

Paulus staggered to his feet and looked around. "No idea. But if he's dead, we should at least carry out his last order. Come along now, before the rest of the wall here collapses around our ears."

They ran along in the ditch for a while until they got to another breach. A single bloody arm projected from a pile of earth, the hand raised as if in a final salute. Lukas paused briefly but had no time to examine the horrible spectacle. Giovanni tugged at him to keep him moving forward.

"There's nothing you can do to help him now," he said as they hurried past. "He is already with God."

"Or in hell," Lukas mumbled. "Who is to know?" All this slashing and killing suddenly seemed so senseless, and he felt a vast emptiness opening up inside him. God could not have wanted this, but if God was not on their side, wasn't this whole war a great evil?

The boys were wandering in a labyrinth of partially collapsed trenches, earthen walls, and natural ravines somewhere in no-man's-land. Cannon and musket balls continued landing around them, raising clouds of dust so that they had trouble following each other. Other soldiers came running toward them now with torn shirts and bleeding faces scorched by gunpowder. Lukas could hear the commands they shouted to one another and was shocked to realize they were Swedes.

"The enemy has advanced farther than we assumed," Paulus whispered. "Well, fortunately we're all so caked with dirt that even my mother couldn't say whether I was friend or foe." He winked at Lukas. "Just keep your mouth shut, and you'll pass for a tiny Swede."

They turned a corner and came upon another deep trench that had recently been abandoned by the soldiers. Only a few smashed muskets lay on the ground, and there was not a soldier in sight. The noise of battle also sounded distant and muffled here.

Through the clouds and gun smoke, Lukas thought he saw at the end of the trench the outlines of a mountaintop with the ruins of a tower. The old castle! His heart started pounding.

"Ha!" Jerome exclaimed. "We made it! Now all we have to do—"

He stopped short as an avalanche of stones and dirt poured over him. With a hoarse cry, Jerome fell to the ground and attempted to protect his head with his hands as more stones came raining down. Overhead, at the edge of the trench, the faces of Kaspar, Karl, Max, and Gottfried appeared, holding clumps of dirt in their fists. It was clear the four servants had intentionally triggered the avalanche.

"Well, look at this. I knew we'd meet again," Kaspar hissed. "Now we've got you! You took our jobs away from us."

Lukas saw that Kaspar had pulled out a scratched pistol and was pointing it at him, Giovanni, and Paulus. Jerome still lay half-conscious under the clumps of dirt.

"Listen, Kaspar," Lukas said, struggling to sound calm. "We have one last important task assigned to us by Zoltan. The Swedes have overrun our fortifications. We must get to Wallenstein to warn him. So please—"

"Splendid! Then we'll do that for you," said Kaspar, who had now climbed down into the trench with his companions. "For you, this is the end of your trip." He sneered as he fumbled with the pistol in his hand. "So, which of you shall I take in my sights first? You, you, or . . . you?"

"You have only one shot, Kaspar," Paulus replied coldly. "So just think about it carefully. Afterward I'll smash you into pulp."

"You're right, big fellow. I think I'll take you, and then—"

Kaspar broke off as a figure approached from the south part of the trench, where the imperial troops were said to be. It was an especially large soldier, and he quickly drew closer.

"Damn." Kaspar squinted to get a better view of the man through the haze of gunpowder, then he calmed down visibly. "His armament appears to be that of a Spanish mercenary—one of us. But don't get your hopes up too soon. Once he's gone, you're next."

Lukas didn't know what astonished him the most: the fact that Kaspar had spoken of a Spanish mercenary or the appearance of the man, whose clothing looked more and more familiar as he approached. When he was just a few steps away, there was no longer any doubt.

The same helmet, the same baggy black breeches . . .

Lukas cringed. It was one of the Spanish mercenaries who had waylaid them at Lohenfels Castle and had abducted his mother and sister—a henchman of Waldemar von Schönborn! He even thought he recognized the face. A scar wound its way like an ugly worm across his right cheek. Lukas felt like screaming, but was choked by the horror of it.

This mercenary was the same one who shot his father with the crossbow.

"God be with you!" Kaspar said obsequiously, raising his hand in a peaceful gesture as he lowered his pistol and walked toward the Spaniard. "It feels good to find a loyal Catholic here on the battlefield. We're just now wiping out these heretical Swedish dogs—"

The mercenary had pulled out his sword almost casually and rammed it into Kaspar's belly. An expression of disbelief spread across Kaspar's face, and his mouth opened in one final question.

"But . . . ," he whispered.

With a sweeping motion, the man stuck his bloody sword back in its sheath and continued past Lukas and the other servant boys as Kaspar sank to the ground, lifeless.

"You accursed rat, you will regret that!" cried Karl. He jumped up, reached for a pistol that lay at the bottom of the trench, pointed it at the mercenary, and fired.

It was a well-aimed shot at close distance, and Lukas watched as the bullet penetrated the mercenary's doublet right between the shoulder blades.

But then, something very strange happened.

The man just kept striding forward.

He didn't stagger; he didn't even quiver. It seemed he hadn't even felt the shot. Suddenly, he turned around, and eyes that looked like glass marbles stared back blankly at the terrified boys. Then he turned around again and stomped up the hill toward the old fortress.

"What in God's name was that?" Giovanni gasped.

One of the frozen! The thought shot through Lukas's head. *God be with us, the Spaniard is a frozen one!*

He thought about everything Senno had told him. Was it possible this Spanish mercenary, the murderer of his father, was invincible? A *frozen one*? Someone who had made a pact with the devil in return for eternal life? A witch?

Someone was shaking Lukas. It was Paulus, trying to shout over the renewed reports of the muskets. "Listen, whatever just happened there, we have to continue! But Jerome's injury is more serious than we thought at first. A large rock hit him right on the head." He pointed back to where their own camp was located. "I'll take him to the field doctor, and you keep moving forward with Giovanni, do you understand?"

Lukas nodded as if in a trance.

Paulus took him by the shoulders and shook him again, while Giovanni had become impatient and already marched ahead a few steps.

"This is the way up the hill to the old fortress!" Giovanni called to Lukas, pointing forward. "We can only hope we don't meet that monster again."

Together they ran along the trench, where they soon saw more shouting and fighting mercenaries. They stumbled over corpses and burning remains of palisades, onward toward the top of the mountain. Lukas felt empty and exhausted. His shirt was torn, he was almost deaf from the constant noise, but above all, he kept seeing before him the face of the Spanish mercenary.

Empty eyes, like glass marbles . . . frozen . . .

Suddenly, they reached the end of the trench, and before them lay open land sloping steeply upward, with a pitched battle in progress. Everywhere around them men were fighting with swords, sabers, daggers, pikes, and bare fists. Up on the hilltop, Lukas could now see the defensive tower with a flag on top riddled with bullets—a red lion on a blue background.

Wallenstein's banner.

"We've got to get there," Giovanni shouted at him, "then we've made it!"

They were about to rush up the hill when Lukas saw a large figure about fifty yards from them. It was the Spanish mercenary, marching steadily up the hill as if being pulled along by a string. Now and then men charged him or shot at him, but the broad-shouldered man continued forward unperturbed. Now, finally, Lukas thought he knew where the mysterious Spaniard was headed.

"He's going to attack Wallenstein!" Lukas cried, half out of his mind. "This monster means to kill the general, and there is no one who can stop him. He is invincible, we've seen it ourselves!"

Giovanni paused, wrinkled his forehead, and rubbed his nose—signs that he was concentrating on something—as he closely observed the mercenary.

"Perhaps you're right," he mumbled, "but he may not be as invincible as we think." He pointed at the old watchtower. "We mustn't waste any time. You run ahead and warn Wallenstein, Lukas, and I'll look after our friend here."

Without further ado, Giovanni dashed off across the battle-field toward the Spaniard. Lukas could see his friend picking up a torch and something else, but then he was swallowed up in the clouds of smoke.

Now I'm all alone, Lukas thought, *just as Zoltan said, but it will be enough if just one of us makes it.*

He drew his sword and ran up the hill. Sometimes he had to jump over a crater, or fight off a soldier with a few blows of his sword. And as he ran on, he suffered some blows himself, and blood was dripping down his cheek, but he felt nothing. He ran on and on, struggling desperately for breath and with the sharp taste of iron in his mouth. Wallenstein's banner high atop the old fortress seemed endlessly far away, and Lukas felt as if he weren't getting any closer. He climbed on, staggering, falling, and struggling to his feet again, until finally, he reached the bare top of the hill with the tower.

An officer on horseback blocked his way, his sword raised and ready to strike.

Lukas dropped his own weapon and raised his hands.

"I'm . . . from the Black Musketeers," he panted with his last ounce of strength, "and bring an important message for Wallenstein."

The officer lifted an eyebrow. "For Wallenstein?" He seemed to hesitate for a moment, but then he pointed behind him, where a single man sat on a large horse, his hands on his sword, his gaze directed proudly forward as if he could view the entire world from the mountaintop.

"There is His Excellency, but— Hey! Stop!"

Lukas had simply run forward. When he reached the general, he fell on one knee and lowered his head. "My lord, the . . . the Swedes . . . ," he panted.

Wallenstein looked down at him severely, and also a bit surprised. His red cape fluttered in the wind. "What is it?" he growled, with a voice as sharp as a blade. "Speak up, lad!"

"The Swedish soldiers have broken through the western lines," Lukas said, his voice fading. "They are on the way to the army encampment. We . . . need reinforcements, now, or all is lost."

Then he collapsed unconscious in front of the great general's horse.

XVII

The first thing Lukas heard when he regained consciousness was a tinkling, like that of little bells. It took a while for him to realize what he heard was the sound of people laughing.

Are they angels perhaps? he thought. *Am I in heaven?*

But the smell was definitely too bad for it to be heaven. He sniffed, then opened his eyes a crack and saw white tent fabric and beneath him a hard camp bed and tucked around him a scratchy woolen blanket. He was in one of the tents in the army camp. Was the battle over? When he carefully turned his head, he realized he was not alone.

Right next to him lay Jerome, surrounded by a half-dozen young girls who were all giggling and feeding Lukas's French friend with slices of apple. One of them was trying to stitch up Jerome's ripped doublet while another was working on his badly battered hat.

"Ah, finally, you're awake," Jerome said when he noticed Lukas's astonished gaze. "And I thought you'd sleep until Last Judgment."

"Where . . . am I?" Lukas mumbled, still confused.

"You're in the field hospital, sleepyhead!" Jerome laughed, and the girls joined in. "But don't worry, they didn't have to cut off your leg. You got a couple of big bruises and stab wounds, but nothing that won't heal. The field surgeon said you were really lucky, considering that you just casually walked through the enemy lines with Giovanni. The doctor got him out of bed yesterday and released him. He's going around again spouting big words."

Lukas looked down and realized now that his arms and chest were bandaged. A heavy bandage was wrapped around his forehead, and his head hurt when he moved.

"What . . . are all these girls doing here?" he asked, sitting up, which gave him a terrible headache.

"Oh, these are just a few of my new friends," Jerome replied with a shrug. He was also wearing a bandage around his head, but seemed already in very good spirits. "They're all delightful maids from the field hospital. May I introduce them? Barbara, Agnes, Magdalena—"

"I think I'd feel better if we were alone for a while," Lukas said hesitantly.

"As you will, you spoilsport." Jerome whispered something to the girls and they left, still giggling.

Lukas looked around a bit. The tent they were in was huge and full of dozens of wounded soldiers, all lying on cots or on the floor. A few attendants scurried around changing dirty bandages. Some of the men groaned or whimpered softly, but most just lay there silently with ghostly white faces. The air smelled strongly of blood, garbage, and herbs burning in clay jars scattered around the tent to dispel the stench.

"Is the battle already over?" Lukas asked.

Jerome laughed. "You're asking if it's already over? Hey, you've been sleeping for two days and nights, and before you ask—yes, we won the battle, also thanks to you. Wallenstein sent three thousand Musketeers to the north side, and they finally repelled the Swedes. Those bastards suffered bitter losses and have withdrawn again behind the Nürnberg city walls." He winked at Lukas. "If Wallenstein doesn't deign to give you a medal, then at least the old grumbler Zoltan should."

"Then he's still alive," Lukas exclaimed with relief. "And I thought . . ."

"That just a single cannonball would kill him? *Sacré bleu*, Zoltan is the commander of the legendary Black Musketeers, don't forget!" Jerome chewed happily on an apple slice. "Just remember our motto. To hell and beyond. Our leader has made a pact with the devil, and he won't die so easily."

Jerome's final words startled Lukas. He couldn't help thinking of the Spanish mercenary in the trench, who had apparently been invincible. Could the murderer of his father really have been a frozen one? What actually had happened out there on the battlefield?

At that moment, a tent flap was pushed aside, and Paulus and Giovanni entered. Both smiled with relief on seeing Lukas well and alert.

"Just look, our hero finally woke up," said Paulus with a grin, "and if I understand the giggling girls out there correctly, the field surgeon didn't cut off anything important down below."

Lukas blushed. At first he wanted to make some sarcastic response, but then he turned to Giovanni.

"What about the Spaniard?" he asked intently. "Were you able to stop him? I must know."

Giovanni's face immediately darkened. "You get right to the point." He looked around carefully, then lowered his voice. "I spoke with a few soldiers who met the fellow on Wallenstein's hill. They all observed the same thing we did. Evidently he wanted to reach the general in order to kill him, and he couldn't be stopped either by bullets or sword blows"—a slight smile played around his lips—"but by something else."

"And what was that?" Lukas asked. "Just stop tormenting me!"

"Fire." Giovanni grinned mischievously. "He was really afraid of that. I noticed earlier on the battlefield how he steered clear of burning wagons and glowing remains of palisades. So I got a barrel of oil, lay in wait, and then poured it over him. It wasn't quite enough to stop him completely, but the very sight of my torch sent him running."

"The murderer of my father is still out there," Lukas muttered.

"The murderer of your father?" Paulus asked, baffled. "But—"

"This Spaniard is one of Schönborn's henchmen," Lukas interrupted. "I recognized him. He was there when they attacked our castle and shot my father with a crossbow. I think he did something to transform himself into one of the frozen ones."

"The frozen ones?" Now it was Giovanni's turn to look at him suspiciously. "Dear Lukas, is it possible the blow to your head was stronger than we thought?"

"I wish that were the case," Lukas replied, and then he told his friends about his conversation with Senno, and for a while, it was silent in the tent.

"White and black magic, talismans, and potions that make you invincible . . ." Paulus shook his head. "Hmm . . . I don't know. That's pretty strong stuff. It's just like the scruffy astrologer, telling you things like that."

"But the Spanish soldier!" Lukas insisted. "You saw it yourself. He was invincible. Think about what Tabea said about the mercenaries who fought against Scherendingen near Augsburg.

They, too, seemed invincible and had a strange look in their eyes. Maybe they were frozen as well."

"Did you consider that our friend might simply have been wearing an iron cuirass underneath his clothing?" Jerome said. "Giovanni thought the fellow looked very muscular and husky. Maybe he was wearing a thin cuirass of Solingen steel strong enough to resist the shot and repel the blows later on."

Giovanni nodded. "I didn't think of that. That would explain a lot. And Tabea was practically out of her mind with fear at the time, so it's no surprise Scherendingen's opponents looked to her like ghosts."

"And how about the wolf and my amulet with the pentagram?" Lukas asked, getting more and more confused. "Ivan also saw the wolf, and the amulet has really felt hot recently. And . . . the blue cloud, when my mother—"

He stopped short when he noticed the pitying gazes of his friends.

"You don't believe me, do you?" he whispered finally.

Giovanni sighed. "I've got to admit, it's hard for me to believe all this magic stuff. Maybe Senno simply put crazy ideas into your head, though it's true the Spanish mercenary really had something strange about him," he added, still pondering the question.

Lukas couldn't help thinking about the man's eyes.

Lifeless as marbles . . .

The mercenary had killed Kaspar with his rapier, like a demon for whom people were nothing more than pesky bugs or useless toy figures.

"What about Kaspar?" Lukas asked, to change the subject. "Is he . . ."

"He's dead." Paulus nodded. "If you ask me, that bastard didn't deserve anything better. But there's good news as well. After the experience in the trench, his three friends are clearly interested in coming to terms with us, and Zoltan offered to take on all seven of us—but not until we've recovered."

"Then let's enjoy ourselves until then as best we can." Jerome clapped his hands. "How about bringing the girls back? I feel that my bandages need to be changed."

The others laughed, and Lukas joined in halfheartedly, but deep inside he could still feel the dead glass eyes of the Spaniard looking at him.

It was a few weeks before Lukas could leave the field hospital on his own, but in the meantime, his friends brought him food they'd been able to plunder after the withdrawal of the Swedes and entertained him with the newest gossip.

Not everyone in the Black Musketeers regiment had been so lucky as he. Almost a hundred brave warriors had fallen on the northern front, the greatest toll in lives of any battalion in Wallenstein's army. Swedish losses were disproportionately higher, however, running into many hundreds. This was not the first time Lukas wondered when all this killing would end. It became harder and harder to make any sense out of all the slashing and stabbing.

Wallenstein had allowed the enemy forces to withdraw from Nürnberg—a decision that was opposed by many of his officers as well as the Kaiser himself.

"He's allowing the Swedes to kill themselves," Giovanni explained to Lukas. "That's his plan. Many of them are sick and suffering from hunger as they wander like beggars through the German Reich. When winter sets in, they'll pull in their tails and crawl back to where they came from."

On the one hand, Lukas hoped his friend was right, but on the other hand, he was afraid that after the victory, Wallenstein's army would be disbanded and he would be sent away. He was still not even one step closer to finding his little sister.

After leaving the field hospital, Lukas was able to return to his work as a servant. He was busy as usual, feeding and brushing the horses, when Giovanni came to him with a serious look.

"The commander wants to see you," he said. "It sounds urgent, and you should get moving at once."

Lukas frowned. Had he done something wrong? Since the battle of Nürnberg, Zoltan had hardly spoken to him. There hadn't even been a gesture of thanks for his warning to Wallenstein of the impending assault. Why all this hurry now?

"I'll be there in a moment," Lukas replied. He set the feed bucket down and headed toward the commander's tent. The stab wound to his left leg had healed for the most part, and he felt otherwise quite well, but he still had some difficulty walking.

As so often, Zoltan was sitting at his desk assembled from old barrels and was signing and sealing some documents. Lukas knew that Wallenstein had high regard for the commander of the Black Musketeers and often used his experienced soldiers for dangerous errands and reconnaissance work. For Zoltan himself it meant a lot of tedious paperwork.

"How I hate this stuff!" he growled without looking up from his work. "Damn! Soldiers are here to fight, not to write and seal documents!" Finally he put his heavy bronze seal aside and regarded Lukas sternly. "Do you know why I sent for you?"

Lukas shrugged. "To be honest, I have no idea, sir. If it's because of the message I delivered during the battle—"

"Aha! You expect a reward, or at least some thanks, don't you?" Zoltan interrupted with a grim smile. "Let me tell you that I'm extremely sparing in my expressions of thanks, especially when a soldier has only performed his damned duty. No, I called you for another reason . . ." He was silent for a moment, and then an almost mischievous look passed over his face.

"I wanted to congratulate you, Lukas. Best wishes on your fourteenth birthday."

"But . . ." Lukas was so surprised that words failed him. In fact, he'd completely forgotten that he'd just turned fourteen. He tried to think back to his last birthday. His parents were still alive then, his sister was an annoying though loveable pain, and he had gone hunting with his father. Was that just a year ago? To him, it seemed like an eternity, another life.

"Your friends told me." Zoltan laughed. "They know you better than you think. I made them promise to let me be the first to offer my best wishes. And in addition, I wanted to give this back to you." He reached under the table and pulled out Lukas's Pappenheim sword. "You lost it in the battle, and I kept it for you." The commander examined the blade. "It's a nice piece, good workmanship. You don't often see something like this. Where did you get it?"

Lukas opened his mouth, embarrassed, but Zoltan waved him off.

"The color of your face tells me I wouldn't want to know. Well, no matter who this sword belonged to before, now it belongs to you. So take good care of it and prove yourself worthy of it." With these words he handed the freshly polished Pappenheim sword back to Lukas.

"As is appropriate for a boy of your age, I have a birthday present for you," Zoltan continued, his voice taking on a more serious tone. "The gift is also intended as an award for your service in the battle. But don't run around telling everyone, or every soldier will expect an award from me just for performing his duty." He picked up a little wooden box, which had been concealed underneath all the letters and documents, and pushed it across the table. "Open it."

Curiously, Lukas opened the cover. He broke out in an exclamation of surprise.

"But . . . ," he started to say.

"It's a wheel lock pistol made in Augsburg," Zoltan explained, "a marvel of technology. It has never missed its mark and has, by God, been through many battles. Take a close look, Lukas."

Lukas's fingers glided over the polished cherry-wood handle, the cold steel barrel, and the well-oiled hammer with the priming pan next to it. Suddenly, he stopped. On the underside of the barrel, a name was engraved. It was a name he knew only too well.

Friedrich von Lohenfels . . .

Lukas's heart raced, and all the blood drained from his face. He felt so weak that the pistol nearly slipped from his fingers. Was it even possible?

"Yes, it's your father's pistol," Zoltan continued in a soft voice. "A few weeks ago, I thought I saw your resemblance to him, and I should have noticed it earlier. The same face, though younger, the same movements, and the same brilliant fighting technique. He taught you all these tricks, didn't he?"

Lukas nodded silently. The pistol in his hand suddenly seemed to weigh tons.

"A few days ago, your friends revealed to me who you really are," said Zoltan. "They said you didn't want to curry favor with me as the son of a nobleman and therefore kept your name secret. I can understand that." He sighed. "You couldn't have known that your father and I were very close. As I've heard, he died recently in the service of the Kaiser . . ." Zoltan paused briefly, and Lukas thought he saw a tear in his eye. "I also knew Dietmar von Scherendingen. Together with Friedrich, we often went into battle. We were like brothers. Back then, Friedrich gave me this one of two dueling pistols. He had the other. We swore never to separate."

Lukas felt dazed and barely able to speak. "But why . . ."

"Why did we finally separate, you want to know?" said Zoltan. He smiled sadly. "Well, why do men separate? Either because of a woman or alcohol. Your father met a beautiful, intelligent girl named Sophia, your mother. And Dietmar fell victim to brandy. But there were times when we were inseparable. One for all . . ."

"And all for one," Lukas finished, his voice hoarse.

Zoltan looked up, pleased. "You know this motto? It stands for great friendship. It seems you have found good friends just as I did then."

"Even if they are always playing tricks on me," Lukas answered with a weary nod. Just a few moments ago, he'd been annoyed with Giovanni, Jerome, and Paulus, but evidently the friends hadn't told Zoltan everything. The commander didn't know how his father had really died, and he also didn't know why Lukas was really here.

"One thing should be clear to you," Zoltan went on now in a coarser tone as he raised his finger. "You may be the son of a nobleman and someone who was once a good friend to me, but I'll treat you like everyone else here. There will be no extra favors, do you understand? And you never received this pistol—at least no one but your friends must learn about it."

Lukas nodded and ran his fingers again along the barrel of the beautifully made present.

"Oh, and one more thing," Zoltan added. "I have heard you met with Senno. Stay away from this quack. I don't trust him at all. Wallenstein's orders are becoming increasingly strange, and I fear we have Senno's influence to thank for that. I consider it a serious error to have let the Swedes simply move on, and I think we shall soon hear from them again. What a disgrace there are no more men like your father." Gruffly, he waved Lukas off. "And now, move along before I start getting sentimental. We should forget about old times. It gets us nowhere."

The next day, the army moved on.

Wallenstein had decided to teach his next lesson to the Saxons, who were allied with the Swedes. For the imperial army, that meant another brutal forced march as summer slowly but surely gave way to fall. Nights were cooler now, and the rainstorms more violent. Lukas's shirt and doublet clung to his body, he shivered and froze, and the smoky campfires in the evening did little to dry out his clothing.

Wherever they went, they came upon scorched wasteland. The few farmers they met who had not fled into the forests and swamps were at the point of starvation. The soldiers made soup out of acorns, animal hides, and grass, or ate rats and mice that didn't scurry back into their holes fast enough. At night, sitting around their campfires, they told horror stories of creatures who visited cemeteries to feed on the dead or who stole hanged men from the gallows to still their nagging hunger.

Their own army also suffered hunger, and more and more soldiers were starting to grumble about their great general.

"Zoltan is right—we should have slaughtered the Swedes at Nürnberg," Paulus grumbled, too, more than once. "The Saxons would have become docile as little lambs, and we wouldn't have to tramp through rain and mud forever. I miss the free life of a performer."

"You can forget about that," replied Giovanni, pulling his hat down over his face to protect it from the stinging rain. "First of all, we promised Lukas to help him search for Elsa, and besides, everyone is tired of all the fighting. Who wants to watch a sword-fighting performance when some drunken soldiers have just killed his family?"

When he thought no one was watching, Lukas took the wheel lock pistol and practiced shooting with his friends in the nearby woods. Soon he learned how best to keep the powder dry, to pack the bullet in the barrel in practically no time, cock the hammer, and then to aim as calmly as possible.

"You shoot really well," Giovanni commented one day when Lukas once again hit a clay jar standing on an overturned tree. "The eye of a hawk and the calm breath of an old stag. The practice really paid off."

"That doesn't do anything to bring my parents back," Lukas said bitterly and loaded again.

Instinctively, he reached for the amulet that still hung around his neck. Even if everything Senno had told him was just non-sense, he somehow felt protected by the talisman. The pentagram had not felt warm for a long time.

That night Lukas had another horrible nightmare. It was somewhat like the dream that had tormented him shortly before Red Sara gave him the amulet. He was surrounded by dense clouds, and behind them, something unspeakably evil was lurk-ing. He knew it, even if he couldn't see it—the huge, black wolf prowling around, its red eyes flashing in the darkness, trying to force its way to him through the impenetrable gloom. The fog lifted, the wolf's eyes flared up like candles . . . and then it jumped.

Directly at Lukas.

Lukas shouted, and someone started shaking him. It was Jerome, looking at him with obvious concern.

"Thanks for waking me up," Lukas gasped. "It was only a dream that—"

"Listen to me. I have to tell you something," Jerome interrupted.

Lukas blinked and saw that the sun had already risen. Cold, damp air came through the entrance to the tent.

"What is it?" Lukas asked, rubbing his tired eyes. "Are the Swedes attacking again?"

"No," Jerome replied softly, "but Karl and fat Gottfried just stopped by. They had to deliver a message to headquarters, and do you know who they saw there?"

Lukas was suddenly wide-awake. He knew Jerome's answer before he gave it.

"Waldemar von Schönborn has arrived at our camp," Jerome whispered. "It's said he wants to look around here for heretics. We can finally pay him a visit."

Lukas nodded grimly. When he got up, the amulet beneath his shirt briefly touched his naked skin, and he cried out.

The talisman was glowing hot.

XVIII

Shortly afterward, the four friends met in an old, half-empty covered wagon off to one side that stank of brandy and gunpowder. They'd often used it recently as a hiding place. It was dark and stuffy, and behind the leaking barrels, they could hear rats squeaking, but at least the friends could speak undisturbed here.

"What exactly did the other servant boys have to say about Schönborn's arrival?" Giovanni asked Jerome excitedly.

"Well, they were delivering a message to headquarters, and just at that moment a large contingent of men on horseback arrived with a high clerical figure in their midst wearing a purple robe. His bodyguards announced him in bombastic words, by name and title, and you couldn't miss it." Jerome grinned. "I told Karl and the other boys that I'd give them my daily meat ration if they could tell me anything about Schönborn. The stuff is always so infested with maggots anyway that I can't stomach it."

"These bodyguards," Lukas asked, "were they perhaps Spaniards?"

"*Bien sûr.*" Jerome nodded. "But Karl and Gottfried couldn't say if our strange invincible friend was among them. They were standing too far away to see that."

"You said Schönborn intends to look for heretics here?" Paulus asked as he restlessly struggled to sit on a barrel much too small for him.

"One of the guards mentioned that," Jerome replied. "Schönborn no doubt intends to find and kill all the heretics in the camp. Prostitutes and Gypsies especially are a thorn in his side. It seems his henchmen have also brought along a cartload of torturing implements."

Giovanni shuddered. "That's horrible! Someone like that is a father confessor to Wallenstein? Then I'd prefer this quack astrologer Senno."

"In any case, the bastard is here, and we can finally get moving," Paulus growled. "First we need to have a look around the camp." He got up and the covered wagon tipped precariously to one side. "Let's hurry over to headquarters before Zoltan notices our absence and gives us extra sentry duties."

The army had set up camp near a small, burned-out town with a mountain range behind it, its highest summits already covered in snow. It was unpleasantly cold for the middle of October, and the soldiers had wrapped themselves in tattered blankets and coats taken from corpses. On their way to headquarters, Lukas saw weary, anxious faces. Many of the men suffered from whooping cough and diarrhea, and Lukas wondered if the sick men would hold out until they arrived at their longed-for winter encampments.

Fortunately, the quarters for the Black Musketeers were not far from Wallenstein's barracks, a short walk for the friends. As usual, the strange building on wheels was surrounded by a circle of white tents where some watchmen were on duty. Carefully, the boys moved forward and ducked behind a withered blackberry bush near one of the tents.

"The last time I made it through with a guard," Lukas whispered. "It doesn't look like we're going to have that much luck today, but at least from here, we have a view of the Spanish mercenaries. The other servant boys weren't lying."

There were about a half-dozen Spanish soldiers, all dressed in their typical baggy breeches with a cuirass, sword, and round helmets. The mysterious mercenary with the bulbous scar was not there, however. Waldemar von Schönborn was not there, either; presumably, he was inside one of the tents, perhaps even with Wallenstein personally.

"Look over there," Jerome whispered. "That's the cart the others told us about."

Behind one of the tents, half concealed, stood a large cart from which two soldiers were unloading a heavy box while others were sorting through bundles of twigs, chains, and thick ropes lying on the ground in front of them.

"Schönborn must be serious about his search for heretics," Giovanni mumbled. "You can only hope that Wallenstein stops him, because if this fellow is looking for a heretic, he'll find one. That's as sure as—"

He stopped on hearing a sound behind them. Shocked, they turned around, but to their relief, they saw a boy about ten years old standing there. He had short, dark hair and a dirty face and was picking his nose as he looked curiously at the older boys.

"Damn, kid, you really gave me a shock," said Giovanni. "So move along, take off. There's nothing to see here, and we have no candy for you."

"What are you doing here?" the boy wanted to know.

"We . . . ah . . . have a message to deliver to headquarters," Paulus replied. "It's important, so don't bother us."

"Then why are you hiding behind a bush?" the boy responded.

Lukas sighed. It was obvious the little fellow couldn't be put off that easily.

"Listen," he said, pulling a tarnished copper button from his pocket with a handsome embossed figure on it. Jerome had found it on the battlefield and given it to Lukas in the field hospital. "This is a valuable piece of jewelry, nothing less than a button from Wallenstein's vest. It's yours if you leave us alone."

The boy took the button and looked at it with interest, then shook his head and gave it back. "That's the head of the Swedish king and doesn't come from Wallenstein's vest," he answered emphatically. "You were lying to me."

"Damn, you little know-it-all!" Paulus said impatiently. "You've got your choice, take the button or we'll beat you up. Which do you prefer, huh?"

"If you hit me, I'll scream," the boy said with a grin, "and we'll see what the guards have to say when they find you here behind the bush."

For the first time, Lukas took a close look at the boy. He was wearing the simple, filthy clothes of a servant, but Lukas saw something mischievous and defiant in his eyes that he found touching, though he didn't know why. The lad was clever. Lukas raised his hands in resignation.

"Very well, you have won. Tell us what you want from us, then leave us in peace."

The boy crossed his arms over his chest and put on a stubborn face. "I'd like to belong to your gang. You're a gang, right? I can tell things like that."

Paulus roared with laughter. "Listen to the little monkey! No taller than my belly button, and he wants to wander through the camp with us. Hey, run back to your mother and hide there. Hurry along!"

"I don't have a mother anymore," the boy replied softly. "She's dead."

For a moment, silence reigned. "I'm sorry to hear that," Lukas said finally, and nodded sympathetically. "What's your name anyway, kid?"

"Daniel," the boy answered after hesitating briefly.

"Listen," Jerome whispered to the others. "This is a waste of our time. We've seen enough, and we're not going to shake off this little mite. Let's come back some other time, all right?"

Giovanni and Paulus nodded, but Lukas kept looking at Daniel, who seemed to be waiting for their decision. "He seems to have no one to watch over him," Lukas whispered. "He's all alone in this camp—"

"There's surely someone around to look after him," Paulus interrupted and tugged at Lukas's sleeve. "Come on now. We really have more important things to do than to look after a little brat like him."

"You're probably right." Lukas sighed and reluctantly went along with them.

Daniel continued standing defiantly behind the bush, his arms crossed. He didn't shout, he didn't cry, and it was perhaps this silence that moved Lukas most of all. The boy's eyes seemed to follow him until he'd disappeared with the others behind the tents.

In the coming days, Lukas remained tormented by the knowledge that Waldemar von Schönborn had finally arrived in the camp. A few times his amulet started to feel hot, always in the hours just before daybreak.

Their marches between encampments were hard and tedious and brought them farther and farther northeast. There was also work to do in the evening, so the boys had no more opportunity to observe the headquarters. They usually fell asleep as soon as they lay down.

On the fourth day, there was another chance when Lukas was sent out to get a barrel of brandy for Zoltan and the officers. This time he got to within a few steps of the headquarters. Hiding behind a moss-covered boulder, he watched the busy comings and goings in front of Wallenstein's barracks. He was just about to turn around when the door opened and out stepped a figure he would never forget as long as he lived.

It was Waldemar von Schönborn.

The inquisitor wore the same cloak he had on when Lukas's mother was burned at the stake in Heidelberg. A monk's cowl covered his thinning gray hair, and his hooked nose gave him an imperious and cruel appearance as he scrutinized the area around the headquarters.

For an instant, Lukas thought Schönborn had seen him, but that was impossible, as he was well hidden behind the rock. Still, he felt the inquisitor's gaze like a knife in his chest. A murderous passion swept over him; he wanted simply to attack Schönborn and slit him open with his sword, but no doubt the guards would stop him first. Besides, then Lukas himself would surely be put to the stake, and he would never learn anything about Elsa's fate.

No, he had to proceed more rationally. But how? As he regarded his enemy now for the first time in more than a year, his plan suddenly seemed unbelievably childish and foolish. Schönborn had taken Elsa with him from their parents' castle and had attached great importance to sparing her life, but did that mean he knew where she was now—and even if he did, how could Lukas ever find out? Should he just go to Schönborn and ask him? That sounded so foolish that he almost broke out laughing, which would have revealed his hiding place. Instead, tears of anger rolled down his cheeks, and he sobbed quietly. Here he stood, only a spear's throw away from his parents' murderer, yet he was completely powerless. He'd never felt so lonely, so small. His whole journey up to now had been pointless.

He sat down on the rock and let his tears flow.

"Why are you crying?" asked a voice behind him. Lukas spun around and saw little Daniel, who appeared to be once again roving around the area. He had to be from a regiment very close by. Strangely, Lukas wasn't angry at all that Daniel had interrupted his snooping again. Looking back one last time at the headquarters, he saw that Schönborn had gone back into the barracks anyway.

"I'm . . . crying because of my parents," Lukas said after a while, wiping his tears away. "They are dead, just like your mother, and I feel so alone." He smiled sadly. "Those are two things we have in common."

"My father is alive, but he never has much time for me," Daniel replied in a flat voice, picking his nose. "Sometimes it's just like he was dead. Except, he can get really angry if I've done something wrong."

Lukas laughed and found he was already feeling better, talking with the child. "All fathers are like that," he told Daniel. "Don't worry too much about it—just nod and look ashamed when he scolds you. The storm passes usually as fast as it came."

Daniel grinned. "Thanks for your advice. I'll try that the next time."

"Does your father know you are wandering around here?" Lukas asked.

Daniel shrugged. "I don't think he cares. He always has so much to do." Suddenly he turned around, frightened. "Oh, I think the guards have seen us."

In fact, two of the soldiers were looking at them suspiciously. "Hey, you kids," one of them shouted. "Why are you hanging around? You have no business being here, so take off!"

Lukas pressed his lips together grimly. "I've got to go," he said to the boy, "but I'm sure we'll meet again."

"Will you ask your friends if they'd take me into your gang?" Daniel pleaded. "Please?"

"I . . . can't promise you anything, but perhaps we can take you along when we go out into the forest to practice sword fighting and shooting."

Daniel's eyes gleamed. "That would be great!" he shouted gleefully. "It's so boring here, and no one wants to play with me. I'm so alone. Like you. But I don't have friends like you do."

"I'll see you soon, Daniel." Lukas gave him a good-bye pinch on his dirty cheek, and then he left, trying to sort out all his feelings. The short conversation with Daniel had made it clear to him that despite all the problems, he'd found something very valuable.

A friend.

His trip, then, hadn't been entirely in vain.

◆ ◆ ◆

"You really want to bring the kid along when we practice shooting?"

Giovanni shook his head in disbelief. They'd just met again in the old covered wagon, and Lukas had told his friends of his recent observations.

"Why not?" he insisted. "How can it hurt to bring him along?"

"Just wait a minute, Lukas." Paulus cast a stern eye at him. "We followed you through half the Reich to find this accursed Schönborn, and now suddenly you want us to care for children? We have other things to do. We should stick to our plan."

"May I remind monsieur we still don't have any plan?" said Jerome. "We're just assuming that Schönborn knows something about where Lukas's sister is, but we haven't the slightest idea how to get him to talk."

"You could ask Senno to cast a spell on the inquisitor for you so he'll let us in on where Elsa is," Paulus said sarcastically. "Then the magician can prove what truth there is to his white and black magic."

The others laughed, but Lukas just sat there thinking it over. Paulus's teasing had given him an idea. Senno had offered him his help before, and Lukas had declined, but now he could use all the help he could get. If the enigmatic astrologer was still around, Lukas decided he'd take him up on his offer.

XIX

For the rest of the week, Lukas used every free minute he had trying to find Senno's tent in the sprawling army encampment, but
no matter who he asked or where he went, no one had seen the
astrologer recently. Was it possible he'd just left? Lukas told his
friends nothing about his search. He knew they considered Senno
a charlatan, only looking out for his own advantage.

No one thought an attack by the Swedes was likely in the
coming cold months, so in mid-November Wallenstein finally
decided to send the army to its fortified winter quarters. There the
boys were busy all the time building tents and log houses, setting
up fortifications, and digging trenches.

The soldiers were relieved for a temporary reprieve from the
constant marching. The army deployed to the smaller cities in the
area, but the Black Musketeers remained close to Wallenstein's
quarters, located for the time being in the city of Weißenfels.
The inquisitor Waldemar von Schönborn and his retinue took
quarters in an abandoned monastery that was already notorious
as a place of horror. Terrifying stories made the rounds about what
now transpired there.

"Every day, his soldiers go to the individual camps, searching for heretics," Jerome told them when he came back from an errand. They held their meetings now in a mill gutted by fire, some distance away between stunted pine trees. "They come and get everyone who looks suspicious to them," Jerome continued. "They take away Gypsies, midwives, young prostitutes, and recently even a baker because it was said he got his flour from the devil. It's dreadful! *Très, très terrible!*" He shook his head.

"And in the cellar of the monastery, they torture their prisoners until they confess they are witches," Paulus added. "Fat Gottfried was near there yesterday, and he says the screams of these wretches can be heard everywhere."

"Why doesn't Wallenstein do anything?" Lukas asked angrily. "He's got to know about it."

"I'm afraid he's so involved with preparations for war that he hasn't heard very much. In any case, it's said he's already on the way to Leipzig." Giovanni shrugged. "Perhaps Schönborn has talked him into believing the suspects really are evil magicians. I've heard the general is receptive to that kind of nonsense. Remember Senno." He paused and rubbed the side of his nose, thinking. "But this miserable monastery gives us one advantage— the building is a partially charred ruin, like a Swiss cheese riddled with holes, and there are many ways to sneak inside unnoticed."

"Isn't that just great," Jerome replied dryly. "If we don't watch out, these strange Spanish soldiers will keep us right there and put us on the rack down in the crypt."

The friends fell into a gloomy silence.

"We have to go back before Zoltan sends someone out to look for us," Lukas said finally. "Who knows, maybe we'll think of something better in the next few days. Meanwhile I've promised

Wanja I'd go over to the blacksmith in Weißenfels to pick up a few horseshoes."

The boys separated, each going his own way. Lukas hurried to the nearby town, where he paid a visit to the smith standing by his glowing forge. As the smith was handing him the horseshoes, Lukas felt a prickling sensation on the back of his neck, as he always did when someone was watching. Cautiously, he looked around and saw Daniel standing between two houses, looking like a little dog waiting for its master.

He doesn't give up, Lukas thought, but he was still glad to see the boy.

"Hey, kid!" he called to him. He'd scared Daniel, however, as the boy dashed off.

"Maybe not," Lukas mumbled, almost a bit disappointed. Then he stiffened. He had better things to do than to run after a little runt like that. If Daniel wanted to ask him something, he'd have to come to him.

On his way back to camp, he heard agitated voices. Lukas hastened his steps and soon came to a large gathering of men standing around the tents and wagons. They were mumbling excitedly, and some had clenched fists and angry faces. A piercing shriek came from somewhere in the midst of the crowd.

"Move aside," an imperious voice shouted. "In the name of the Church, move out of the way or I'll have you all arrested along with this heretic woman!"

The horseshoes slipped from Lukas's fingers. He'd heard this voice before, and the very sound of it caused his blood to freeze. Back then, the inquisitor had spoken almost the same words when his mother was arrested.

The inquisitor's threat had its effect. The crowd of people parted, and Lukas saw a group of Spanish soldiers taking away a whimpering young woman in chains. Alongside them, atop his dappled gray horse, rode Waldemar von Schönborn.

"This woman is guilty of witchcraft," he thundered. "There are witnesses who have seen how she cast a spell on a newborn calf that then grew two heads. Anyone who helps her is likewise guilty of witchcraft."

"By God, the calf came into the world like that, I swear!" the girl cried, trying to tear herself away.

Only now did Lukas recognize her. She was the daughter of the butcher traveling with the army, and he'd had some pleasant chats with her from time to time. With her black hair and impudent look, she reminded him a bit of Tabea. At that moment, the father arrived, wringing his hands.

"Oh, my lord!" he pleaded with Schönborn. "She speaks the truth. I myself saw the calf when it was born. It had two heads! Please release her—she is my only daughter."

The inquisitor brought his horse to a halt and scrutinized the man with tears running down his face.

"You say you witnessed the birth of the calf as well?" he asked in a sharp voice.

The butcher nodded emphatically. "Yes, my lord, I swear—"

"Then you are also suspected of heresy," Schönborn interrupted. He turned to the soldiers. "Seize him. We'll soon bring the truth to light."

The soldiers grabbed hold of the man, who was shouting loudly and desperately attempting to reach for the girl. He lashed out in all directions, but they tied him securely with heavy ropes.

"You devils, you devils!" he kept screaming. "God knows I speak the truth!"

"Well, then you have nothing to fear from me," Schönborn said with a smile. "By the time you are tied to the stake, God will recognize his own."

The people grumbled, but no one dared to resist the soldiers. Lukas was still hiding behind the crowd so that Schönborn couldn't see him, but a fury was building inside him so enormous he could scarcely restrain himself. Could these men simply do as they wished? Someone had to act, or this girl and her father would be put to the stake and burned just like his own mother.

Lukas bent down and picked up one of the horseshoes on the ground. It was heavy, and if he aimed well it could be a deadly weapon . . .

"If I were you, I wouldn't do that."

Lukas flinched. The voice came from right behind him. He turned around and saw the warning gaze of Senno, who had leaned over to whisper in his ear.

"I can understand your anger, lad," the astrologer said, "but it will get you nowhere. If you want to do something about this outrageous injustice you must proceed differently—cleverly and deliberately."

Lukas couldn't understand how the elegantly dressed man with the waxed goatee had been able to approach him so silently. He lowered the horseshoe. "Where were you? I looked for you everywhere."

Senno smiled. "Well, now you've found me. Have you changed your mind and will you now tell me more about yourself?"

"Indeed, I really need your help," Lukas blurted out. "But I have no idea whether there is anything you can do to help me. It's about—"

Senno placed his fingers to his lips. "This is not a good place for our discussion. It would be very inauspicious if Schönborn found me here."

"Then you are not friends?" Lukas asked.

Senno's laughter sounded like the ringing of a far-off bell. "No, we're not friends, certainly not. I suggest we continue this conversation this evening. My tent is east of Weißenfels near the mass graves of the plague victims."

"But I was looking for you there just yesterday."

"It seems not carefully enough. That's where you'll find me."

Without another word, Senno turned away and soon disappeared in the crowd.

The soldiers had led away the butcher and his daughter, whose pitiful screams could still be heard. The figure of Waldemar von Schönborn, sitting proudly upright on his dapple-gray horse, was visible for a long time from a distance.

After some deliberation, Lukas decided not to tell his friends anything about his meeting that night with Senno. If they knew, he was sure they would try to talk him out of it. He could always tell them about it later.

As night descended over the camp, he donned a hood and a warm black cloak he'd bought with the pay he'd received just a few days earlier. There was a new moon, and the sky was cloudy, making Lukas almost invisible in the darkness. He slipped easily past the guards, who were careless anyway in performing their duties here in the winter encampment.

As soon as he was outside the camp, Lukas headed toward the little city of Weißenfels, whose charred ruins stood out in the night sky like dragon's teeth. The plague cemetery, where many who'd died in recent years were buried, was a ways outside town. Just recently Lukas had looked around there for Senno's tent and was thus all the more surprised to find it there, along the wall of the cemetery. It was still a shimmering bluish black, but a warm light shone out through the entrance flap, as if to suggest this tent was the only living creature in an otherwise dead world. Directly behind it lay the cemetery with its many fresh grave mounds as testimony to the fact that the Great Plague continued unabated here in Weißenfels as well.

Cautiously, Lukas approached the entrance to the tent. The other tents and wagons were located at quite a distance, perhaps out of respect for the dead, so that Lukas didn't have to fear being observed. As he was about to reach for the tent flap, he heard Senno's melodious voice from inside.

"Come in. I have been waiting for you."

Lukas frowned. Evidently, he had not been as quiet as he thought. On entering, he saw Senno sitting at the table strewn with ink-stained documents and rolls, just as on his last visit. A single lantern cast a warm glow over the room, and the silk flags along the walls with their strange symbols and signs rustled softly in the breeze.

Senno smiled and motioned for Lukas to sit down.

"It's much better for us to have our conversation here, don't you think?" The astrologer leaned forward, and once again Lukas felt as if he were being examined by invisible fingers. "You said perhaps I could help you. Tell me about it, lad."

Lukas hesitated briefly. For a long time, he'd been pondering how much to tell Senno about himself. At the moment, the astrologer seemed the only person who could help him with his questions, so he decided not to hold back anything.

"I believe my mother was a white witch, a good witch, if there really is such a thing," he began. "The inquisitor Waldemar von Schönborn killed her and my father and abducted my little sister, Elsa. Since then I have been searching for my sister. Can you help me find her?"

Senno's right eyebrow quivered slightly, but otherwise, Lukas couldn't detect any reaction.

"I'm afraid you'll have to tell me a bit more if I am to help you," the astrologer replied finally.

Lukas began to tell everything, starting with his thirteenth birthday, then the abduction of his mother and death of his father, and his own flight. When he got to the burning of his mother at the stake in Heidelberg, it was hard for him to hold back his tears.

"And you are quite certain you saw a blue cloud above the execution site?" Senno asked.

Lukas swallowed the bitter taste in his mouth and nodded. "She spoke to me, very clearly, and she did it a second time. She . . . said Elsa would need me and I was to look for her. That's why I came to this camp."

He continued telling about his nightmares in which he was followed by a huge black wolf, and about the good-luck amulet Red Sara had given him, which recently had turned hot a number of times. Now he had Senno's full attention.

"He seems to take a great interest in you," he murmured.

"Who?" Lukas asked.

Instead of answering, Senno started rifling through the documents on his table, looking for something. Finally he took out an old, tattered parchment roll. "Ah, here it is," he exclaimed with relief. "I was afraid I'd lost it." When he spread it out in front of them, Lukas saw some characters unfamiliar to him and the image of a wolf.

A large black wolf with eyes like glowing coals.

"The wolf in my dream!" cried Lukas. "That's how it looked."

"That's what I suspected." Senno looked at Lukas for a long time, and at last resumed speaking. "This says that black witches have the gift of sending their spirit on journeys to search for someone. To do that, they often choose the figure of a wolf in a nightmare. Sometimes this wolf can also appear in physical form, but for everyone else, it remains invisible."

"A Spanish mercenary mumbled something during our exhibition fight in Augsburg," Lukas recalled. "Then the wolf suddenly appeared and attacked me. Later, mercenaries attacked our camp."

"They wanted to be certain it was really you. *He* wanted to be certain." Senno nodded, lost in thought and rubbing his face with his well-groomed fingers. "He tried to find you, he sent his men out to bring you back, but the amulet protected you. No matter how hard he tries, you're invisible to him. And the reason the pentagram has been so hot lately is that he's so close to you now." Senno leaned back in his chair, pleased with himself. "All the pieces fall together. I was right when I suspected there was something special about you."

Only now did Lukas begin to understand. Despite the warm glow of the lantern, a shiver ran down his spine. Could that be possible?

"You . . . think Schönborn has been looking for me," he asked, "with the help of this black magic? But I always thought . . ."

"He is a man of the Church?" Senno smiled wearily and waved him off. "Once, perhaps, he was, but he hasn't been one for a long time. I assume Waldemar von Schönborn, as an inquisitor, really did find a witch. Since then, he has a compulsion to learn as much as possible about white and black magic in order to someday become a powerful warlock himself. It appears he has already learned some things." Senno gave a deep sigh. "For a long time, I've been collecting evidence against him to put an end to his evil machinations, but Schönborn is sly, he enjoys the trust of Wallenstein, and until now, I have not succeeded in exposing him."

"There's something else I wanted to ask," Lukas said. "Do you remember the frozen ones we spoke about the last time? I think I've actually seen one, and if I'm not mistaken, Schönborn sent him."

Then he told Senno about the strange Spanish mercenary that he and the other servant boys had met in the battle near Nürnberg.

After Lukas had finished, Senno twirled his waxed beard for a moment, thinking. "If that's right, then Schönborn has gone further than I could imagine in my wildest dreams."

Lukas frowned. "What do you mean by that?"

"Well, I've learned that Schönborn wants to overthrow Wallenstein. You must know that the general has powerful ene-mies—the Bavarian elector and now perhaps even the Kaiser himself. For many noblemen, Wallenstein simply has too much influence, and they want to do away with him. As Wallenstein's father confessor, Schönborn sees his own hopes being dashed, and secretly, he would like to switch sides. It would appear that Schönborn sent this mercenary to kill Wallenstein." Senno laughed softly. "And a ragtag bunch of pimply army brats prevented that at the last moment. Who would have thought that possible?" The astrologer paused and seemed to be pondering something else. "Why not?" he mumbled. "It would be worth a chance."

Suddenly, he leaned forward so close that Lukas could smell his perfumed breath. "Can you read?"

Lukas cringed. "Me? Yes, but why—"

"Schönborn must have documents somewhere that would expose him," Senno continued, lost in thought, almost as if he were talking to himself. "Surely, there are revealing letters to the Kaiser, the electors, or others . . . If I had these letters in hand, I could convict him. I could demand from him whatever I wanted. First, he'd have to release all those poor souls awaiting their execution in the infamous monastery. And then he'd have to tell us where your sister is."

"But who is to say that Schönborn really knows where Elsa is?" Lukas asked. "Maybe I'm just pursuing a will-o'-the-wisp."

"Nonsense!" Senno slapped the table so hard that the documents flew in all directions. "Listen, Lukas! This man has a strong compulsion to find you, even if I don't know why. I'm sure he is this wolf that has been terrorizing you, and there is certainly some reason why he took Elsa back then. He will know where she is."

"Back at Lohenfels Castle, Schönborn wanted to have me killed," Lukas interjected. "Why should he be looking for me now?"

"He must have learned something that makes it necessary for him to find you." Senno's gaze was almost pleading. "Lukas, the very first time I saw you I knew there was something very special about you. Perhaps it has something to do with your mother—I don't know. But now fate has brought us together. If you help *me*, I will help *you*."

"And how can I do that?" Lukas asked impatiently.

Senno grinned. "By breaking into the monastery and looking around for compromising documents."

"You want me to break into the monastery?" Lukas shook his head, bewildered. "But I'm just a boy, and a simple servant. Why don't you look for a capable soldier to do this dirty work?"

"First of all, I can't trust anyone here in the camp," replied Senno, rubbing his waxed beard with embarrassment. "My reputation is, ah . . . not the best, as you probably know. And secondly, if Schönborn is looking for you so urgently, there's something about you he fears. It seems there is more to you than one might assume."

Lukas clenched his teeth, and thoughts flashed through his head like tiny fireworks. Everything Senno had just told him was so insane, so bizarre that he just wanted to get up and leave. But hadn't he also had some bizarre experiences lately? Even if Senno's stories about black and white magic were just nonsense, it could still be true that Waldemar von Schönborn was a traitor with plans to kill Wallenstein. If they could find some incriminating documents, it might be possible to extort him and to find out where Elsa was, if she was still alive.

Lukas was still sitting opposite Senno, petrified. The flickering light of the lantern seemed to set the animals on the flags dancing, and the whole room started to spin. At last, Lukas began to speak.

"Very well, I'll do it," he said. "I'll walk into the den of the lion, but only under one condition."

Senno raised his eyebrows. "And that would be . . . ?"

"I'll take my friends along—one for all, all for one. Perhaps that's not a magic formula, but at least it's something just as powerful."

The astrologer began to chuckle.

"You may be right, lad, friendship is indeed a magic bond."

XX

"You want us to break into Schönborn's monastery and steal some documents for this crazy astrologer?"

Giovanni stared wide-eyed at Lukas, and Jerome and Paulus opened their mouths in astonishment. They'd come together before dawn in the ruins of the old mill. All night, Lukas had been wondering if it was really a good idea to have his friends along on this dangerous mission, but he finally decided to tell them his plan. He needed all the help he could get.

"I don't even know myself if we can trust Senno," Lukas admitted, "but at the moment, I have no other way to learn more about Elsa. Senno intends to extort Schönborn—"

"And found a few stupid minions like us to help him," Paulus interrupted. "It doesn't matter if we get caught and tortured, we're just a bunch of kids from the baggage train. Lukas, I really don't know what to say about that, apart from the fact that it's a suicide mission. Even if we manage to get inside the monastery, we have no idea where to look, and the place is probably teeming with all these eerie Spanish mercenaries."

Lukas stared through one of the smudged window openings, where dawn was beginning to break. As so often in recent days, the countryside was wrapped in dense white fog. Inside, they were sitting on worn, moss-covered millstones with a single torch they had brought along for light, which made Lukas feel even more despondent. Paulus was right! The whole idea was more than risky. He still hadn't told his friends that Schönborn was perhaps a real sorcerer; it was difficult enough already to convince them of his plan.

"Then, like it or not, I'll have to do it alone," he muttered.

"Wouldn't that suit you just fine!" Jerome said. "So you can have all the martyr's laurels to yourself. No way—we're coming with you!"

"Really?" Lukas asked timidly.

Giovanni grinned. "Of course, you idiot. To even have a chance of success, you'll need my intelligence . . ."

"And my strength," Paulus grumbled. "Too bad it's not a cloister with young, pretty nuns—then we would have some use for Jerome."

"Hey, what do you mean—" Jerome burst out. But at that moment, they heard a commotion in front of one of the windows. Paulus put his finger to his lips, ran to the window, reached through the opening, and pulled in a struggling, kicking creature by the back of the collar.

It was Daniel.

"Let me go right away, you . . . you fat monster!" the boy shouted, pummeling Paulus in the side.

"And what if I don't?" Paulus replied, lifting Daniel up in the air. "Are you going to call the Swedish king to help you?"

"Let him down, big guy," Giovanni said. "You're going to choke him. Make him tell us what he's doing here."

"Well then?" said Jerome, rolling his eyes. "It's obvious this annoying kid is looking for someone to play with again. Since he knows where we hide out now, this little leech won't let go."

Paulus set the boy down on the ground roughly. Daniel crossed his arms defiantly and glared at the older boys. Despite the unfortunate situation, Lukas had to admit to himself he was actually a bit happy to see Daniel.

"Ha! I listened in on you," the boy snarled. His face was just as soiled with dirt as the last time they'd met. "I know what you're going to do."

"It was only a game," said Lukas, trying to calm him down, fearing that Daniel would blurt out their secret in the army camp. "Nothing you heard was meant seriously."

"You're lying!" Daniel shouted. "I know you're going to break into the monastery and look for something there, and if you don't let me help you and your gang, then I'll . . . I'll . . ." He hesitated.

"What will you do?" asked Paulus in a threatening tone.

Daniel was silent, but his eyes flashed like a wild animal at bay.

"Naturally, you can stay with our gang," said Giovanni, who was also trying to calm the boy down. "I have a suggestion. We'll go to the woods with you tomorrow to practice shooting—"

"No, I'm going with you to the monastery," Daniel interrupted.

"You're doing *what*?" said Lukas with disbelief.

"I'm going with you to the monastery. I can help you."

"Well, isn't that a great plan!" Jerome clapped with feigned enthusiasm. "A little kid like you smuggles us past the guards and guides us to the strictly confidential documents of Wallenstein's father confessor. Why didn't we think of that ourselves? An ingenious plan!"

"There's a changing of the guard every two hours at the monastery," Daniel replied in a serious tone. "For a short time, the back door is unguarded. Of course, you have to sneak past the mercenaries in the hallway. And, ah, yes . . . if you're looking for documents, they are probably in the archive on the second floor."

For a long time no one said a thing. The four friends just stared at Daniel as if he were a ghost.

"How do you know all that?" Lukas finally asked. "Or did you just make it up?"

Daniel shook his head. "I'm in the monastery every day, and I know every room there, from the cellar to the attic. You won't find a better guide than me."

"Do you belong to Schönborn's retinue?" Paulus inquired. "Are you a baggage carrier for his soldiers?" When Daniel nodded, Paulus tore at his hair and groaned. "Damn, why didn't you say that before? It would have saved us a lot of trouble."

"Nobody asked me," Daniel replied coolly. "So do you think I can come along?"

"Not so fast," Jerome said, turning to Daniel. "Listen, kid. I believe now you're telling the truth and you really are part of Schönborn's retinue. Perhaps you work there in the kitchen or something like that. But this is no easy matter. Why don't you tell us everything you know about the monastery, and—"

"Either you take me along or I won't say anything more," Daniel declared.

"Good Lord, did anyone ever tell you that you're a real nuisance!" Paulus shouted. "If I were your father, I'd beat you black-and-blue at least three times a day."

Daniel grinned. "But you're not my father."

Lukas had to smile as well. In many ways, Daniel reminded him of his sister. He was about to turn back to the boy when he heard a noise outside in front of the mill, and he suddenly fell silent. It sounded like the voices of many men.

"It looks like we have visitors again," Giovanni whispered. "Isn't there ever any peace and quiet here?"

He crept to the window opening and peered out into the early light of dawn. Quickly he withdrew, then turned to the other boys, his face as white as chalk.

"What's the matter?" Lukas asked.

Giovanni's hands began to tremble as he pointed toward the window. "See for yourself."

Now the others came running to the window. Lukas squinted and recognized a group of soldiers creeping through the forest nearby in the early morning fog. Though they were speaking softly, it was audible, and what they spoke was not German.

They were Swedes.

"What are *they* doing here?" Jerome whispered. "I thought King Gustav Adolf had taken his troops to their winter quarters, just as we have."

"Apparently not," Giovanni replied. "This looks like a reconnaissance party, and wherever there is a reconnaissance party, there's an army not far behind."

"Do you think the Swedes are going to attack us *now*—at the start of winter?" Paulus stared at him. "But . . . but . . ."

"That doesn't make any sense at all, I know." Giovanni nodded grimly. "And that's just the reason they're attacking us now—because we don't expect it. You've got to admit, it's a stroke of genius. We've got to go and warn our men as soon as possible, or Wallenstein's army will be wiped out!"

More and more Swedish soldiers appeared from behind the dark pine trees and fanned out in the forest. Lukas had long ago stopped counting them. There were dozens, probably even an entire company. A smaller group now proceeded straight toward the mill.

"If they find us here, then it's over for us," Jerome groaned, "and I'm afraid it's already too late to circle around them."

"Then, like it or not, we'll have to break through their lines," Paulus responded, reaching boldly for his saber.

Lukas pointed at Daniel, who was standing next to them with an anxious expression on his face. "And how about the kid? We can't just leave him here alone."

"We'll bring him along and take the troops by surprise in front of the mill," said Giovanni, also drawing his sword. "The fog outside is pretty dense, and if we're lucky, we can get through their lines without being caught." He took a deep breath. "At least we'll have the element of surprise in our favor. On three, we'll attack. One, two, *three* . . ."

Paulus kicked at the rotted wooden door, which burst open with a crash, revealing a handful of astonished Swedes.

"Together against death and the devil!" Jerome roared.

"To hell and beyond!" cried Lukas, Giovanni, and Paulus all at the same time.

Holding little Daniel by the arm, Lukas ran toward the Swedish soldiers. The fog had gotten even thicker, billowing over the land, enveloping much of it like a white shroud. The soldiers had recovered from their initial confusion and were running toward the friends with drawn swords. Behind them in the fog, other soldiers became visible. Holding Daniel firmly with his right hand, Lukas lashed out with his Pappenheim sword. He could feel his blade sliding through something soft, then he heard a groan, and now he was past the first line of Swedes. The others ran alongside him toward the forest, still enveloped in darkness, where the first outposts of Wallenstein's winter camp were located. If they could get that far, they would be safe.

More soldiers came running toward them. There was a loud bang, and through the white fog Lukas could see the flash of a gun muzzle. He cursed himself for not having loaded his own pistol earlier, but now it was too late.

The bullet had obviously missed them, as he could see Giovanni, Jerome, and Paulus, along with Daniel, still running next to him. Slashing with their swords, the friends fought their way through, and the Swedes withdrew, cursing angrily. Another shot followed, and this time Lukas heard a shout of pain.

Giovanni stumbled forward a few steps before collapsing.

"Giovanni!" Lukas cried. He wanted to run over to help, but he also had to care for little Daniel, who was clutching his hand so hard it was almost as if they were bound together.

"Giovanni!" Lukas cried again, as he continued stumbling through the forest. Out of the corner of his eye he could see Jerome bending down over their injured friend. For a moment, Lukas was distracted. There was a sound of something whistling through the air as he was attacked from the side, and only at the last second was Paulus able to come between them and ward off the blow from the Swedish soldier.

It had missed Daniel's head by a hair.

"Run ahead with the kid!" Paulus called to Lukas. "I'll take care of Jerome and Giovanni . . . Hurry!"

Paulus ran back to his two friends, around whom a dark cluster of Swedish soldiers had gathered. Lukas could see there were far too many—his friends would never make it—and he got only a quick glimpse of Paulus before a cloud of fog passed over the scene.

Lukas ran on with Daniel, who was clinging to him in terror. It couldn't be much farther to the clearing. Lukas thought he could make out a lighter area in front of them with a red glow of individual campfires. Their winter quarters! He continued running, with the shouts of the Swedish soldiers right behind him.

When they had almost reached the clearing, suddenly another Swede rose up directly in front of them out of the fog, like a phantom. Grinning, he approached Lukas and Daniel with a raised pistol.

"Förbaskade skitstövel," the Swede cursed as he aimed.

There was a flash, and for a brief moment, Lukas saw blue stars before his eyes. Assuming the flash came from the pistol, he fell to the ground, pulling Daniel down with him. Above them, the Swede shouted. It sounded as if he was in great pain. Lukas looked up cautiously and saw the soldier whimpering and rubbing his eyes. Had he injured himself with the shot? Everything around Lukas was gray, and he couldn't make out anything. Then something strange occurred to him.

I didn't hear a shot . . . How is that possible?

There wasn't any time left to think. He scrambled to his feet, took Daniel by the arm, and ran on until he finally reached the edge of the clearing. Before him in the fog, Lukas could see the first campfires in the Kaiser's winter quarters, and the angry shouts behind him faded away. He stumbled toward the nearest fire, where a sleepy watchman squinted at him.

"Say, lad, what's going on?" the guard grumbled. Then he yawned and got to his feet. "You look like you've seen a ghost."

"Not a ghost," Lukas panted. "The Swedes! They're coming! They're already—"

Gunshots could now be heard in the forest. Lukas turned around and saw his three friends running toward the campfire.

Paulus had thrown the injured Giovanni over his shoulder like a sack of potatoes, and Jerome was right behind them. Again there were flashes of light at the edge of the clearing, then the report of a gun, but the shots missed their target. More and more Swedes appeared out of the fog, black dots in a line, but they didn't yet dare leave the cover of the forest.

Out of breath, the three boys finally reached Lukas, Daniel, and the watchman, who clutched his spear, clearly confused.

"Quick, you idiot," Paulus cried, "sound the alarm! Or do you want the enemy to rouse us from our dreams with their swords and muskets?"

At last, the soldier began to understand. He reached for his horn, blew it loudly, and soon other horns answered from the other campfires—a wild cacophony that could be heard for miles, as the sun slowly rose in the east.

The Swedes had arrived.

Grim-faced, Zoltan entered the tent in the field hospital where the five boys were taken after their confrontation with the Swedes. "It looks like I have to thank you boys for the second time."

Outside the tent, the noise of thousands of soldiers could be heard hurriedly preparing for the battle to come.

A bullet had grazed Giovanni's left leg. It hurt, but fortunately was not life threatening. Paulus and Jerome had gotten off with a few bruises, though they'd had to fight like tigers against more than a dozen soldiers. No doubt the dense fog had saved the three of them.

"They were actually Swedish scouts you scared off," Zoltan continued. "Their army is not far away from us." The commander cursed and spat on the ground. "These incredible dogs don't abide by any ordinary guidelines, they just go ahead and attack during the winter. But they'll pay for this! Now that we know their plan, we'll throw all our resources into the battle against them."

"But aren't our men scattered for miles all around?" Giovanni asked. "And General Pappenheim's army was recently sent back to Halle. How can he come to help us that fast?" Giovanni's face was still pale, but evidently he hadn't lost too much blood—in any case, his mind was functioning perfectly once again.

"We've already sent messengers to Pappenheim," Zoltan replied, "but you are right. We can only pray that the general and his men arrive in time. Meanwhile, Field Marshal Colloredo will hold off the enemy here while the Black Musketeers head for Lützen, where we shall meet up with the other parts of the army. That's a small town, around ten miles from here. We'll meet the Swedes there for our last great battle." He looked at them earnestly, one by one. "I expect to see you in the front line, as is appropriate for the Black Musketeers. Except for Giovanni, of course, who will stay here in the hospital tent. And . . ." Only then did Zoltan appear to realize there was a fifth boy among them. Daniel had been sitting quietly in the background, still terrified by the strange encounter with the Swedish scouts.

"What's this little rascal doing here?" Zoltan asked, puzzled. "He's not one of us."

"Eh . . . that's Daniel, from the baggage train of the inquisitor Waldemar von Schönborn," Lukas explained. "He got lost in the woods when the enemy came."

"Aha! Lost . . ." Zoltan squinted suspiciously. "Then send the little runt back to Schönborn. I've heard that Wallenstein's father confessor is staying here in the monastery. I'll be glad when I can get rid of that troublemaker. I was afraid I'd have to watch a few poor sinners get burned at the stake." He clapped impatiently. "And now hurry up! The next time the horn blows, we march off. Don't disappoint me."

With one final, emphatic nod, Zoltan left the tent, leaving the boys alone. They could already hear the sounds of muskets and cannons going off, and it was clear that skirmishes had already broken out nearby.

"Did you hear that?" Giovanni whispered, after the commander had left. "This is our chance."

"Eh?" Jerome frowned. "What is our chance? Too often you speak in riddles."

"Good Lord, how can anyone be so stupid!" Giovanni exclaimed. "The army is leaving, and only Schönborn is staying behind in the monastery. That means the building will practically be unguarded. If we want to steal these documents—now is the time."

"You forget Schönborn's guards, the Spanish mercenaries," Paulus grumbled. "Surely, they'll stay here with him."

"I can get you past them," Daniel said, apparently having recovered from his fright. "I know a hallway that—"

Jerome groaned. "*Mon dieu*, I'd completely forgotten that our esteemed leader reaches just up to my navel. Perhaps we should take off for Lützen right away and fight in the front line. Then at least I'll be killed by a bullet and not have to die in the inquisitor's torture chamber."

"I've made up my mind," Lukas said. "I'm going to the monastery with Daniel. Giovanni is right—we'll never have a better chance. Who knows if Schönborn isn't already preparing to leave?"

"But what about our oath?" Paulus asked. "We are Black Musketeers, don't forget. We have sworn always to follow the orders of our commander. You heard Zoltan, and he won't put up with any nonsense."

Jerome nodded. "We are Black Musketeers, we don't just run away. And besides—"

"I also swore an oath to my mother!" Lukas interrupted brusquely. "And for me, that carries more weight than any soldier's vow. I'm going to look for Elsa, and by God, I'm going to find her," he declared, staring stubbornly at the others. "Besides, for a long time I've been wondering about the point of this war. At first, I thought it was all about protecting the German Empire from its enemies—the Protestants, the Danes, the Swedes . . . But who really is our friend, and who is our foe? Wherever I look, all I see are victims, on both sides!"

His face contorted in pain, Giovanni sat up from his sickbed. "I agree with Lukas. This is a war between great powers, and the farmers have to suffer for it. I'm sick of extorting every last penny from the poor so that our baggage train can keep eating its way through the country. If we just keep on like this, the war will never end."

"That's nonsense," Paulus argued. "We can destroy the Swedes here and now. Then we'll finally have peace."

Giovanni nodded grimly. "The peace of the dead—until the next battle, and the next . . . How long has this war been going on? Ten years? Twenty? I've stopped counting."

"If everyone thinks like you, we'll be an easy target for the Swedish king," replied Jerome. "I can't forget that my parents were murdered by Protestant mercenaries loyal to the Swedes."

"A few of the men out there saved my butt at Nürnberg," Paulus growled, straightening up to his full height. He, too, seemed to have made his decision. "I can't let them down now, not in this decisive battle."

"But you can abandon Lukas? Is that what you're saying?" Giovanni hit back.

"Damn! I don't even know his sister, and none of us even knows if she's still alive." Paulus pointed furiously at the entrance to the tent. "But the men out there I know, and they're still alive."

"Stop!" Lukas shouted. "Just stop your quarreling because of me. I didn't want any of that. You're my friends, aren't you?"

An embarrassing silence followed. Just as Giovanni was about to reply, a horn sounded outside the tent.

"The signal to march off," Jerome murmured, and he looked down at the ground.

Paulus cleared his throat. "I'll check the horses over there," he grumbled. "Some of them need to be saddled. We can talk later, can't we?" He looked at Lukas, who smiled back at him wearily.

"It's all right, Paulus, just go. We'll meet again, I'm sure."

Jerome, too, headed slowly toward the exit. "I'll go and help Paulus. Until later then, Lukas."

Jerome winked at Lukas, trying to appear confident. But it didn't look genuine; it was as if he were wearing a mask. Then he went outside with Paulus, where the noise of the departing baggage train could be heard. Lukas, Giovanni, and Daniel remained behind, alone.

"Surely, they'll be back soon, and then . . . ," Giovanni began to say, trying to console Lukas, but he shook his head sadly.

"They're right, Giovanni. They're heading off to their war, and I'm going off to mine."

"Whatever happens, you can rely on me," Giovanni replied. He tried to get up, but fell back onto his bed with a groan. The injury troubled him more than he'd first admitted.

"Damn!" he cried. "Why couldn't the bullet have gone just a bit farther to the left?"

"It could also have gone a bit farther up, then you would be dead," Lukas replied as he got to his feet. He buckled on his sword, reached for his pistol, and put on the leather straps attached to the pouch of gunpowder and bag of bullets.

"Where are you going now?" Giovanni asked, pearls of sweat on his brow.

"Where else? I'm going to the monastery with Daniel. We'll find those documents and take them to Senno, and then I'm going to pray that my sister is still alive."

"I'll pray with you, Lukas," Giovanni promised in a faltering voice. Once again he tried to sit up, but fell back, moaning. "You must forgive the others," he said. "They've experienced terrible things in this war, and they think they're doing the right thing."

"Everyone in this war thinks they're doing the right thing," Lukas replied gloomily. A bitter taste rose in his mouth. He took Daniel by the hand. Until then, the boy had been listening silently to the friends' conversation.

I mustn't cry now, Lukas thought. *I'm no longer a child, and I have a mission to fulfill.*

"Come, boy, it's time to go," he murmured, leading Daniel to the exit.

"I wish you luck with all my heart," Giovanni called to them.

"I'll need it," replied Lukas. "Farewell, my friend."

Then he turned and headed out with Daniel into the noisy army camp.

XXI

For a while, Lukas perceived his surroundings as if through a veil. The laughing and singing soldiers, the neighing horses pulling heavy cannons toward the battlefield, the distant gunfire . . . Everything seemed muted and gray, just like the winter sky with its deep-hanging clouds.

A nagging feeling came over Lukas that he'd just lost the only real friends he'd ever had. Once again, he was alone, and no one could say who would survive this battle or what awaited him in this accursed monastery. Lukas had come to a crossroads, and now there was no going back.

He had to find Elsa, even if this attempt should cost him his life.

The sounds of musket fire brought him back to earth. The first skirmishes were beginning nearby, and he had to take care. He grabbed Daniel firmly by the arm and ran toward the little city of Weißenfels, from which a long line of soldiers wound its way. Here some of the larger buildings were burning, among them the old castle that the soldiers had likely set on fire when they left. The city gates were wide open, and the air was full of the odor of smoke, gunpowder, and death. Lukas decided to avoid the wide main road in order to meet as few soldiers as possible. They ran through deserted alleys and lanes, encountering from time to time a horse that had broken free or a wandering cow. Thundering cannons could be heard outside the city walls.

"You have a sister?" Daniel asked after they'd wandered around awhile.

Lukas nodded dreamily. Only now did it occur to him that he hadn't told Daniel anything about Elsa.

"Yes, I have a sister," he said, "but I've lost contact with her during the war. When I saw her the last time, I promised I'd keep looking for her, and since then, that's what I've been doing. I'm hoping I'll learn more about her in the monastery."

"I had a brother once," Daniel replied. Suddenly he appeared very tired and confused. "But that was a long time ago. I can't remember him—he probably died."

"Well, I don't know about my sister," said Lukas, "but something tells me she's still alive—at least I hope she is. Her name is Elsa."

"Elsa?" Daniel stopped and smiled. "A nice name. I think—"

An earsplitting blast made Lukas flinch, and he dropped to the ground, pulling Daniel after him. A moment later, huge rocks and rubble came flying over their heads, smashing through the roof of a house. There was another loud crash, and splintered rafters fell all around them. When Lukas looked up cautiously, he saw that part of the castle had been destroyed. Evidently the withdrawing soldiers had blown up large supplies of black powder.

"I'm afraid we have no time now for conversation," Lukas panted as he turned to Daniel. "Show me how to get into the monastery unnoticed. You said you know the way."

"Come." Daniel took his hand and led him on through the silent lanes until they came to a stop in front of a dark, towering, box-shaped building. For a moment, Lukas thought he heard a desperate cry coming from inside.

"The monastery," Daniel announced, with childlike innocence. "This is where I live."

Shuddering, Lukas looked up at the mighty walls, blackened by the soot of centuries. It might have been a splendid building at one time, but the war had left its mark here, too. Gutted windows stared out at the two boys, and the upper part of the steeple had collapsed, but the monastery building behind it seemed to be in better condition, with gardens and a cloister. Daniel led Lukas past the monastery into a narrow lane.

"Where are we going?" Lukas asked, surprised.

Instead of replying, Daniel led him to a small stone bridge over a trickle of water that might at one time have been a brook, though now the bed was muddy and almost dry. Daniel pointed to a rusty grille directly under the bridge.

"I found this grille some time ago when I was playing," he said proudly. "It's easy to lift up."

To prove his point, he climbed down into the smelly streambed and pushed the rusty grille aside. Lukas followed, but was disgusted to find himself up to his ankles in mud. He crawled over a dead cat, then stooped down and squinted into the dark passageway.

"And this passage really does lead to the monastery?" Lukas frowned. "Are you sure?"

"It doesn't take long," Daniel tried to assure him. "I've already used it a couple of times when I wanted to run away for a while. Come on!"

The two boys crawled on all fours through the knee-high tunnel that stank of mold and garbage. It was so dark that Lukas couldn't even see his hand in front of his face. Again and again, he reached out and touched something disgusting and slimy. He didn't even want to know what it was. And a few times his shirt ripped against sharp corners and edges. Fortunately, Daniel was telling the truth, as the tunnel soon ended in front of another grille hanging loosely on its hinges. Behind it Lukas could just barely make out a large room.

"The wine cellar," Daniel whispered, carefully opening the grating. His face was even grimier than usual now. "From this point on we need to watch out for the guards."

As quietly as possible they sneaked past the huge barrels. A bit of daylight shone through the slits in the walls so that Lukas could see a door at the other end of the cellar. Daniel put his finger to his lips and pressed on the door. It swung open, revealing a hallway lit by a few torches that soon branched in two directions. To the right, the stairway led up, and to the left . . .

A long, agonizing scream came from that direction, and Lukas knew at once where that corridor led. He hadn't been wrong earlier.

The torture chamber! he thought. *Surely, that's where they took the butcher and his daughter. We have to help these people before they suffer the same fate as my mother.*

He was about to turn left, but Daniel tugged at his sleeve to hold him back.

"There are too many guards that way," he whispered. "They'll catch us right away. You want to search for papers, don't you?"

Lukas nodded reluctantly. Even if everything in him wanted to resist, he had to admit that Daniel was right. And he'd have to trust that Senno had told him the truth. If they had the documents, they'd be able to extort Schönborn, and then he would have to release the prisoners.

Again a piercing cry echoed through the dark corridors. Lukas clenched his teeth, then followed Daniel, who had already scurried up the worn stairs to the ground floor. Suddenly, the boy stopped and motioned to Lukas to be silent. With bated breath, Lukas pressed his back to the wall, trying to make himself as invisible as possible.

They could hear footsteps coming, and Lukas caught a glimpse of three Spanish mercenaries patrolling the wide hallway. They were talking quietly, and he was relieved to see that the frozen man with the scar was not among them. Nevertheless, if the guards turned their heads just a bit, they would discover the two boys on the stairway, and Lukas didn't even want to think what would happen then.

He didn't dare to breathe again until the mercenaries had gone by.

"That was close," he whispered.

"But good for us," Daniel said with a smile. "They're making the rounds. After they pass us, they go first to the cloister and then to the sleeping quarters, so the way up to the library is clear."

"What do you actually do here that makes you so familiar with this place?" Lukas whispered.

But Daniel was already hurrying down the hallway toward another stairway leading up to the second floor. At the top of the stairs, he ran straight toward a wooden double door.

"The library," he said. "If you are looking for documents, this is the right place. Besides, he always works here."

"*He?*" Lukas gasped and stopped suddenly. "Schönborn? You mean Waldemar von Schönborn works in there? But if he's now—"

"Now he's over in the church celebrating mass," Daniel cut in. "He always does that around this time." The boy had already opened the door and motioned for Lukas to enter. "Here," he said, smiling with pride. "The library. We have time until the next bell rings, when the mass is over."

Reverently Lukas entered the high-ceilinged, wood-paneled room. Books, folios, and rolls of parchment rested on shelves reaching up to the ceiling. In the middle of the room was a large oak table with stacks of documents piled on it, and behind the table, a chair whose wooden frame and high back were richly decorated. Grotesque demonic figures with devil's horns seemed to grow out of the wood. Many had their mouths wide open; others writhed in pain or seemed to be casting evil glances at the observer.

The inquisitor's throne. The thought flashed through Lukas's mind: *This is where he probably signs his death sentences.*

He reached for the amulet hanging around his neck, which until then had at least given him a feeling of being protected. But it was missing. He stared at his torn shirt in shock.

"The amulet!" he cried. "It's gone!"

Once again he felt around his neck, under his shirt, and in his pockets, but the talisman had disappeared.

"I must have lost it down in the stinking sewer," Lukas said. "It got caught on something. Damn!"

He felt an irresistible urge to run back into the cellar to look for the amulet, but naturally he knew that would be foolish. They should feel lucky they made it into the library at all, and there was no proof the talisman really offered any protection. Perhaps it was all just pure superstition. Here in this room, he didn't need any magic, just a clear head.

He walked along the bookshelves. Where should he start his search? Senno had spoken of documents that would bring Schönborn's treachery to light. Letters, messages, hastily scribbled orders . . . He saw nothing but endless rows of books and parchment rolls. Randomly he began taking some heavy tomes off the shelves, but all were written in Latin. Now he was annoyed he'd spent most of his time staring out the window during the old chaplain's Latin class, unlike Elsa, who could read Latin verses out loud by the time she was six and had always been interested in books. He put the books back and moved on to some other shelves. The works here were more interesting, full of symbols, pentagrams, and signs like the ones he'd seen in Senno's tent. One of the books was lavishly illustrated—a male goat dancing around a young maiden wearing a wreath in her hair, for example, or a snake coiled around a five-pointed star. Curious, Lukas took the book and began to leaf through it. He probably wouldn't find any proof of Schönborn's treachery here, but it did seem like a kind of magic book. Was Senno right—was Schönborn really a black witch?

"The *Grimorium Verum*," came a voice just behind him. It was Daniel.

Lukas jumped. For a moment, he'd completely forgotten he wasn't alone in the room.

"It's very old," Daniel continued. "It describes how to conjure up demons. I like the pictures because the animals look so real, but the Merseburg Incantations are even better."

"What . . . ?" Lukas was at a loss for words and·just stared at Daniel in amazement. "You know all these books here?"

"Well, not all of them, but most. Whenever I'm bored, I leaf through them, and I'm often very bored."

Lukas pointed at the endless rows of shelves and shook his head. "But there are hundreds of books here! How can you say you know all the books in the monastery? You've only been here a few weeks."

"Not here in the monastery." Daniel winked at him. "He always takes them along, well protected in boxes. When he has time, he even reads them to me out loud." He closed his eyes and whispered almost inaudibly, *"Eiris sâzun idisi, sâzun hêra duoder, suma heri lezidum . . ."*

"He reads to you?" Slowly it was dawning on Lukas that Daniel was perhaps not a simple servant boy as he and the others had assumed. "It seems you know the inquisitor quite well," he mumbled.

"I'm not so sure." Daniel shrugged. "He rarely has time for me, even though he sometimes says I'm the most valuable thing he has. He wants me to call him Father, though he really isn't." The boy glared at Lukas. "He locks me up like a precious gem. Now this is what he gets for doing so little to take care of me. That's why I play tricks on him."

Lukas seized Daniel by the arm. "Listen, Daniel. I really have to know now what you have to do with Schönborn. This isn't any joke—it's important."

"Hey, you're hurting me, stop!" Daniel tried in vain to squirm away. "Just wait!" he snarled. "When he learns about this, he'll punish you, you'll see!"

"Then he can just go ahead and do it, but first you're going to tell me why you know all about these books here, how it is you can read Latin, and why you mumbled those words before."

"He taught me how to, he taught me everything . . . and if you don't let me go right away, I'll show you what else I learned from him . . . you ruffian!" Daniel squirmed and whined, but Lukas kept a firm grasp on him.

"Let me go!" Daniel shouted again. "Or you will regret it . . . *Let me go!*"

At the very moment Daniel raised his voice, something strange happened. Directly in front of Lukas, there was a blinding flash of blue light, so brief it might have been his imagination, but Lukas's eyes hurt as if he'd looked right into the sun. He cried out, let Daniel go, and placed his hands in front of his eyes. He recalled when he'd seen that flash of light before. It was just that morning, when he and Daniel had fled from the Swedish soldiers into the forest. A soldier had been blinded, just as he had been now.

By Daniel?

"Who are you?" Lukas gasped as the pain in his eyes subsided. "What's between you and the inquisitor?"

At that moment there was a creaking sound as the double door to the library swung open. Lukas looked up and saw as if in a dream Waldemar von Schönborn standing in the doorway, a smirk on his lips. He was wearing a wide black cloak with a high collar, and a crimson cap covered his thinning hair.

"What a wonderful surprise," exclaimed Schönborn as he entered the room, his cloak fluttering behind him like a pair of leathery wings. "I thought I heard something, that is, I felt your presence, Lukas. I could sense you were very close by, but I didn't know you would come to visit me so soon."

The inquisitor motioned toward Daniel, who was standing in a corner, pouting. "And I see you've already met my impudent protégé. I ought to really give her a good spanking, but on the other hand she led you to me."

"*She?*" asked Lukas, still slightly blinded, in a rasping voice. Everything seemed to start spinning around. "But why . . ."

"Yes, *she*." Schönborn's lips twisted into a diabolical grin as he continued smugly. "I hope you still recognize Elsa. She may have changed a bit, but she's still just the same impudent and insufferable know-it-all as she was more than a year ago. A real nuisance, but very . . . well, yes, *talented*." He laughed softly and clapped his hands as if he'd just pulled off a successful magic trick. "What a joy! So now brother and sister are finally united again."

XXII

Lukas had to catch his breath. The shock was so great he thought for a moment he'd pass out. Had he misheard? This boy in front of him was really Elsa? Still slightly dazed, he stared at Daniel, who was clearly as confused as he was. Only now did Lukas recognize features in Daniel's dirt-covered face that seemed strangely familiar to him—the dimple on the chin, the freckles, the small gap between teeth . . . But the boy in front of him had short, dark hair, and Elsa's was long and blond, and furthermore—

"Your sister was always a tomboy, as you surely know," said Schönborn, interrupting Lukas's thoughts. "She really did everything she could to be accepted among the boys following the army. She cut her hair short and dyed it so she could move through the army camp unmolested. With all the dirt on her face, I would even have had trouble recognizing her. Beyond that, your sister, as I said, is extremely talented. She has learned a few tricks that were even difficult for me."

The inquisitor stepped forward a few paces and turned to his protégé. "Elsa, *demonstra veritatem*!" he demanded in a booming voice. The impertinent, defiant child, whom Lukas had for so long thought of as Daniel, suddenly seemed very weak and fragile. Hesitantly, she held her hands up to her face and lowered her fingers, and it was as if she were stripping off a mask.

"My God," Lukas gasped. "How is that possible?"

Standing in front of him was his little sister.

Lukas didn't know exactly what Elsa had done as she passed her hands over her face. It was still the same dirty face, the same short haircut, and the same black hair, but now her features suddenly looked softer, more like a girl's. The changes were small, but taken together they transformed the strange boy into an all-too-familiar girl.

"Lukas . . . ?" she asked hesitantly, as if awakening slowly from a bad dream. Her familiar voice was back as well.

"Not bad, eh?" Schönborn said with a smile. "She inherited her mother's talent, but even now she's better than her mother, much better. Someday she will be a very powerful witch. I have woven my magic around her so she no longer remembers her family, but it appears the bond between the two of you is stronger than the shackles of my magic. I shall have to cast another spell. *Veni Nebulae!*" Again, Schönborn's voice thundered, and he waved his hand in a peculiar gesture.

Elsa staggered, as if struck hard by something, and seemed to fall into a trance. She closed her eyes, opened them again, and stared at Lukas, but this time her gaze was blank.

"Who . . . are you?" she murmured.

Lukas could no longer hold back. Tears ran down his cheeks, and he embraced the little sister he had been seeking for so long. And all that time she had been so close!

"It's all right now, Elsa," he whispered. "I promised not to let you down, and now I am finally back with you." Everything was all right, he'd said, but he knew deep in his heart that was not true.

"How touching," Schönborn said. "Little brother and little sister in each other's arms. Too bad that your parents are no longer here to see it."

"You devil!" Lukas yelled. He released Elsa and reached for the loaded pistol next to the sword on his belt.

"You devil!" he cried again, aiming at Schönborn. "I don't know what game you're playing here, but one thing I do know— you'll pay for this, for the death of my mother and father, and for everything you have done to my family."

Waldemar von Schönborn didn't flinch. "If you kill me now, your sister will be lost to you forever," he said ominously. "I can make sure she never remembers you again, and that she remains forever in the same world of dreams she is in now. If you calm down, however, I give you my word of honor I will let you both live."

"The word of honor of a warlock and a murderer!"

Schönborn grinned. "Perhaps, but still, my word of honor. That's the best I can offer. So what do you say?"

Reluctantly, Lukas lowered the pistol. His sister had fallen to the floor, curled up, and seemed to be sleeping.

Schönborn nodded with satisfaction. "Good children, both of you. Now put down the pistol, remove your sword, and come closer."

Lukas obeyed. Unarmed, he approached Schönborn, who had taken his seat on the throne adorned with demonic wood carvings and was looking at him with an almost paternalistic smile.

"You're surely wondering what this is all about," he began. "Let me say first that your sister's well-being is very close to my heart . . ." He paused for a moment. "Perhaps more than you can imagine."

"What did you do to her?" Lukas growled. "What happened to Elsa since you took her away?"

Schönborn sighed. "Always this childish impatience! I'm afraid that to explain it, I have to go back a bit further." He pointed to the shelves along the walls. "Have you looked at the books here?"

Lukas nodded. "They're books of magic, aren't they? Then you really are a sorcerer."

"Call it what you will, I myself have never liked that word. It reminds me too much of pitch and sulfur and cheap tricks performed at country fairs. Let's say I investigate powerful things that cannot be explained."

"Things you use to send other people to the stake," Lukas cut in.

Schönborn dismissed the thought with a wave of his hand. "They are sacrificed on the altar of truth, and sometimes I acquire ancient knowledge from them. Midwives and Gypsies, especially, have preserved knowledge that goes far back to Roman times."

"To the druids," Lukas replied.

"Aha! You know about them?" Schönborn chuckled. "Let me guess, my old adversary Senno told you about them, didn't he? Did he also send you here? You must watch out for him just as much as you do me. If he knew my little secret, he'd do exactly the same as I do, I'm sure. He's been looking for it almost as long as I have."

Lukas frowned. "What secret?"

Once again, Waldemar von Schönborn pointed at the books on his shelves. "Most of these books aren't worth much," he said wearily. "They're just cheap works of random charlatans. Some contain perhaps a grain of truth, but it's very difficult to find." Lost in his thoughts, he fondled the demonic figures on the armrest. "There is only one work that truly deserves to be called a book of magic. It's so powerful that if properly used it could change the world forever." He sighed. "Unfortunately, it is not in my hands. Not yet. It is called the *Grimorium Nocturnum*, the *Book of the Night* . . ." His last words were hardly more than a whisper, but the room seemed suddenly to cool down, and Lukas's flesh began to crawl.

"No less a person than Taliesin, the famous English bard, was said to have written it," Schönborn continued. "The gates of the world stand open to anyone who can read and apply the teachings of the *Grimorium Nocturnum*—nothing can stop him. For centuries the book was hidden away in Bohemia, in a monastery in Prague, and I've spent half my life trying to find it. I almost got my hands on it." He pounded his fist on the table while Elsa tossed restlessly about in a corner, moaning in her sleep.

"But then the war came, and the abbess at that time had the book taken away. She entrusted it to a young nun blessed with a strange gift. She was a white magician, one of the last great witches. With this book, she could have turned the world upside down!" Schönborn raised his hands toward the ceiling as if pronouncing a benediction. "But this stubborn woman used the *Grimorium* only for trivial miracles—healing peasants, making wells flow again, and causing rain to fall when the crops were suffering from a drought."

Lukas groaned. "My mother . . . this young nun was my mother."

"Sophia von Lohenfels, indeed." Schönborn nodded. "Beautiful, intelligent, just as hard to control as her daughter.

She married some good-for-nothing knight. It took me two years to find her. But Sophia was strong, and I couldn't wrest the book from her." The inquisitor sneered. "Then the pope made me his tool, with all the power and authority of a witch hunter. Your mother was one of the first suspects I was able to . . . question. Still, she wouldn't tell me where she'd hidden the book. She remained silent to the very end." Schönborn shook his head, almost sadly. "What a waste! Together we could have done so much."

Once more, Lukas thought back to his mother at the stake, the blue cloud, the stars, and he could hear her voice within him again.

Have no fear, my son. I will always be with you . . .

"My mother is dead," Lukas said in a soft voice, "so what do you want from me and Elsa?"

"Now we are getting to the heart of the matter." Schönborn leaned over the table, examining Lukas like a rare insect. "Even though your mother remained steadfast on the rack, I could coax at least one sentence from her. Only her two children could lead me to the hiding place . . . those were her last words. At that time, I had only one child, the other had fled, and I used every power I had to try to find him."

The wolf, Lukas thought. *Senno was right. Schönborn sent the wolf to find me!*

"Someone gave you a piece of jewelry protected by a magic spell," Schönborn went on. "I assume it was a talisman—a pentagram, wasn't it? It made you invisible to me. But it appears you no longer have the amulet, and I could pick up your trail again. When I was over in the church, I clearly felt your presence." He grinned. "Now the secret can finally come to light."

"I know nothing," Lukas replied and looked around anxiously at his sister, still in a deep slumber. "If you intend to torture me and Elsa, then—"

"Who says I will have you tortured? No, I have something much better for you."

"*¡Ven!*" Schönborn called loudly, turning toward the door, and in stepped three Spanish soldiers. Their eyes were empty, their movements erratic, like puppets on a string, and one had a bulging scar on his cheek.

The frozen one, Lukas thought. *The man who murdered my father! My God, Schönborn has created more of these monsters.*

The soldiers, each carrying a long knife, walked slowly toward Lukas and Elsa, who was still lying on the ground.

"Keep still, Lukas," Schönborn said gently. "It won't hurt—at least not more than absolutely necessary. My search is finally at an end."

The soldier with the scar raised his knife.

XXIII

Lukas dodged the knife, but a second soldier slipped in behind him and held him in a viselike grip while the first one raised the knife again to strike. Out of the corner of his eye, he saw the third frozen man approaching the sleeping Elsa.

This is the end! he thought. *They'll slit our throats like lambs in a slaughterhouse. My search was all in vain.*

To Lukas's great surprise, the razor-sharp blade only scratched his scalp. There was a pulling and tugging, and that was all. It took him a moment to realize that the man was merely cutting his hair off. Then he did the same with Elsa. What was Schönborn planning to do?

Lukas could do nothing but watch as his dark locks fell to the floor, one after the other. Elsa lay there bald as an egg, groaning in her sleep, but she didn't stir. Lukas was trying to struggle free again when he noticed something.

There was a pattern on Elsa's bare scalp.

It looked like an illustration, a rough black-and-blue sketch, and since Elsa continued sleeping without moving, Lukas had time to study it. Lines truncated at regular intervals, then joined together again, formed a strange figure:

"I see you have noticed," Schönborn said. "Astonishing, isn't it? I had to stop and study it myself when I saw it for the first time. Elsa cut her hair off about four weeks ago, and that's when we saw the pattern. It's a drawing that someone must have etched into her skin. I've had a sketch made of it, and since then, I've been pondering what it might be."

Lukas stared at Elsa's shaved head, but no matter how intently he studied it, he couldn't make any sense of it. The lines appeared just as a blur.

In the meantime, the two frozen men had cut off his own hair, and one of them, still holding him in an iron grip, swung him around to face Schönborn.

The inquisitor clapped his hands with glee. "Just as I thought!" he exclaimed. Then he approached Lukas.

"Even if I don't know yet what it is, I think I know who is responsible for it," Schönborn said. "I'm sure this is what your mother meant when she said on the torture rack that the only way to find the *Grimorium*'s hiding place would be through her children. I have pondered this a long time, but I knew Elsa's tattoo was only one part of the secret. The other part . . ." He ran his fingers over Lukas's scalp, and a chill ran down Lukas's spine. "The other part is, as expected, on your scalp."

Lukas flinched. Was there a tattoo on his head? How was it possible he didn't know anything about it?

"I presume your mother had these tattoos made long ago," Schönborn declared, as if in answer to Lukas's silent question. "She could have given you a mild sleeping potion so you suffered no pain and it would remain a secret. It must have been shortly after Elsa's birth." His face darkened. "And I can imagine why it was at just that time." He closed his eyes, as if viewing a mental image. Then he stared again at Lukas's shaven head.

"Curse her!" he snarled. "I thought the second image would offer the solution to the riddle. But I'm no closer now than before." He seized Lukas and started shaking him. "What is the meaning of these images?" he shouted. "Talk! You know something! You must know something!"

"I know nothing!" Lukas protested, his eyes flashing. "And even if I did, I'd never tell you. Not at any price!"

"Oh, don't say that. I'm fairly good at . . . shall we say, getting information out of people. You'll soon learn that for yourself. But first I must take care of something else here," he said, turning away. "And for that I need my creatures." He pointed at the three Spanish soldiers standing like mute giants behind Lukas. "Rodriguez, Juan, Carlos . . . I think they turned out very well, don't you?"

"The frozen!" Lukas growled.

Schönborn looked at him curiously. "I see you know. Nothing can injure the frozen ones. They are made of clay, ready to kill anyone who gets in the way of either me or my plans. It took a long time for me to master this magic. There were many"—he grimaced—"failures."

"But they are people whose souls you have stolen!" Lukas shot back. "Creatures without a brain or a heart."

"Bah! Who needs a heart anyway?" Schönborn shrugged. "In return I have given them immortality. I didn't even have to force them to take part in my experiments—they all did it willingly."

Trembling, Lukas stared at the three Spaniards standing there with empty eyes and pale, paper-like skin—toy soldiers ready to carry out Schönborn's next command. Lukas remembered the men he saw at his father's castle. At the time, they'd still seemed normal, even the soldier with the scar, the murderer of his father.

"My servants and I have one last mission to carry out, and then I can devote my attention completely to you and your sister," Schönborn said. He turned to the three soulless creatures. "Take the children down to the dungeon," he commanded, "and then we will head off for Lützen. It's time to turn the tables in this war."

Silently, Schönborn turned around and stared out the window, where the mist was drifting by like shrouds. In the distance they could hear the cannon fire.

The soldiers seized Lukas and his sleeping sister and carried them like heavy baggage down to the cellar, from which mournful cries could again be heard.

Not long after that, Lukas was staring at a small, barred window, through which a tiny beam of light fell into the dungeon. Their prison was a square, low-ceilinged room whose cold stone floor was sparsely covered with stinking straw. In one corner stood a jug of water and a tin plate with some crusts of bread and hard cheese, which he hadn't touched.

He heard crying from time to time from the adjacent cells and thought he heard the voice of the butcher's daughter, though he couldn't be sure. How many poor victims had Schönborn locked up down here? How many were waiting to be tortured and put to death at the stake?

Lukas stood up and rattled the door, but it was made of solid wood reinforced with iron. There was no possibility of escape, to say nothing of freeing the other prisoners.

His gaze wandered over to his little sister, who was still sleeping on some straw in the corner. She appeared to be slowly awakening from her trance, as she was moaning and writhing about. Lukas hurried over to her and dabbed her sweaty face with the corner of his dirty shirt.

"I'm here with you, Elsa," he murmured. "Whatever happens, I'm here for you."

Elsa sighed but did not regain consciousness. Soon Schönborn would return, and then even her big brother would no longer be able to help her. It was even possible she wouldn't remember him.

He had failed.

Moments became minutes, and finally hours, and in order to while away the time, Lukas studied the lines and pattern on Elsa's skull until his eyes were virtually spinning. The diagram reminded him of something, but he couldn't say what. Just when he thought he was on the right track, the memory was swept away, like autumn leaves in the wind.

Long winter nights in the castle . . . A game . . . Laughter and the odor of wild roses . . . "Let's play hide-and-seek, Mother . . ." Hide-and-seek . . .

Instinctively, he reached for his shorn scalp. Did it have a similar pattern? He had no mirror to check. Before Schönborn left the monastery, he'd made a sketch of Lukas's tattoo, but Lukas had found no chance to examine the sketch more closely.

"Lu . . . Lukas? Are you there?"

Elsa's voice woke him from his reveries; his sister had opened her eyes. She looked exhausted, but her gaze was clear. Evidently, she knew who he was.

"Elsa!" Lukas breathed a sigh of relief. At least this magic spell appeared broken. "Yes, it's me, your brother. Do you finally recognize me again?"

Elsa nodded, at first hesitantly, then more and more vigorously. Lukas looked at his sister lovingly. She'd been only nine years old when Waldemar von Schönborn abducted her, but despite her young age, Elsa appeared strangely grown-up now, and great wisdom seemed to shine in her eyes—wisdom she must have somehow acquired just in the last year.

"I . . . I remember," she said haltingly. "That morning in the castle the day after your birthday . . . You said we should go and hide in the keep. I didn't want to, I was so angry at you—"

"Waldemar von Schönborn had our mother arrested as a witch," Lukas interrupted. "I had to flee. Do you remember? I swore then that I'd come and find you."

"What happened to our parents?" Elsa asked.

Lukas felt a stabbing pain in his chest. *She doesn't know. Schönborn never told her!*

"They . . . they are both dead, Elsa," he said after a while. "Schönborn was responsible—and he did it just because of a book."

Elsa did not cry; she just looked at him sadly, and for a while, neither of them said a word.

"Tell me what happened," she said finally.

Lukas began with their last morning together at the castle, then the death of their father and how Lukas had followed their mother to Heidelberg. He told of the blue cloud and the voice inside him when their mother died. And finally he told of his time with the exhibition fighters, and the Black Musketeers, and how he'd found her.

"Isn't it so strange?" he concluded. "I went looking for Schönborn, and at the same time, he was looking for me! All because of this bizarre tattoo! Do you know what it all means?"

Elsa ran her fingers over the lines on her scalp, trying to remember. "He told me I was something special, and that the drawing would make me even more powerful than I already am."

"Powerful?" Lukas frowned. It was hard for him to imagine that his sister could somehow be *powerful*.

Elsa sighed. "I can hardly believe what you have told me about Schönborn, even if I know it's the truth, now that he's thrown both of us into this dungeon. You must know . . ." She paused. "Schönborn was never unkind to me. He was . . . like a father. That's even what I called him."

"Elsa!" Lukas shook his head in despair. "This man is a monster, he killed our parents, he tortures and burns people. What else do you need in order to be able to hate him?"

"Please understand! I had no memory of all that. He said I was an orphan he'd saved from a deserted village. He took care of me and made me into what I am now."

Lukas held his breath. There was one thing he'd hesitated to asked, but now he did. "And who, or what, are you now?"

"He tells me there is a mighty power dormant in me. He has taught me how to read the old books, and since then I know things no one would believe possible. About magic."

Lukas remembered the blue flash that had blinded the Swedish soldier, and later even himself, and how she'd been able to change her appearance with just a wave of her hands. What else had this warlock taught her?

"Doesn't it trouble you," Lukas asked bitterly, "that he extorts this knowledge from poor people like the ones in the cells next to ours, waiting for their execution at the stake?"

"I swear I knew nothing about that, Lukas. I thought these people were evil witches and sorcerers, and that we, Schönborn and I, were the good ones. Now everything looks so different..."

Elsa broke off and began to cry. Suddenly, she was a ten-year-old child again who needed consolation. Lukas took her in his arms and caressed her.

"Tell me how you do this magic," he said, trying to calm her down. "I'd like to understand it."

Elsa sniffled. "Once you know how, it's really very simple—you just need to say the right words. Certain words strike a chord in me, and then it happens."

"But before, when you changed your face, you didn't speak," Lukas said, "and you didn't when you blinded me, either."

Elsa smiled. "Once you have mastered it, it's enough just to imagine the word in your head. It's the same with all the magic potions, talismans, and other things. Their only use is to help your imagination."

Lukas paused. "You mean the amulet that seemed to protect me—"

"Did protect you, because you believed in it, and because someone first had cast a charm on it by using the ancient words to transform it into a powerful magic object. Schönborn says the ancient words are the decisive thing. The druids had no system of writing but passed down everything to their pupils by word of mouth. For this reason, most of it was lost when the Romans persecuted and killed the druids." Elsa sounded now like an eager little schoolgirl. It was easy for Lukas to imagine how Schönborn had taught her all that knowledge. She had always been much better than he was at memorizing and studying.

"Only a few wise old men wrote down the words," Elsa continued, "a few druids as well as Roman scholars, and thus the magic words have survived. There is, however, only one book that contains them all."

"The *Book of the Night*," Lukas murmured, "written by the bard Taliesin. Schönborn mentioned his name before."

"He was supposedly a minstrel at the English court around the time of the legendary King Arthur," Elsa said. "Some think he was the last druid. With Taliesin's death, the druids' knowledge was lost forever. All that remained were fragments—and the *Grimorium Nocturnum*, of which only a single copy remains. Whoever possesses it will be the master of all witchcraft."

"It is believed the book was hidden for years in a Bohemian monastery," Lukas murmured, adding what he had learned from Schönborn. "Our mother was a young nun there and must have taken the book with her . . ."

"It seems I've inherited her talent," Elsa said. "Schönborn thinks there are only a few of us left. We are the last of the white magicians, the last in a long chain of druids. He looked for years to find someone like me."

"Now he has you, and soon he will also have the book." Lukas clenched his fists. "Don't you understand, Elsa? You are only a tool for him, just like these soldiers whose souls he has stolen. He intends to use you to become the greatest sorcerer of all times. Who knows what other plans he has in store."

Suddenly, Lukas remembered Schönborn's final words before he had both of them thrown into the dungeon.

My servants and I have one last mission.

What sort of mission could that be? What did the inquisitor have in mind that was so important he even had to put aside the search for the *Grimorium*?

The sun had now set, darkness had fallen, and an oppressive silence fell over the small cell in the dungeon. Lukas thought of the butcher's pretty daughter, locked up along with her father somewhere in one of the neighboring cells. He wanted to help them, as now they were no doubt both awaiting execution here.

After a few uneventful hours, Lukas finally managed to fall asleep. In his tangled dreams, the great black wolf was pursuing him again as he ran on and on through an endless labyrinth while behind him the panting of the beast became louder and louder. He saw the faces of his parents, who seemed to be calling to him, but he couldn't understand what they were saying.

When he opened his eyes, gasping for breath, it was already early morning. Elsa wiped the sweat from his brow and looked at him intently, running her fingers over his face as if trying to comprehend her brother again.

"I looked at your tattoo," she said, "and it's a pattern just like mine."

"That's what I'd assumed," Lukas replied, rubbing the sleep out of his eyes, "but unfortunately I can't figure out what it means, either."

His stomach growled loudly. Now he was glad to have the crusts of bread, the hard cheese, and the jug of water that the guards had put out for them. But when he heard the wailing and crying from the next cell, Lukas put the cheese down again. He had lost his appetite. Again, time passed slowly, interrupted only by occasional sharp cries.

"Isn't there any magic you can use to help these poor souls?" he asked Elsa.

Elsa shrugged. "If this were a normal cell, it might be possible to escape and free the others, but Schönborn cast a powerful spell on the entire dungeon when he locked us up here. I tried earlier, when you were asleep."

"Then it seems we are lost," Lukas said, "we, and all the others here. We'll never . . ."

He paused on hearing a faint sound on the other side of the door. Someone was coming down the hall.

Lukas tried not to shiver. The time had come, and Waldemar von Schönborn had returned to get them. He would torture them just as he had tortured their mother. It would probably start on the rack, or with the glowing tongs, or the thumbscrews. How long would Lukas manage not to scream and beg for mercy? Fear washed over him like a mighty wave.

A key was inserted in the lock, squeaking as it turned, and the heavy door swung open. Lukas held his breath and reached for Elsa's hand.

"Whatever happens, Elsa," he whispered, "I will always be your brother, and you my sister. At least they can't take that from us, even if . . ."

His jaw dropped, and he stared at the figure in front of him.

"But . . . but," he stammered.

"Close your mouth. That really looks stupid," Paulus growled. "Especially when you don't have any hair on your head." Behind him, grinning, stood Jerome and Giovanni as well, with a fresh bandage on his leg.

"Greetings, Lukas," Giovanni said with a wink. "Did you seriously believe we'd let you down?"

"What have they done to you two beautiful people?" Jerome asked, rubbing his nose. "You looked like freshly polished cannonballs. And who is this girl anyway?" he asked, turning to Elsa. "I'm not sure, but somehow the little brat looks familiar to me."

Lukas was so relieved he didn't know whether to laugh or cry. For a while, he could hardly move; he just stood there staring at his friends.

"This kid is my sister," he finally managed to say. "I'll tell you everything else when we're finally out of this stinking hole."

One after the other, he embraced his friends. He'd never needed them as much as at this moment.

◆ ◆ ◆

Minutes later, they were standing out in the hallway, where Giovanni was holding a large ring of keys and hastily opening the individual cells.

"Did you really believe we'd let you go off on this adventure alone?" said Jerome in a feigned tone of severity.

"I would have understood," Lukas replied softly.

"Nonsense!" Paulus slapped him so hard on the shoulder that Lukas had to cough. "When we returned from the battle and Giovanni told us you'd already set out for the monastery the day before, we naturally came after you. One of the guards up on the first floor kindly offered us his keys." He paused. "Well, when I think about it, he didn't actually offer them."

"But . . . how did you get past all the rest of them?" Lukas asked.

Jerome winked. "Oh, there weren't all *that* many. Schönborn took most of them with him to Lützen, and the servants and maids ran off long ago because of the fighting. And the rest of the guards, well . . ." He played with the handle of his sword. "Never pick a fight with the Black Musketeers."

The doors to the cells squeaked as they opened, and around a dozen emaciated figures came staggering out. Many of the prisoners had bloody scars or burns on their backs, and others had an arm hanging limply at their side as if their shoulder had been dislocated. All of them looked as if they could hardly believe their good fortune in escaping their tormenters. In the back of the group, Lukas recognized the butcher and his daughter, smiling at their liberators. The girl's dress was torn, her black hair dirty and stringy, but otherwise, she appeared uninjured, like her father.

"You must be angels!" she gasped.

"Oh, we have too many earthly needs to be angels," Jerome responded, eyeing her approvingly. "I could show you for example how—"

"We really don't have any time for that," Giovanni interrupted with annoyance. "I'll assume Lukas has some things to tell us." He pointed at Elsa. "Above all, about his sister."

Lukas nodded. "How much time do we have until Schönborn shows up here?"

"At the moment, Schönborn is the least of our problems. The Swedes are coming." Paulus ground his teeth. "We've overtaken their advance guard, and the rest should be here in a few hours."

The butcher's daughter waved a grateful good-bye to Lukas as the prisoners hurried toward the stairway and the exit. Lukas felt a sudden desire to follow her with Elsa and forget everything he'd experienced in the preceding hours, but then he straightened up and turned to his friends.

"I suggest we get to the library right away, where we can talk. We've taken care of one job," he said, "but a much larger one awaits us."

XXIV

Soon after, the five were sitting upstairs in the dusty library. The friends had brought a few blankets for Elsa and Lukas and, most importantly, something to eat and drink from the deserted monastery kitchen so they could warm up and satisfy the worst of their hunger.

"What actually happened in Lützen?" Lukas wanted to know.

Jerome cleared his throat. "It was just as you predicted—one long slashing and beating without a clear winner. The Swedes had almost won, but at the height of the battle their king fell and they retreated."

Lukas was stunned. "King Gustav Adolf is dead?"

"No one knows exactly what happened," Jerome said. "He was supposedly shot at close range even though he was well protected. It seemed like witchcraft."

A bitter suspicion welled up in Lukas. He thought of Schönborn's last words just before he set out for Lützen.

My servants and I have one last mission.

Was it possible that one of the frozen men killed the Swedish king? Was that the last mission? But why? Schönborn had just sent his henchmen out to fight Wallenstein. What sense would there be in killing Wallenstein as well as his greatest enemy?

"But there are more important things to talk about than the battle and the sad fate of the Swedish king. What happened to the two of you?" Giovanni asked. He looked at Elsa, who was sitting in a corner, leafing through one of the many books. Then he turned to Lukas. "Why did they shave your heads, and what's the meaning of these strange tattoos? And where is Daniel?"

Lukas pointed at Elsa. "She is Daniel."

Paulus scowled. "What nonsense! Is this a joke? We don't really have time for that."

"I know . . . it's hard to understand. I can barely understand it, either." Lukas sighed, then he told his friends what he'd learned the day before in the monastery. When he was finished, the others stared at him incredulously.

"Let's see if *I* understand this," Paulus said. "It wasn't just your mother who was a white witch, but also your little sister, who can change herself just like that into a boy? And these tattoos can lead us to a magic book, in fact, the most powerful magic book there is?" He snorted. "This Schönborn is pulling a trick on you just like the quack Senno, and you're falling for it again!"

"Just look at Elsa," Lukas pleaded. "She was Daniel. Just look what she did with her face. That was magic!"

"What I see is a little girl with her head in the clouds, and that's all," Paulus replied. "God knows what happened to Daniel, but in any case, he's not here."

"Elsa?" Lukas turned to his sister. She still seemed engrossed in Schönborn's magic and not really following the conversation. "I'm afraid we have to clarify things for my friends," he said. "They won't help us until we can convince them. Can you do that again?"

"What?" Elsa asked, looking up from her book.

"Well, turn yourself back into Daniel."

Elsa shrugged, looking bored. "If that's all you want . . ." She got to her feet, placed her right hand over her face, and lowered her fingers slowly. Paulus, Jerome, and Giovanni gasped.

Before them stood Daniel.

Elsa passed her hand again over her face, and now Lukas saw his little sister before him. She changed her appearance a few more times in just seconds until she was finally Elsa again.

"Is that all you want?" she asked.

"That . . . is simply unbelievable," Paulus said. "How did you do that?"

"Do you also want to see how she can set off a blinding flash of light in your head?" Lukas asked. "Or how she—"

"Thanks, I don't think that's necessary," Jerome said, raising his hand. "We are . . . uh . . . convinced."

Giovanni shook his head. "Real magic! Who would have thought that possible? My apologies, Lukas. We were beginning to wonder if your imagination was running away with you."

"You don't have to apologize," Lukas replied. "For a long time I didn't believe it myself. The important thing now is to keep the *Book of the Night* from falling into Schönborn's hands."

"There's nothing simpler than that." Jerome clapped once. "Let's just get out of here. Without the tattoos, Schönborn won't find the hiding place of the magic book. Voilà!"

"You idiot!" Giovanni growled. "Can't we assume Schönborn has made copies of both images?" He turned to Lukas, who nodded. "So, we have to solve the riddle before he does."

Paulus groaned. "You are the one responsible for the deep thinking." He cracked his knuckles. "My job is breaking bones."

Jerome pointed to a corner of the room, where Lukas's sword and pistol still lay on the floor. "At least you've been thoughtful enough to leave your weapon there, but if we get into a fight—"

"Damn, don't you understand?" Lukas interrupted. "What good are all the weapons in the world if Schönborn has this book? You saw that frozen man in the battle at Nürnberg. Just imagine what would happen if Schönborn created hundreds of them with the help of the *Grimorium*. He could win any battle! We must prevent that."

"But first we have to solve this riddle. Hmm . . ." Giovanni took a quill and ink pot, sat down on the chair with the demonic carvings, and motioned for Elsa and Lukas to kneel down in front of him. "Let me first draw both tattoos. Perhaps it will help us to understand this." With the skilled hand of a former monastery schoolboy, he sketched the patterns on a thin piece of parchment. Now the two images stood side by side.

"They are similar, yet not quite the same," said Giovanni. "The lines go in different directions, even though both are circles with a dot in the middle."

Once again, Lukas thought he remembered something, but the longer he looked at the lines, the more they seemed to blur before his eyes.

"What in God's name is it?" he murmured. He blinked, and now he saw tiny letters running along the bottom of the circles, spelling two words, though neither of them made any sense.

H-R-U-P-L-T-N-S O-T-S-A-A-I-U

"Hrupltns and Otsaaiu?" Jerome giggled. "What language is that? Arabic, Coptic, or perhaps idiotic?"

"Most likely it's not a language at all, but a code," Giovanni replied, rubbing his temples as he contemplated the images. "But what sort of code? I once read a Greek book about coding, but that was a long time ago."

Elsa, too, leaned down to look at the parchment, then turned to the boys. "It's actually rather simple," she said with a shrug.

"Rather simple?" Giovanni looked up at her. "What do you mean by that? Do you know the solution? I hardly think that's possible, so don't get in our way now with your precocious words."

"If you needed any proof that she's Daniel, now you have it," Paulus said, grinning. "Both are just as impudent."

Elsa stuck her tongue out at him, then she continued, as defiantly as Daniel. "I don't know the solution, but at least I know how to escape from both labyrinths." She ran her finger along the lines to the middle. "This way, then that way, then this . . . As I said, it's really very simple. But you boys are probably too dumb to see it."

For a while, no one said a thing, and they just stared at Elsa.

"What's the matter with you?" she asked. "Did I do something wrong again? If you don't need my help, I'll just keep quiet."

"Labyrinths!" said Lukas, slapping his forehead. "Of course! How could we be so dumb. They're labyrinths! Elsa's right. Our mother often drew mazes like that for us, and that's what these patterns made me think of."

"Indeed, you're right," said Giovanni, running his finger over the lines again. "They're labyrinths." He laughed. "Sometimes you can't see the forest for the trees."

"Or because of the magic," added Lukas, realizing the lines no longer looked blurry now that Elsa had revealed the truth.

"Very well, so they're labyrinths," Paulus said. "Now when we're bored, we can always play guessing games on their heads. But what does that all have to do with the book of magic?"

"Maybe the tattoos are trying to point to some other labyrinth," said Giovanni.

Jerome rubbed the side of his nose. "I don't know anything about labyrinths—you only find those in the castle gardens of noble people, and people like us never get invited to those places."

Lukas bent down again over the sketch. "Let's have another look at these letters," he suggested. "Our mother always liked to play word games with us. Maybe we can figure it out." He turned to Elsa. "Can you make any sense of this?"

"Aha, do you need my help now after all?" She crossed her arms. "I don't have any other suggestions."

Lukas groaned. "Oh, come now, don't be so touchy."

But Elsa refused to talk.

"Damn!" Giovanni said. "These letters have to mean something. We can't sit around forever waiting for an idea." Outside, loud cannon fire could be heard. The battle was clearly continuing here and there around Weißenfels. Lukas looked out the window anxiously. It wouldn't be long before plundering soldiers broke into the monastery.

"Our mother thought that only Elsa and I together could lead the searchers to the hiding place," he said. "That makes the matter even more difficult. Why are there two labyrinths? There can be only one hiding place, isn't that right?"

"You're right." Giovanni nodded. "Just the two of you together, but—"

He stopped short, then quickly started ripping the parchment sheet down the middle.

"Hey, what are you doing?" Jerome protested. "Now we have to do it all over again, and we don't have time for that."

But Giovanni had torn the document in two so that there was now just one labyrinth on a page.

"Wait," he whispered excitedly. "I have an idea. You need to put the two of them together to get the meaning . . ."

Carefully, he laid one document precisely on top of the other. The parchment was so thin that the part underneath was visible. Lukas was the first to notice.

"The lines!" he shouted. "They come together to form a single new labyrinth, and just look at the letters—they suddenly make sense."

HORTUS PALATINUS

The letters in the first tattoo fit exactly in the gaps of the other, forming two Latin words.

"Hortus Palatinus," Giovanni exclaimed. "That means the Palatine Garden. We're getting close." He turned to the others. "Have any of you ever heard of a Palatine Garden?"

"Oh, in the Palatinate, there are lots of beautiful gardens," Paulus replied calmly. "Orchards, flower gardens, vineyards, vegetable gardens . . ." He stopped, looking at Lukas, who had turned pale. "What are you thinking? Do you know which garden it means?"

Lukas nodded silently. It was so obvious. Even when he saw the tattoo the very first time, the thought had flashed through his mind, but he had pushed it aside. Now it came back with striking clarity.

A game . . . Laughter and the fragrant odor of wild roses . . . "Let's play hide-and-seek, Mother . . ."

"The garden in the Heidelberg Castle," he said. "I went there a few times as a child with my mother. It's a beautiful place, like something out of another world, with statues, fountains, hedges clipped in the shape of strange beasts, and—"

"A labyrinth!" Paulus groaned. "Do you really think that's the garden we're looking for?"

Lukas nodded. "It's called the Hortus Palatinus. I remember now how Mother sometimes spoke of it. She loved the place. Jerome gave me the clue that I needed. He said he'd heard of such labyrinths only in castle gardens."

"Ha!" Jerome puffed out his chest. "And everyone says I can only look good but don't know how to think. Now you can take that all back."

"You're the most handsome, smartest, and above all, most egotistical of the four of us, Jerome." Giovanni grinned. "In any case, Schönborn will be mad as hell he didn't figure that out." He stood up and wiped the ink from his hands. "Let's go then."

Lukas stared at him. "You don't really—"

"What should we wait for?" Paulus broke in. "For Schönborn to come back and roast us over his grill? Of course we'll come along with you and Elsa to the Hortus Palatinus. Your trip began in Heidelberg, and with our help, it will end there, too."

"It's almost three hundred miles to Heidelberg," Lukas said. "Are you really sure you want to go on this long trip with me and Elsa?" Elsa's eyes widened at the mention of her name, but now she seemed too stunned by the turn of events to speak.

"One for all and all for one. Did you forget that?" Paulus tossed Lukas's pistol and sword to him and headed for the exit. "Who knows what awaits us in this labyrinth? You'll be glad to have me and my sword."

"But what about Zoltan?" Lukas asked. "We would be deserters, and didn't you and Jerome say that you wouldn't let down our comrades-in-arms?"

"We've sent a message to Zoltan that we're not deserting, but just taking an indefinite leave from the regiment," Giovanni replied. "Anyway, when the old man saw you weren't in Lützen, he drew his own conclusions. I think he'll understand." He headed after Paulus, then hesitated. "All right, I think he'll give us hell when we come back. But for us, you're worth it."

XXV

They rode as if the devil were on their heels.

That very same day, after leaving the monastery, they'd stolen five horses in a poorly guarded stable of the army camped nearby. In the days following the Battle of Lützen, the entire region was in turmoil, and not much attention was paid to the theft. Carts full of groaning men wounded in the battle rolled along the muddy roads, some regiments marched to the beat of drums and playing of flutes toward their winter quarters, and looters destroyed the few remaining villages and cities. Wherever Lukas looked, he saw burning houses, smoking church steeples, and wailing peasants fleeing from the soldiers with their few remaining possessions.

This is hell on earth, he thought. *Will this war never end?*

The friends rode through the wind, hail, and rain, stopping only occasionally to rest, water their horses, or have a bite to eat themselves. For the first few days, Elsa was very tired, and it appeared that Schönborn's magic had an aftereffect not unlike that of a slowly dripping poison. Eventually she regained her strength and was able to keep up with the others on her small pony.

Lukas, however, became increasingly tired and pale and dreamed again of the huge black wolf that pursued him night after night through billowing clouds of mist, watching him with its red, glowing eyes.

And now Lukas no longer had the amulet to protect him . . .

"It's Waldemar von Schönborn," he mumbled to himself after the third restless night. "The inquisitor is looking for us, and I have the feeling he will soon find us."

They were sitting together in the forest alongside a small, flickering fire that gave off little warmth. The last of the provisions they had brought with them from the monastery were now gone, and all they had for breakfast were a handful of beechnuts they had gathered in the forest the night before.

"Maybe we should have let Zoltan in on our plans," Paulus said. "He might have helped us. As it is, we're nothing but deserters and outlaws that any officer who comes along can put on the gallows."

"Zoltan wouldn't have believed a word we said," replied Giovanni. "Aside from that, if Schönborn really can use his magic to find us, even the legendary Black Musketeers can't help us. Not even Zoltan."

"But there's something else that can help us," Elsa said. She'd been sitting by the fire carving a tiny figure. Now she put the wooden angel in Lukas's hand. She also had similar gifts for Giovanni, Paulus, and Jerome. "Here, take this."

"What's it supposed to be?" Paulus asked suspiciously. "A toy? I'm too old for that, child. I'd prefer a homemade cudgel."

"They're figures that can make us invisible to Schönborn," Elsa said earnestly. "I've cut them for you from linden wood and have put a magic charm on them. It doesn't really matter what they represent, but I like the angel most. Do you like them?"

"Eh, oui, très belle," said Jerome. He took the clumpy figure with the two crooked wings in his hand. "And what shall we do with it?"

"You must always carry it with you, day and night." Elsa gave them all a stern look. "This is very important! If I know Schönborn, he's raging mad and will do everything he can to find us. If he does, then God help us."

"And these little puppets will protect us?" Paulus asked skeptically. In his big hands, the angel looked like a fragile matchstick.

Giovanni spoke up. "The fact is that Schönborn is looking for Elsa and Lukas, and perhaps by now he has solved the riddle himself. Then he'll also come to the Hortus Palatinus, and these puppets won't do us any good." Impatiently, he looked up at the overcast sky, where the first gray light of morning had appeared. "We should get started again soon. We still have a long way to go."

After they'd been riding for almost two weeks, the first flakes of snow started falling, though it was just the end of November. A white cover now lay over the destroyed houses and the corpses still lying at the roadside. The air got colder and colder.

"Can't you conjure up some fire to keep us warm while we're riding?" said Jerome, turning to Elsa with chattering teeth. "N-not even a small one I can put in my pocket?"

Elsa smiled wearily. "Believe me, if I could, I would have long ago used my magic to bring back the summer, but unfortunately, I'm not as powerful as you think. My magic works only on small things."

"But how about that blue flash you used to blind the Swedish soldier?" Paulus asked, leading his robust stallion alongside Elsa's pony. "That was real magic as I imagine it."

"And it took a great deal of my strength. For hours afterward, I was completely exhausted." Elsa shook her head. "People always expect great things from us witches, but basically all we can do with our words and gestures are trivial things. Schönborn believes that with the help of the *Grimorium*, however, we can do more."

"God help us if he gets his hands on the book of magic," Giovanni observed grimly. "I'm afraid then this war will go on forever."

"Hasn't it already? And I can't see any end in sight," said Lukas. He spurred his horse to a gallop as it sloshed through the snow, neighing. "Sometimes I think it will last a full thirty years."

After another week of hard riding, they finally reached the Palatinate, by now in Swedish hands. Here, in enemy territory, they had to be even more careful. A few times already during their trip, they'd had to fend off minor attacks, but after a few well-placed blows and a shot from Lukas's pistol, the attackers usually ran off. Only once had there been a battle with a large band of robbers, but Paulus held them off with his sword, giving the friends a chance to escape.

Now they proceeded only in the early morning hours or at twilight. They wore dark coats, and the fog and falling snow-flakes were their best companions. Through the trees they could see shadowy outlines of destroyed villages from time to time, but steered clear of the few people they saw on the slushy roads. Whenever they could, they found nourishment in nuts, as well as the last of the shriveled autumn apples, and caught rabbits and partridges in the forest with snares and traps.

Lukas's stomach growled constantly, and the first signs of frostbite appeared on his fingers, but an unwavering will drove him onward. His hair, as well as Elsa's, had grown back a bit, so that the tattoos were concealed now under a covering of fluff, but he could sense it there, stinging slightly.

One foggy morning as it was snowing lightly, they arrived in Heidelberg. Lukas remembered leaving this city more than a year ago; he'd been a child then, anxious and completely alone. His mother had died here, and Lukas's trip through the German Empire had begun.

Now he returned as a warrior.

Heidelberg had been overrun by the Swedes the previous June, and in the morning light, the destruction of the walls, tower, and church steeples was clearly visible behind the city wall. On the steep hillside the famous Heidelberg Castle stood in solitary splendor, but here, too, gutted windows stared down into the valley, one of the towers had been blown away, and in some places, bare, charred beams could be seen where there once was a roof.

"And now?" Jerome asked, rubbing his cold hands. "We can hardly go riding into town with our weapons and politely ask directions to the Hortus Palatinus."

"I assume that our friend here knows exactly where this magical garden is located," said Giovanni, turning to Lukas. "Is that right?"

Lukas nodded and pointed to an area to the left of the castle, though it was still too far away to see anything in detail. "The garden, or what's left of it, is on the west side of the castle," he said. "To reach it, fortunately, we don't have to go through the city, we can just circle around it and approach the castle from the mountainside. I'm certain we'll find a breach in the wall up there, and the castle does not appear heavily guarded."

They rode along a little farther out of sight of the city walls before dismounting and leading the horses up a forested slope. Now, in the early morning, it was calm, no one was visible, and clouds of mist drifted over the snowy forest floor. After a short search, they reached a moss-covered wall with several breaks in it.

"The rear wall of the castle," Lukas announced. "Probably it was stormed by Tilly's troops many years ago and not repaired since." He motioned to his friends, then climbed over the low wall. "Follow me."

They crept through the sparse bushes until they came to another wall with a steep drop on the other side. Down below was a wide area bounded by the castle ruins to the west and the mountain above Heidelberg to the north. The area seemed so strange and magical that it briefly took their breath away.

"This . . . is unbelievable!" Giovanni finally said. "A wonder of the world!"

Lukas nodded. "That's what they once called the Hortus Palatinus. It was said there was no more beautiful garden on earth. Now it may be overgrown and partially destroyed, but I clearly remember the flowering arbors and bubbling fountains when my mother took me walking here."

There were endless rows of hedges in the garden, which used to be trimmed but now were wild and tangled, and between them, many marble statues, small fountains, hidden niches, arbors, and grottos decorated with shells and semiprecious jewels. The grounds had a number of levels connected by stairways. A fine white layer of frost had settled on the bushes and hedges.

It took Lukas a while to realize what this image reminded him of. *The garden is sleeping,* he thought. *When war came over it, it began its winter sleep, and now it will never awaken again.*

Once more, he saw in his mind the image of himself, Elsa, and their mother strolling past the fragrant rose beds. His sister had been too young for her to remember it now, but as she stared at the garden below, she, too, was spellbound by the magic emanating from the Hortus Palatinus, even after all these years.

"Somehow everything here looks like a damned labyrinth," Paulus grumbled. "Which of these labyrinths was your mother thinking of when she had the tattoos put on your heads?"

"The Sorcerer's Labyrinth." Lukas pointed to an area at the back of the garden directly bordering the steep slope of the mountain. "That's what we called it then, anyway. I'm sure that's where the hiding place is."

The labyrinth Lukas pointed to was an overgrown, rounded area with concentric circles inside, interspersed with small gaps. At the center stood a solitary, run-down temple.

"The Labyrinth of the Sorcerer." Giovanni grinned. "A suitable name for the hiding place of a magic book. The labyrinth does indeed resemble the tattoos on your heads."

"Except that it's now somewhat overgrown," Jerome noted. "We'll need our swords and knives to cut our way through there. Very well, let's get to it!"

It took a while, but finally the friends found an old willow with branches long enough to shinny down into the garden. Once they were on the ground, they walked past a number of overgrown evergreen boxwood bushes that at one time had been fashioned in the shape of animals. Lukas could make out a stag, a fox, a boar, and a hare with laid-back ears, but the bushes hadn't been trimmed for years and the animals seemed strangely deformed. They had monstrous heads, hunched backs, and their green coat of leaves seemed to mushroom out in all directions.

Shivering, Lukas pushed his way through the thicket to look at the huge garden before them. On their left was a dark grotto guarded by a stone god sitting by a well. Long icicles hung from his beard, and he seemed to be eyeing the friends suspiciously. As Lukas turned away, he briefly had the feeling the giant would rise and follow them through the garden, but a quick look back reassured him the giant was still sitting beside the fountain.

"Am I imagining it, or is it really a lot colder here than out in the f-forest?" Jerome asked, his teeth chattering again, as he wrapped his coat more tightly around him.

"You're right," Giovanni replied with a frown. "It's as if winter has settled in here in the garden. It could just as well be January."

In fact, a hard white crust of ice covered many of the tree trunks, the hedges seemed frozen, and drops of ice hung like white pearls on the withered leaves. The closer they came to the rear of the garden, the colder it became. Lukas glanced at Elsa, who had a worried look.

"Can you explain that?" he asked.

"Perhaps it really is the book," she murmured. "It can sense that we are coming, and like an anxious creature, is showing its teeth."

"Well, isn't that just fine," Paulus grumbled. "Then let's go and see what else this book has in store for us."

A while later, they passed some niches in the rock decorated in shells, with a copper statuette inside, cracked and covered with verdigris. Lukas examined a flute player with goat horns, and a fat, naked child grinning and thrusting his hips toward a ballerina. Giovanni stopped, fascinated.

"These are surely the so-called automatons," he explained. "I've read about them in a book. They move just by the power of water and steam. I assume that the figure on the left could once play a flute, the beautiful girl could dance, and the fat child, well—"

"Was peeing on someone!" Paulus interrupted with a grin. "I always knew that princes had a very strange sense of humor. But now let's move along quickly before I freeze solid."

It had become so cold that Lukas could feel the frost creeping into every pore of his body, and when he breathed out, a white cloud rose up. The crunching of his friends' footsteps in the snow seemed to be the only sound in the entire garden.

They passed by another weathered fountain and were now standing at the entrance to the labyrinth at the back of the garden. Dark, withered hedges formed a natural wall eight feet high.

"The Labyrinth of the Sorcerer." Lukas pointed toward an overgrown entrance that had at one time no doubt been a portal of roses. "We can only hope that our sketch is correct. I wouldn't want to get lost in there when it's as cold as this."

Giovanni took out the thin parchment sketch he'd drawn, which he'd kept carefully tucked inside his coat. He turned it carefully until it was aligned in the right direction.

"It appears we are here," he said, pointing to a spot on the perimeter of the map. "If we follow these instructions exactly, we should soon arrive at the middle."

"And how do we know that's exactly where the book is?" Jerome asked.

"Do you have a better idea?" Giovanni snapped back. "From up above we could see there was a temple in the middle of the labyrinth where something could be hidden. Besides, a labyrinth always leads you to the middle—that's the way the ancient Greeks designed them."

He pushed aside an icy twig and disappeared into the labyrinth, and the others followed.

As Lukas stepped into the tangle of tall hedges, suddenly, as if by magic, the light of day vanished. Though he could still see a narrow strip of the gray winter sky above him, the sun didn't seem to reach the ground. Everything was bathed in twilight, as if night were falling. Narrow, shadowy paths disappeared into the frosty darkness. Giovanni walked ahead, holding the map, now and then stopping to think before heading down another path.

"Everything here is so overgrown you really don't know if it's a path or just an animal trail," he complained. "It's so easy to lose your bearings!"

"Just keep trying," Paulus urged him. "My hands are almost frozen to the hilt of my sword."

Paulus raised his saber and kept looking around suspiciously. Lukas also had an uneasy feeling that someone was lying in wait for him behind every hedge.

Or something, he thought. *Maybe the bearded guard at the fountain really is following us . . .*

The bushes became thicker, and the space between them was sometimes just shoulder width. Thorny branches reached out and tugged at Lukas, and ice-cold, sharp-edged leaves scraped across his face. Now the light had almost completely disappeared, and their frozen coats crackled in the cold.

Once again, Giovanni found himself at a crossing and studied the map.

"Don't tell me we're lost," Jerome groaned. "Pretty soon my feet are going to fall off."

Giovanni looked up from the map. "You can try it yourself, if you want. There actually should be another passage, but I can't find anything here. We should be almost there." He sighed. "I'm at a loss, damn!" Angrily he kicked a pile of icy leaves, and at that moment, Lukas shouted.

"There's the path! Do you see it?"

Behind the pile of leaves, an opening appeared that until then had been hidden. Lukas pushed the pile aside and crawled on his knees through the hole. Suddenly everything around him became brighter, pale sunlight was visible, and it became noticeably warmer.

A clearing appeared before him with a few dead linden trees and a small wooden building in the center. The roof had partially caved in, the columns adorned with wood carvings were tilted and bent, and ferns and ivy hung down the sides of the building.

"The temple in the middle of the labyrinth!" Lukas shouted. "We actually found it."

Now the others also crawled through the hole and stepped into the clearing.

"I was here with my mother once," Lukas said excitedly. "We stopped to rest at this temple."

He rushed into the building, whose walls for the most part were rotted and had collapsed. The stone floor was covered with moldy foliage that Lukas quickly pushed aside, hoping perhaps to find a stone slab with something buried beneath it. But the foundation was smooth and all of one piece.

"Where could your mother have hidden the book?" murmured Giovanni, who was now standing beside him, looking around. They examined the columns and the roof, but couldn't find anything unusual. In the meantime, the other friends and Elsa explored the temple surroundings.

"There's nothing here," Jerome finally announced. "I'm telling you, the book is somewhere else. Perhaps this isn't even the right labyrinth."

"But it is," Lukas replied. "The hiding place has to be here somewhere."

He closed his eyes and brought back memories of the past.

"Let's play hide-and-seek, Mother . . . please . . ."

He had run off to hide here somewhere, but where? Lost in his memories, he walked around the clearing.

"Just drop it, Lukas," Jerome said. "There's nothing here. Let's try instead—"

"Shh!" Giovanni interrupted. "Can't you see he's thinking?"

"How would Jerome know that?" Paulus said. "He doesn't even know what it means to think."

"If I wasn't so damned cold, I'd have rapped you over the head with my rapier, you idiot," Jerome replied.

"Stop this arguing at once!" Elsa shouted. "Or shall I cast a spell and give you all long noses?"

Her threat worked. Grumbling, the two separated. Jerome leaned against one of the crippled linden trees, pouting, while Lukas kept walking back and forth in the clearing.

Where did I hide then? he was thinking. *Where . . .*

"Merde!" Jerome sputtered, looking up at the gray sky, from which a few snowflakes were falling. "If I were a rabbit or a badger, I could at least crawl into my warm, comfortable burrow, but now—"

"The badger hole!" Luke cried out. "Of course! How could I have forgotten?" As excited as he was, he still couldn't help laughing. "This is the second time Jerome has put me on the right track. If this continues, he'll become even smarter than Giovanni."

He ran toward the astonished Jerome, still leaning on the linden, and brushed aside a knee-high pile of icy foliage, twigs, and mushy snow that had formed against the tree. Behind it was a twisted, dead root, and beneath that a small burrow. His heart pounding, Lukas knelt down and reached into the opening.

"When I was here with my mother, I was so small I could hide in this place," he declared. "It's no doubt an old badger's burrow."

"Just make sure there's no badger in it now," Paulus warned him. "Those beasts can really bite."

Lukas pulled his hand back, but when he didn't hear any snarling or hissing, he reached in again. The hole was so large he couldn't feel the back of it with his fingers, so he got up his courage and crawled head-first into the opening.

The stench of wild animals and dung made him gag. He held his breath for a moment, then pushed forward until his hips were also inside the earthy burrow. Roots and leaves scratched his face. Back then, he had gotten his whole body inside the hole, and he still remembered the tingling feeling when his mother walked past the tree and couldn't find him at first. It had been a perfect hiding place.

Also the perfect hiding place for a book . . . ?

"Well?" Lukas could hear the muffled voice of Giovanni outside. "Is there something there or . . ." His voice trailed off as Lukas crawled deeper into the hole.

Frantically, Lukas searched the pitch-black space with his hands. He could feel dry straw, rock-hard feces, bones, and scraps of fur. The stench was so bad that his eyes began to tear up, and he wouldn't be able to stand it here much longer. Again, he searched the darkness for the book, for anything, but nothing was there.

He'd been wrong.

As he started to back out again, his right hand touched some hard object in a corner. It seemed to be made of wood and was about the size of a jewelry box. He could feel the cool iron of a padlock.

"I found something!" he shouted. "A little box. This is it."

But his friends didn't answer. Holding the little box in his hands like a fragile egg, Lukas pushed backward toward the surface, where he could feel the cold winter wind blowing over his legs. His lungs filled with fresh air. Hurriedly he pulled the box out behind him and turned to his friends, beaming with joy.

"Finally, our trip is—" He stopped short, as if someone had suddenly grabbed him by the throat, and the box clattered to the ground.

Before him stood Waldemar von Schönborn.

The inquisitor smiled broadly. His crimson cloak was the color of fresh blood, and a thin layer of snow covered his cap. In the background, the three Spanish mercenaries with the dead eyes were waiting. One of them was holding a knife to Elsa's throat and had clapped his other hand over her mouth as she struggled to free herself. The two other creatures had drawn their swords and were pointing them at Giovanni, Jerome, and Paulus, who were silently staring at Lukas and the box, helpless with rage.

"How nice to see you again, Lukas," said Schönborn. He stooped down and picked up the weathered wooden box. With his long, slender fingers, he tenderly stroked the cover, secured by a rusted padlock. "Of course, it's much nicer to have finally arrived at my goal and realized my greatest dream—and I can thank you for that."

Lukas suddenly felt the world turn colder.

XXVI

For a while, they stood there silently looking at each other, and then Schönborn began to speak again.

"So it was worth waiting for," he murmured. "You probably thought you could escape from me, but you forget that in this accursed Reich, I still wield great power. Fresh, fast horses await you at every inn when you travel with the seal of the pope." With a smile, he raised his right hand with a golden signet ring on his finger. "All doors are open to me."

"He caught us by surprise," Giovanni said. "We were so excited about what you found in the hole. I'm sorry, Lukas."

"You mustn't feel sorry," Lukas replied softly. "I knew that it wasn't over yet." He turned to Schönborn. "How did you find us? Was it magic?"

Waldemar von Schönborn shrugged. "I must confess, at first it was harder than I'd expected. There was a protective magic, but that didn't stop us for long."

"Curses! Elsa's wooden angels!" Paulus ground his teeth and stared sheepishly at the ground. "I lost the ugly thing right away somewhere in the forest. I swear, I'll never say anything against handmade toys again."

Schönborn seemed confused for a moment, then continued. "Well, in the end, I could cast a stronger spell anyway." He reached under his cloak and pulled out two puppets that looked like they'd been made from thin, finely woven thread. "Your hair, Lukas, and Elsa's as well. Do you remember? You were kind enough to leave some of it behind. These puppets finally set me on your track. When I saw you were heading for Heidelberg, I put two and two together. A few days ago, we overtook you, then patiently waited for you here."

"So you also solved the riddle," Lukas said. "I didn't think you could do it." He sounded as defiant as Elsa.

Schönborn smiled. "Yes, the riddle, but we couldn't find the hiding place. You knew something that your mother didn't tell me, not even on the rack in my torture chamber, though she screamed like a stuck pig."

Unspeakable anger consumed Lukas, and he reached for his sword. But he immediately put it back down again when Schönborn pointed at Elsa and his friends. "Careful, not so impetuous, young friend. You surely don't want anything to happen to them."

"We'll make easy work of your mindless henchmen here," said Jerome, advancing a pace. "It would be best for you to leave, monsieur, before an even greater misfortune occurs. Or have you forgotten that we are Black Musketeers?"

Schönborn laughed. "So young, and already such a fresh mouth. I certainly don't doubt that you young fellows can strike a few blows on my men. But as you surely know, the frozen can't be killed with weapons, and sooner or later you'll get tired or inattentive in your fight, and that will be your downfall. Is that what you want?"

When there was no answer, Schönborn nodded. "Precisely. Do you see? You have your whole life still ahead of you, so don't throw it away frivolously." Then he pulled a dagger out from beneath his cloak, picked up the rusted lock, and broke it open. He lifted the moldy cover, and a smile of relief spread across his face.

"Finally!" he exclaimed. "The *Grimorium Nocturnum*, the *Book of the Night*. Now it is finally mine."

He took out an unassuming book about the size of his palm and bound in black leather. For a moment, Lukas felt sure that Schönborn was mistaken. That was the most powerful book of magic in the world? He'd imagined something much larger and more illustrious, a heavy tome bound in gold leaf with colorful letters. This looked more like a cheap, old prayer book that could be found in any village church.

Schönborn cast the empty box aside and ran his hands reverently over the worn leather.

"So many wars, so many dead, so much sorrow because of a book," he murmured. "Imagine everything the *Grimorium Nocturnum* has seen—the bloody battles of the Romans and the Gauls, the fall and the burning of Rome, Attila the king of the Huns, princes, kings, emperors . . . Now all its wisdom will be mine. Oh, *Book of the Night*, reveal your secrets to me!"

Schönborn closed his eyes briefly and took a deep breath.

Then he opened the book.

Lukas thought he heard the faint sound of a bell somewhere. At the same time, an icy wind began to blow, rustling through the pages of the book, and there was a scraping and squeaking as if somewhere nearby a huge, invisible door were opening. Startled, Schönborn attempted to close the book again, but he could not.

The Grimorium Nocturnum . . . *It's like a living creature,* Lukas thought. *It's fighting back!*

Lukas thought of the unnatural cold in the garden, and he was sure it had gotten even colder since Schönborn had picked up the little box.

For heaven's sake, what powers have been awakened in this book?

Waldemar von Schönborn also seemed to sense that he was in trouble. Desperately, he struggled with the pages that flew back and forth, faster and faster, making a hissing sound like a snake. Suddenly, Schönborn screamed as if something had bitten him. The book slipped from his hands and fell to the ground.

Now several things happened all at once. Giovanni, Paulus, and Jerome drew their swords, attacking two of the Spanish mercenaries. Lukas lunged forward, toward the inquisitor, who screamed again as he looked at his hands that were glowing red, as if they'd been burned by fire. And Elsa made use of the confusion to escape the grip of the third mercenary.

Then she reached for the book.

It was lying right in front of her, and later, no one could say how it had gotten there. Had it flown through the air? Had it simply slipped a few paces in the confusion of the fight? Whatever the explanation, Elsa's fingers closed around the book, and immediately the wind died down.

Then she ran back toward the labyrinth with the *Grimorium.*

"Elsa, wait!" Lukas shouted. "Don't go in there alone."

Just a moment ago, he was about to attack Schönborn, the murderer of his parents, but now he saw Elsa disappearing between the hedges and was overcome by an unspeakable fear of losing her again. He backed away from Schönborn and followed Elsa into the labyrinth.

At once, he found himself surrounded again by the high evergreen walls of boxwood trees. On his left he heard hurried footsteps, so he turned that way at the next opening, but no one was there—just paths leading off in different directions.

"Elsa!" he cried in despair. "Elsa! Where are you?"

It was so cold that Lukas, wearing thin leather shoes, could hardly feel his feet anymore. Now he realized he'd run off without Giovanni's map. If he got lost, he'd surely freeze to death.

Something reached out and grabbed his leg, and he stumbled. As he fell, Lukas could see a slender branch wrapped around his ankle. He tried to pull himself loose, but a second branch shot out and wrapped itself around his neck. Lukas gasped and choked, and colored dots appeared before his eyes.

Schönborn! he thought. *This is his doing!*

With the last of his strength, Lukas drew his sword and slashed at the branch wrapped around his neck. It wriggled and twitched like a worm and finally fell to the ground. With another well-aimed blow, he cut through the branch on his leg, jumped up, breathing heavily, and ran away. Behind him, he could hear a rustling of dry leaves that sounded like the whispering of a hundred voices.

Lukassss . . . Stay, Lukassss . . . You cannnnot esssscape ussss!

Other branches reached out to grab him, but Lukas had been warned. He dodged them and ducked beneath them, waving his sword back and forth. He danced through the dark passageway like he'd never danced before. *Prime, seconde, tierce . . .* As he slashed left and right, the branches fell to the ground. All the exercises of the last year came back to him as he hacked his way like a whirling shadow through the thicket of branches while the voices around him continued rustling like dry leaves.

Lukassss . . . Lukassss . . . Lukassss . . .

He heard a weak cry.

It was Elsa, and she was crying for help!

Lukas ran on and on, but he had completely lost his bearings, and all the hedges and pathways looked alike. When he came to a fork, he was sure he'd been there just a moment ago.

I'm lost! He panicked. *I never should have run off without Giovanni's map. I should have—*

"Lukas!"

This time, the cry seemed to come from close by. Maybe Elsa was just behind the next hedge. He thought he saw a shadow through the thicket of branches with little icicles hanging on them. Was it Elsa? Desperately he sought a way over to the other side. There . . . between the hedges . . . was a small passage. He forced his way through and entered another narrow, shadowy pathway smelling strongly of molding foliage.

Just a few steps away stood Elsa, clenching the book in her hands—but between him and Elsa, one of the three Spanish mercenaries rose up like a mighty tower, his back turned to Lukas, pointing his sword at Elsa's throat, with the other hand reaching out for the *Grimorium.*

"*El libro,*" he demanded in a monotone, "*dámelo.*" When Elsa did not respond, the sword nicked her throat, and a thin stream of blood trickled down her neck. Only now did Elsa see Lukas, and her eyes widened with surprise and joy. The mercenary, noticing her gaze, hesitated.

"*¿Qué pasa?*" he growled. "*¿Qué—*"

Without hesitation, Lukas drew his sword and rushed at the broad-shouldered man, who was at least three heads taller than himself. The mercenary seemed to have expected the attack and spun around in one fluid movement. As the two blades clashed, Lukas noticed the scar on the man's face.

Before him stood the murderer of his father!

The mercenary had enormous strength, and his sword swept Lukas's own weapon aside like a twig. Suddenly, the man lowered his sword, then pulled it back, waving it in a semicircle. The razor-sharp blade would have sliced Lukas in two had he not leaped to the side at the last moment. As he jumped, he lunged forward, striking the mercenary right in the crook of the elbow.

It was a perfect blow. The blade slipped past the cuirass, cut through the skin and muscle, and remained stuck inside.

But the man just grinned.

He stepped back a pace, and the blood-smeared blade slid out of the wound, as if nothing had happened.

By now, Lukas knew this would be the hardest battle of his life. The man before him was not only an excellent fighter, he was practically invulnerable, imbued with demonic powers. But Lukas remembered that in Nürnberg, Giovanni had driven away this very warrior with fire. How could he quickly light such a fire here?

The frozen one prepared to strike again, and Lukas kept moving backward until he stood with his back to one of the hedges, the thorns piercing him like little daggers. Elsa, who was behind the mercenary, had sunk to the ground, her hands still clutching the book, staring wide-eyed in terror at her brother. It seemed as if all her strength had failed her.

Lukas remembered how Elsa had blinded the Swedish soldier recently with her magic. A similar trick now would be their salvation, but she appeared too terrified to act. Or was it something else that sapped her of all her power? At that moment, she was not a mighty sorceress, but only a little ten-year-old girl who was terribly afraid.

And Lukas could not protect her.

"Run, Elsa!" Lukas shouted. "Run! I'll hold off this monster in the meantime."

But Elsa just shook her head. "Not without you," she whispered, "not this time. This time we'll stay together."

Elsa's words awakened new, unimagined strength in Lukas. He thrust his sword with lightning speed, delivering attacks, ripostes, thrusts, and blows. It became clear what good teachers he'd had—first his father, later the sword master Dietmar von Scherendingen, and finally Zoltan, the commander of the Black Musketeers. Each had taught him something he could use now in this fight to the death. From his father, strength and speed; from Scherendingen, tricks and feints; and from Zoltan, courage and the indomitable will to overcome any situation, no matter how hopeless.

And God knows, this was a hopeless situation.

Lukas swung a high cut, then riposted, jumped back, and prepared a thwart cut that sent the mercenary tumbling backward. As Lukas advanced, his blade struck the sword arm of his opponent, but once again, the frozen one didn't even flinch. A wide grin spread across his face as blood dripped from his wound onto the ground.

Then came the next attack.

The two opponents had continued moving backward as they fought and were now standing beneath a latticework bower made of rusty iron bars intertwined with climbing vines and a few withered rosebushes with long icicles hanging down.

Lukas was hot from the fighting, and despite the biting cold, sweat poured down his forehead. Gasping and red faced, he awaited the next attack. His opponent, on the other hand, didn't appear at all tired. As if savoring his advantage, he took his time, approaching Lukas slowly, sword raised.

Lukas used the slight pause to look around. Where was Elsa? He couldn't see her anywhere. But he did see something else. Some of the icicles above him were unnaturally thick and long, as if some magic power had formed them into deadly weapons. They looked almost like spears.

Spears . . .

A thought stirred in Lukas's mind. The frozen man might be invulnerable, but he wasn't made of iron. He could be stopped . . . at least for a short while.

Lukas acted as if he were exhausted, staggering a few steps back and luring the mercenary farther into the dark arbor. Grinning and showing his teeth, the mercenary approached closer and closer, with a vacant, glassy look in his eyes, like a puppet.

"¡Pequeño bastardo!" he growled. *"Vete al diablo."*

Now the man stood directly beneath the icicles. Lukas lowered his sword, as if surrendering, closed his eyes, and knelt down.

The mercenary raised his sword for the final, fatal blow.

"Vete al . . ."

At the same time, Lukas jumped up like a tightly wound spring suddenly released and swung his sword in a half circle, so the icicles in front of him came clattering down like sharp arrows on the frozen one, who reacted too late. His grin turned into a grimace of horror as dozens of icicles rained down. As they bored into his arms, legs, back, and neck, he stumbled, dropped his sword, and fell to the ground, riddled with icy daggers.

"This is for my father," Lukas declared as he shoved his sword back into its sheath. "Think about that the next time you confront a Lohenfels."

He knew he didn't have much time. No doubt the man would get back on his feet soon. Without looking around, Lukas ran down the pathway until he stood between the hedges again, where he'd last seen Elsa.

"Elsa!" he cried. "Where are you? We have to get out of here!"

He heard a whimpering and looked down to see his little sister lying between two withered rosebushes, trembling and looking very small. Gasping, he bent down to her.

"We must go," he implored her, "fast, before this monster gets up again."

Elsa stared at him with empty eyes, still clenching the book tightly as if she was afraid it might open by itself.

"The *Grimorium Nocturnum*," she whispered. "Its words have been echoing in my mind, as if it wanted to crawl inside me like a viper into its den."

Lukas pulled his sister to her feet. "Listen, we must flee! Leave this accursed book here, and then—"

Elsa shook her head. "I cannot. I am . . . the last."

"The last what?" Lukas asked.

"The last of the white sorcerers. That is what the book told me. There are none after me, and it ordered me to guard the ancient wisdom. I cannot leave the *Grimorium* here, as I am its new guardian."

"Then just bring it along," Lukas replied impatiently. "I saw a bright spot back there between the hedges, and I believe there's a way out. All we have to do . . ." He hesitated as he suddenly realized he'd forgotten his friends in all the excitement. Giovanni, Paulus, and Jerome had to still be there in the clearing with Waldemar von Schönborn and the two other frozen guards. He couldn't abandon his sister, but the same held true for his friends who had saved his life so many times. He looked at Elsa. What should he do?

"Listen, first I'll get you out of here," he told her, "then I'll go back to the clearing and help the others. If I don't come back—"

"I'm coming with you," Elsa said.

"It's too dangerous. We can count ourselves lucky that we even found the way out."

"Without me, you won't find your way back to the clearing," Elsa replied, defiant as always.

Lukas frowned. "If I couldn't, then how could you? Remember we no longer have Giovanni's map."

"But we have the book, and the book will lead us. Come!"

Elsa turned and ran back toward the center of the labyrinth. Lukas followed, and soon they were again immersed in the gloomy thicket. But unlike Lukas, Elsa seemed quite sure of herself and which paths to take. She stopped from time to time to put the book to her forehead, and it almost looked as if the *Grimorium* were speaking to her. Then she headed off in another direction. Her exhaustion appeared to have given way to absolute concentration. Now and then, it seemed to Lukas that the twigs and branches were once again reaching out to seize them, but when Elsa ran past, they withdrew, scurrying like rats back into their holes.

After they had been running through the labyrinth for a while, Lukas again heard the sound of swords clashing, and he also thought he could hear Jerome or Giovanni calling for help. He ran faster. They had to be close to the center of the garden now, and he took Elsa by the hand and turned. At the end of the passage, they came to an ivy-covered archway with weathered stone columns that he assumed faced the clearing.

Just as Lukas was about to run toward it, a black whirlwind emerged from between the columns—thousands of tiny dots, like a buzzing swarm of flies. The dots darted wildly in all directions, as if each was looking for its place. Slowly, an image formed, one that Lukas knew all too well.

The black wolf of his dreams.

It glared at him with fiery eyes, and a deep growl came from its wide-open jaws.

"You should not have returned. Who knows, perhaps the two of you would have had a small chance." It was the voice of Waldemar von Schönborn, who now appeared from a side alley of the labyrinth. Confident of his victory, he smiled at Lukas and Elsa. "But I knew you would return to help your friends. Friendship is a firm bond, yet sometimes it can be a deadly shackle." He approached them at a leisurely pace while drawing strange lines in the air with his right hand, like a painter with an invisible paintbrush.

He's drawing the wolf, Lukas realized. *He's painting the wolf with his hand, and the monster is taking shape before our eyes!*

"You recognize this wolf, don't you, Lukas?" Schönborn continued. "A handsome beast, even if no one but you can see it. It feeds on your fear, and cherishes the nightmares it prowls through in order to find you. And sometimes, when your fear is greatest, this monster also takes shape, as it has now."

Lukas tried in vain to suppress the shivers running though his body and stood there, paralyzed, staring at the apparition crouched on the ground between him and his friends. Clashing swords and cries could be heard in the distance. How long would his friends be able to hold out before the frozen ones finally crushed them? Lukas wanted to run to them, but his fear of the wolf was greater.

"If you so much as harm a hair on my brother's head, I'll tear your magic book into a thousand pieces!" cried Elsa, running between Lukas and Schönborn. "He told me what a monster you are."

"And you believe him? How disappointing." Schönborn's face took on a saddened expression. "Have I not always cared for you, Elsa? Have I not taught you everything you need to be a true white sorceress? Before that, you were nothing, but I opened your eyes." He extended his hand that was still dark red from the burns inflicted on him by the *Grimorium*. "Now be a good child and give me the book, will you? You know I'd never do anything to hurt you."

"As if Elsa meant anything at all to you!" Lukas called out, trying to summon up his courage. "All you want is the magic book. Nothing else matters to you." The wolf was crouched on the ground just a few steps away and glaring at him, as if ready to pounce at any moment, but its image seemed to be gradually fading. Lukas pulled his sword, ready to fight and hurry over to help his friends, but he was still trembling too much to move.

"Are you so sure of that, boy?" Schönborn stared at Lukas and pointed casually at Elsa, who glared back at him. "Take a closer look at her, Lukas. You have dark hair, just like your parents. Elsa, on the other hand . . . well, she is blond." He grinned and briefly raised his cowl, revealing a bald head with a fringe of graying blond hair. "Like me."

Lukas lowered his sword. Elsa, too, appeared confused. "Just what . . . are you trying to say?" she finally asked.

"I'll show you something," Waldemar von Schönborn replied. "Look at this." He pulled up his right sleeve and pointed to a thumb-sized birthmark in the shape of a falling teardrop near his elbow. "It's called a witch's mark," he explained, "and it's found on witches and magicians. At least that's what people believe. As you may imagine, I've avoided as much as possible showing it to other people. Even Elsa is seeing it now for the first time. But she recognizes it because . . ."

"Because she herself bears such a mark," said Lukas, completing the thought. His grip on his sword weakened as the awareness hit him like a bolt of lightning. He had seen this mark on Elsa years ago when they were being bathed in a washtub in the castle, and he had seen how some servants had looked at Elsa suspiciously—her blond hair, the freckles, the birthmark. *A bastard,* one of the servants had whispered. At the time, Lukas didn't understand the meaning of that word.

Now he understood.

"Elsa is my daughter," Schönborn declared, savoring the moment. "The first time I arrested your mother on suspicion of witchcraft, I immediately noticed her beauty. She was beautiful, bright, and had something about her that I couldn't get out of my mind. She never confessed, but I knew already. She was a powerful witch—a white witch. I had to possess her, and I took her, and in that night, Elsa was conceived. I assume your father knew, but he kept it to himself. The shame was too great. Yes, Elsa is my daughter, and for that reason I never wanted any harm to come to her."

Lukas's heart was pounding wildly. He remembered the day more than a year ago when he fled from Schönborn's henchmen. What had Schönborn called out then?

Bring me the girl alive, quickly, but kill the boy.

Now, he finally understood why. Schönborn had spared Elsa because she was his daughter, and so he had cared for her like a father. He had taught her everything . . . reading, writing, magic . . .

The wolf under the archway seemed to have grown into a giant shadow lurking between the weathered columns. Lukas shuddered. Everything was as in his dreams, his surroundings faded away, and the cries of his friends behind the archway sounded muffled. Even Elsa, at his side, appeared to be in another world. She had rolled up her sleeve and was staring transfixed at the birthmark as if she still didn't understand.

"Elsa," Schönborn continued gently. "It's true, I am your father. You are the child of an inquisitor and a white witch, and both my powers and those of your mother are united in you. Together we can turn the world upside down." He extended his hand once more. "Now, finally, give your dear father the book. You see he needs you. Alone, I cannot use the *Grimorium*. You are the last of the white witches, and I need your help. Together we are the most powerful magicians since the ancient druids Mug Ruith and Cathbad."

Elsa, still clutching the book, trembled and turned pale, but now she raised her hands and, as if in a trance, took a step toward Schönborn.

"No, Elsa, don't do it!" cried Lukas.

Lukas's fear of what would happen to Elsa was greater than his fear of the wolf, and he lunged at Schönborn, but at the same moment, the wolf growled and came between them. Lukas shouted and attacked it with his sword, but the weapon passed through its body as if through a cloud of smoke. Lukas staggered and fell to the ground, and his sword slipped from his hands as the beast opened its jaws to seize his throat, coming closer, inch by inch. Lukas's fear grew beyond measure, as did the wolf towering over him. He reached out again for his sword and gripped the handle, but he knew that the weapon could not help him this time.

Nothing could help him anymore. It was over, the wolf would seize him by the throat, and then—

At that moment, he heard a voice . . .

Have no fear, children. It is only fear that allows evil to prevail.

Lukas was stunned, and then his heart leaped for joy. From the surprised expression on Elsa's face, he realized that she, too, had heard the voice.

The voice of their mother.

The tender words gave Lukas new strength. He looked at the wolf with a steady gaze, trying to concentrate on what his mother had just said.

Have no fear . . .

"I have no fear, I have no fear," he kept murmuring to himself, as if praying. "*We* have no fear."

The wolf recoiled and began to contract like a balloon when the air is released.

"We have no fear!" Lukas shouted. *"No fear!"*

Then he laughed right into the beast's face.

The wolf's contours began to blur, and the individual dots scattered like bees in search of nectar. Soon all that was left of the great beast was a thin gray cloud.

For the first time, Schönborn seemed uncertain, and he turned to Elsa, who was still standing before him holding the *Grimorium.*

"I am your father," he said in a firm voice, "and I order you to obey me. Now give me the book."

Elsa reached out her hand holding the *Grimorium.*

"Do you see?" Schönborn said with relief. "You're a good girl. Now all you have to do—"

Elsa opened her mouth and spoke:

"OMAR PARTUIS SENTA GRAVA. FORAMEN PORTABILIS."

The words came from her mouth, but they didn't sound like those of a little girl. They sounded like a deep, dark voice from the depths of hell, as if a dragon had been awakened, now soaring up to the heavens to destroy the earth with its fiery breath.

"*Foramen portabilis!*" Elsa shouted again.

A storm arose, sweeping across the clearing, and the book in Elsa's hands began to flutter, faster and faster. Small bushes and hedges were uprooted and flew past Lukas.

Then the world began to spin, more and more wildly, like a bowl on a potter's wheel.

"No!" Lukas could hear Schönborn screaming from some-where. "No, Elsa! Stop! You are my daughter—you . . . are . . . my . . . *No!*"

The scream suddenly broke off, and everything around Lukas turned as black as a starless night sky. Schönborn, Elsa, the frozen, and his friends had all disappeared. He heard a faint hissing that gradually got louder, as if a heavy object were falling down from a great height.

At the same moment, Lukas sensed that it was he himself that was falling.

XXVII

When Lukas opened his eyes, the fall abruptly stopped.

He seemed to be lying on something hard, but it was not the frosty ground of the garden labyrinth. The smell was different, too. The fresh winter breeze had vanished; only the stench of moldy straw, rat feces, and decay remained. He noticed he was still clenching the Pappenheim sword, and the pistol was still tucked under his belt. Wherever he might be, at least he was not unarmed.

He struggled to get to his feet and realized that despite his precipitous fall, he hadn't broken anything. Everything around him was still dark, but after he'd blinked a few times, he began to recognize some vague outlines. Light fell through some tiny cracks above him, forming a square.

A trapdoor, he thought.

When he reached out with his hands, he felt a hard stone wall, mold, and slimy moss.

This is a cell, and I'm a prisoner! But where, in God's name, is Elsa? What happened?

"Elsa," he cried into the darkness. "Elsa! Are you here somewhere? Please, Elsa, say something."

A terrible fear swept over him—but the fear he had lost Elsa again, and his friends, too, seemed to have vanished. Was he all alone in this sinister dungeon?

Not far from him, he heard a groan, and he crept toward it on his hands and knees. He could feel cold arms and legs, and finally a face bathed in sweat. He breathed a sigh of relief. He didn't need light to recognize it was his sister lying there. Elsa was breathing fitfully, still holding the leather-bound book of magic. Lukas bent down over her and tried to warm her with his body.

"Elsa," he whispered, "everything will be all right. I am with you."

"I . . . know, Lukas." She coughed. "You are my big brother, and big brothers have to watch over their little sisters, don't they?"

Lukas laughed. "Yes, that's what they're supposed to do, but you have to at least tell me what happened and where we are."

"It was anger." Elsa's lips were now very close to his ear, and she trembled as if she had a fever. "When Schönborn said I was his daughter, the book and my anger simply swept me away. I wanted only to leave, to escape this monster who is my father." She was crying softly.

"Do you mean you cast a spell that took us to another place?" Lukas asked.

Elsa was silent. Lukas felt her face and realized it was wet from the tears running down her cheeks. "It's a very powerful spell," she said finally. "All my hate was needed to pronounce the words, and it brought me to the threshold of death. I felt something dark reaching out for me with its claws."

"But where are we?" Lukas asked again. He looked up, where he could now clearly see the outlines of the trapdoor. "It looks like your spell put us in a cell. Are we back in Schönborn's dungeon?"

"No, Lukas. It's another cell." She coughed again. Laboriously, she took hold of Lukas and pulled herself up. "I hope, at least, that it is."

"But which one?" Lukas asked.

"It's the place I first thought of when I spoke the magic words," Elsa said, carefully getting to her feet. "The place where it all began."

Suddenly, it dawned on Lukas, and his heart skipped a beat. "Do you mean . . ."

"It's the cell in the keep of Lohenfels Castle," she finished for him. "You left me here alone then, when Schönborn took our mother away. I was so afraid. I climbed up the ladder, and you were standing there looking out the embrasure, your eyes wide with fear. I knew at once that something dreadful had happened. It was like . . ."

"Like the end of our childhood," Lukas murmured. "I know. I also felt something like that."

"You ran away and left me behind. I cried for days until Schönborn's magic finally made me forget everything. Now the memory has returned." Elsa began climbing up the ladder. "Let's see what awaits us up there."

"Elsa, wait! We don't know who is up there—maybe Schönborn's henchmen, or someone else."

Lukas hurried up the steps after her, but she had already lifted the trapdoor and crawled through the opening. He found her in a corner of the drafty keep, staring out through a jagged opening in the wall.

The sight took his breath away.

The keep had been blown up so that only two of the original tower walls were standing. Outside, an icy wind was blowing. Below them lay what was once their parents' castle—charred ruins, the caved-in roofs of the stables, a castle wall shot to pieces . . .

the courtyard where they once played hide-and-seek as children, with rubble scattered everywhere. Lukas was so shocked that for a while, words failed him.

"The Swedes must have done this," he finally said. "Lohenfels was one of the last castles loyal to the Kaiser. My God, they haven't left one stone unturned here."

Suddenly, between the ruins, he spotted something moving. A broad-shouldered figure white with stone dust rose to his feet. His shirt was torn and his hair disheveled.

One of the frozen! Lukas realized at once. *They followed us here. Now we are finished!*

Elsa let out a loud cry, but then a deep, grumbling voice spoke up.

And cursed in a very familiar way.

"What the hell happened? Damn, I feel like I've been rolled over by a thousand-pound cannon. Damn, damn, damn!"

Then two other forms emerged from the rubble. They stumbled around, but it didn't appear they were injured.

"Paulus, Giovanni, Jerome!" Lukas cried out. "My God, I thought it was Schönborn!"

"Can someone pinch me so I know I'm no longer dreaming?" Giovanni mumbled. "Where are we, anyway?" he asked, looking around. "And where the hell is the labyrinth?"

Jerome knocked the stone dust from his shoulders. "It doesn't matter where we are. In any case I can't let the girls see me in this outfit," he wailed. *"C'est terrible!"*

Despite the devastation all around them, Lukas had to laugh. "My God, you three look like really pathetic castle ghosts." He pointed at the destruction everywhere. "Well, if you still need proof that my sister can cast spells, here it is. Welcome to Lohenfels Castle."

Jerome stared at him in amazement. "You mean this pile of rocks is your father's castle? And your sister cast a spell to bring us here?" He turned to Elsa. "Couldn't you have found something a bit more pleasant? Venice, for example? Or Paris, with its pretty girls and good wine?"

Elsa smiled weakly as Lukas led her down the keep's partially destroyed outer stairs to the courtyard. "I'm sorry that I'm not even half as good at being a witch as you'd hoped for. I'm happy anyway that my spell was good enough to get not only me and Lukas, but you three as well, out of the Heidelberg Castle gardens."

"What happened to Schönborn and his frozen ones?" Giovanni asked cautiously.

"The magic whirlwind was strong enough to carry them off," Elsa replied, "but where it took them, I can't say, unfortunately. I only hope it's far, far away."

Paulus spat out a tooth he'd evidently lost in his fall. "I'm afraid there's no place far enough away for that monster. If Schönborn ever sees us again, he won't have too many kind words for us."

"And neither will his henchmen." Jerome grinned. There was a bloodied cut across his forehead. "Considering they're invulnerable, we sure kicked the hell out of them. Do you know how I—"

They heard a sound coming from down in the stables. Jerome and Giovanni reached for their swords while Paulus grabbed a large rock and crouched down, ready to attack. But it was only an old woman in a torn dress, probably looking for something in the ruins. With a cry, she dropped her bag and fell to her knees.

"Oh, my lords, do me no harm!" she pleaded. "I have only come to look around for some of my former belongings. Never would I—"

"Agnes!" Lukas shouted with joy when he finally recognized the old woman. She was his former nurse who had given him her grandson's clothes when he fled from Lohenfels. In the year since then, her hair had become almost white. "It's me—Lukas! Don't you recognize me?" Then he pointed at Elsa. "And here is my sister. We are back! The others are friends of mine, and you have nothing to fear from them."

For a moment, the old maid looked as if she were seeing ghosts. Her jaw opened and shut silently, like a fish's, and then she sighed deeply.

"Thanks be to Jesus, Mary, and Joseph, miracles still happen. The young lord and Elsa have returned, and now everything will be fine!"

Sobbing, she fell at Lukas's feet, and it took him a while to calm her down a bit so she could relate to him and the others what had happened at Lohenfels Castle in the last year.

"Right after you fled, the horrible Spaniards took over here," she told him excitedly. "They exploited us so mercilessly that we were almost grateful when the Swedes finally attacked the castle in the summer. But they were not one bit better, and with their firearms, they shot everything to pieces. I only wanted to see if there was anything useful under the rubble. People in this area are in great hunger."

"If there's anything still left here, it probably moldered away long ago, or the rats ate it," Giovanni muttered. "I can't imagine any place drearier than this."

Lukas gazed at the forlorn castle with its charred beams and courtyard strewn with blocks of stone. Giovanni was right. His parents' castle was a desolate, uninhabitable place. Strangely, though, this thought did not make him sad, but defiant. He stood up straight. "Things really look bad here," he said in a low voice, "but nevertheless, it's my home. Our home," he added, turning to his sister, who stood silently alongside him.

Elsa frowned. She was still holding the *Grimorium* in her small hands, as if it were all that could protect her from the surrounding chaos. "What are you trying to say? Do you want to stay here, amid all the rubble?"

"Well, so far as I can see, the hall is still in fairly good condition," he replied. "The roof over the ground floor did not collapse, and the left wing of the building seems quite livable. If the chimney isn't obstructed—"

"Wait a minute." Paulus rubbed the side of his nose. "You really intend to *live* here?"

"Why not?" Lukas shrugged. "I've had enough of war and destruction. This is our home, and I am the heir of Lohenfels. Eventually, the Swedes will leave. Now, after the death of their king, it can't be long before they also disappear from the Palatinate, and then I will rebuild this castle, bigger and more beautiful than ever."

The old nurse beamed. "Oh, young master, would you really do that?"

Lukas nodded earnestly. "As sure as my name is Lukas von Lohenfels. For now, keep this secret to yourself, Agnes. I don't want us to have uninvited visitors up here. But when the time is right, I'll ask the men of the surrounding villages to help me rebuild the castle."

"You don't know what that would mean to the people here," Agnes replied with radiant eyes. "It would be a glimmer of hope that this war cannot destroy everything."

The old nurse bade farewell, warmly embracing Lukas over and over. Then she hobbled away with her stick through the badly damaged castle gateway, turning around again and again to wave to Lukas and Elsa.

"You are crazy, do you know that?" Shaking his head, Giovanni leaned against a damaged stone column, staring at the rubble all around. He was silent for a while, but finally laughed out loud. "But by God, I just love crazy people!"

Elsa smiled at Lukas. She, too, seemed much more confident after the conversation with Agnes. "The more I think about it, the more I like the thought of staying here," she said. Then she winked at the others. "And it's really possible to make this place a bit more comfortable."

"Can you perhaps conjure up a nice, warm room with a fireplace, deer antlers, and wall tapestries?" Jerome asked hopefully. "That would be a spell that finally suits my taste."

"Well, sometimes one does not need a magic spell. Filthy lucre can do the same thing." Elsa grinned, pulling a leather purse out from under her jacket. They heard a suspiciously familiar sound inside. "Before we left the monastery, I looked around again in Schönborn's study and found *this* inside a book that had been hollowed out." She opened up the purse, and a shower of gold coins spilled out onto the snow-covered ground. "I knew that Schönborn stashed little sums of money everywhere in order to bribe important people when needed," she explained. "It didn't take me long to find it."

Paulus groaned. "And you're only telling us that now? With this we could have been traveling like princes all last month."

"And you would have certainly attracted attention and been robbed," Giovanni replied with a shrug. "Elsa was right to put the money aside for an emergency. With all those gold ducats, you can probably build an entire castle, and it will at least be enough for a few cozy winter months with hot mulled wine and a suckling pig roasting on the fire. I've spent worse times in winter quarters, and I'm sure Paulus and Jerome have, too." He looked at the others, waiting for their response. "Haven't you?"

"Hmm, in fact, *c'est vrai*." Jerome nodded. "And there are fleas and lice everywhere."

"Does that mean you . . . really want to stay here with Elsa and me?" Lukas asked, surprised.

"Well, if you two thought you could bid us farewell so soon, you're wrong," Paulus grumbled. "You'll need a few strong arms to make a halfway decent home out of this ruin, and besides . . ." He lowered his voice. "If Schönborn should ever come back again and find you, you'll be happy for every swordsman you can get. Especially if Elsa really wants to keep this magic book." He looked at her. "Is that what you want?"

"I don't know," Elsa murmured. "Destroying it doesn't seem like the right thing to do. It has chosen me as its keeper. And I don't know what would happen to me if I actually tried to burn it. It's . . . like a living creature, and above all, a very angry one."

"You have time to think it over," Lukas replied, "and until then, we should no doubt be looking around for a heavy chest to hold the money, with many padlocks."

They were standing in the middle of the courtyard when Lukas, on a whim, drew his sword and held it up in the air.

"One for all," he said in a firm voice.

The three friends likewise drew their swords and held them tip to tip with his. Elsa raised her arms, holding the *Grimorium* so that the worn leather cover touched Lukas's sword handle.

"And all for one!" they all cried together.

For a brief moment, the gray winter clouds parted, and the sun shone down. A few of its rays reflected on the blades, and the five friends, all so different from one another, were united for this moment in a brilliant red blaze of light.

And despite the cold winter, Lukas felt a warm wave of friendship flooding over him.

EPILOGUE

It took many weeks to make something resembling a home out of the ruined castle. They cleared away the rocks and broken beams in the courtyard, opened the well, and built new floors and ceilings in some of the rooms that had been gutted by fire. In the end, a half-dozen rooms were renovated sufficiently to be halfway comfortable.

Their pride and joy was the great hall with the fireplace on the first floor that became the focal point of their lives during the cold, dark winter months. There was always a warm fire burning there, the window openings were covered with parchment to keep out the cold, and heavy rugs and furs on the walls and floors ensured pleasant hours in which they ate, drank, played dice, or simply talked.

"I must admit I never thought it could be so comfortable here," said Paulus, cutting himself another slice from the steaming leg of mutton. "When I think what it must be like in Wallenstein's winter quarters now, *brrr* . . ."

"Still, my conscience troubles me that we left Zoltan without saying good-bye," Jerome said. "That's not done among honorable men."

"At least we sent him a message," Giovanni replied. "And something tells me we'll see Zoltan and the Black Musketeers again someday. And perhaps Waldemar von Schönborn," he added gloomily.

Elsa looked up from the book she'd been reading as she sat in a corner wrapped in thick furs. It was still hard for her to accept that Waldemar von Schönborn was really her father, though the freckles, the blond hair, and, above all, the birthmark left little doubt. In the past few weeks, Elsa had taken refuge with the books in the castle library, which had been at least partly spared from destruction.

"If my father really believes he can come and get me and the *Grimorium*, he's mistaken," she responded coolly. "I'm the last white witch. He'll see what it means to cross swords with a real witch."

Lukas looked at his sister with a mixture of respect and also a bit of fear. For her ten years of age, she was sometimes almost incredibly grown-up, as if her year with Schönborn had aged her unduly. But perhaps it was on account of the *Grimorium Nocturnum*, that *Book of the Night*, that lay in a chest in the castle cellar for safekeeping. Sometimes, at night, Lukas heard Elsa climbing down the stairway, and he could hear strange, mumbling sounds. He assumed it was Elsa talking with the book. Or was it perhaps the *Grimorium* whispering something in her ear? He shuddered. There were some things he didn't want to know about.

Old Agnes had apparently kept her word and told no one that Lukas and Elsa had returned to the castle, so for the most part they remained undisturbed except for occasional thieves that they quickly drove off.

Now and then, Lukas rode out to inspect the area, and he learned that the Swedes were still occupying Heidelberg but were slowly withdrawing from the surrounding region. It wouldn't be long before they could start properly rebuilding the castle. The gold coins that Elsa had stolen from Schönborn would help them greatly to get started and possibly employ workers from the surrounding villages.

Sometimes Lukas thought of the traveling artists, those whose lives had been lost—the sword master Dietmar von Scherendingen, strong Ivan and his bear, the musicians Bjarne and Thadäus—as well as the Jannsen Brothers with their acrobatic tricks and, naturally, Red Sara and Tabea. Lukas hoped fervently they had reached Augsburg safely. What if Tabea came to stay with them for a while? Would she like the way Lukas had changed? In recent weeks, he had become happier. It was as if his dead parents had decided to give him the freedom to go his own way. He dreamed of them occasionally, and they were pleasant dreams that brought back no bad memories.

Lukas was warming his hands on a cup of hot mulled wine and letting his thoughts wander when he heard an energetic hammering. Someone was pounding on the door of the great room.

Paulus jumped up and grabbed his sword that was leaning against the hearth. "If those are plundering mercenaries, they are very polite," he growled. "Nevertheless, I'm afraid I'll have to make them a head shorter."

The others also hurriedly picked up their weapons. Carefully, with drawn sword, Lukas went to the door that had been reinforced with strong oaken beams just a few weeks ago.

"Who goes there?" he asked loudly.

"A friend who has been looking for you for a long time," replied a voice that sounded oddly familiar. Lukas hesitated a moment, then a surprised smile spread across his face.

"Senno!" he cried. "Is it really you?"

"In person. Now open the door, lad. I'm alone."

Lukas was about to pull the bolt aside when Paulus held him back.

"Do you really trust this charlatan?" he asked.

"Why not? If armed men were standing out there, Senno wouldn't have needed to knock. We're not strong enough to withstand a siege, so let's see what he wants here."

Lukas opened the door, and a cold wind blew in. Indeed, Senno was standing there, and he seemed to be alone. Behind him, a black horse was tied up by the wall, nibbling on a few sparse patches of moss, and Senno himself was wearing a black, snow-covered cape. His moustache was just as well waxed and twisted as when Lukas had met him the first time.

"It took some doing to find you," he began while peering past Lukas into the room. "Ah, and here are your friends I've heard so much about. Hmm, and the girl with the books is your sister, Elsa, isn't she? How delightful to see you all unharmed."

He was about to enter when Giovanni stepped in front of him.

"Why do I have the feeling you are keeping something from us?" he asked. "You surely didn't travel many hundreds of miles just to say hello."

Senno smiled broadly. "Hardly. The trip is too difficult just for that." He pointed at the stool by the fireplace. "Would it be possible for me to present my concern inside? I have a strenuous ride behind me."

Giovanni looked at Lukas, and when Lukas nodded, he stepped aside and Senno took a seat by the fire.

"Actually, I wasn't looking for you at all, at first, but for Schönborn," he began, rubbing his cold, reddened hands together. "When he suddenly left Wallenstein almost three months ago, I was afraid he'd finally found what he'd been seeking for so long."

"The *Grimorium Nocturnum*," Lukas said. "So you've heard of the book."

Senno nodded. "Naturally, I'm familiar with it. I've been searching for the book almost as long as Schönborn has, with the distinction that I want to use it for good purposes, and Schönborn for evil."

"That's what they all say," Giovanni noted sarcastically.

"Schönborn wanted to use the *Grimorium Nocturnum* to lengthen the war," Senno continued, unperturbed. "Because only in war does the fear and lawlessness prevail that he needs for his nefarious purposes. That's why he had the Swedish king killed by his henchmen. He stirs up hatred and misery, on both sides."

Lukas bit his lip. "Then I was right after all," he murmured. "That's why Schönborn left us behind in the monastery at first. His frozen men killed King Gustav. He died by black magic."

"I knew for a long time that a white witch was the last owner of the *Grimorium* and had hidden the book somewhere," Senno said, turning to Lukas. "When you told me about the fate of your mother, and when it became clear that Schönborn was looking for you, I had a suspicion. But you wouldn't trust me, Lukas."

"For good reason," Paulus interjected. "Zoltan and many others always warned us of you, and I'm still not sure whose side you're on. Perhaps you only look out for yourself."

"I shall no doubt have to continue living with my bad reputation." Senno shrugged. "In any case, after Schönborn and Lukas had disappeared, I made inquiries and learned about this strange child Schönborn had adopted, and I set out in search of her. I tracked Schönborn to Heidelberg, but then the trail went cold. It seemed almost like he had been swallowed up by the earth. Did you have anything to do with that?" Senno twisted his beard and looked at them closely. When there was no reply, he went on. "It might interest you to know I heard about him just a few days ago. It seems he turned up in Rome, was granted an audience with the pope, and he may even be made a cardinal." He laughed bitterly. "Well, they say a cat has nine lives."

Lukas was stunned. It was just as he had feared—Schönborn was not dead, and it appeared he was even more powerful than before! How long would it take Schönborn and his henchmen to find them?

"But Schönborn is not important," Senno said, interrupting Lukas's thoughts. "The only important thing is the book." Suddenly, he scowled. "You have it, don't you?"

"And if we did," Elsa spoke up for the first time, "why is that any of your business?"

"This book can do great harm, but it can also do good," Senno explained. "I only want to know it has fallen into the right hands." He sighed. "But I fear I have come too late. The book has already chosen a new man as its owner. Or rather, a new woman." He looked at Elsa questioningly. "It's you, isn't it? I can feel a very powerful aura emanating from you." Senno shook his head. "A child! If only dear old Merlin knew that, he'd turn over in his grave."

"Who is Merlin?" Elsa asked with curiosity.

Senno waved dismissively. "Forget it. It's an old story. What we do now with the book is more important."

"We?" Lukas frowned. "Why we?"

"Well, it is what it is." Senno drummed his fingers on the table. "One of the most powerful books in the world is in the hands of a ten-year-old girl. To take it away from her would have dreadful consequences. I assume you know what I'm speaking of." The astrologer glared at the friends. "If I can finally convince you of all the good things this book can do, and what I intend to do with it, I'll need your help."

"Do you mean we can fight evil in the world with this book?" Lukas asked. "But just how would we—"

"Don't you see how we're falling into a trap?" Paulus interrupted gruffly. "The best thing for us to do would be to throw him out, then we'd finally have some peace and quiet."

Senno raised his hands, professing his innocence. "First, just listen to what I have to say, and then you can decide."

"Very well," Jerome said, reaching for his wineglass. "We don't have anything to do at the moment, and these winter evenings can be really boring. So tell me, monsieur, what do you intend to do with the book?"

Senno smiled, crossed his legs, looked at them for a long time, one by one, and finally began to speak. "Let me tell you about the legendary imperial sword of Charlemagne. It has been lost to history for many years, and I fear that dark forces have taken possession of it."

"Hmm, a sword?" Paulus raised his eyebrows. "And not just any sword, but one belonging to the famous king? This is getting interesting. Tell us about the sword. Is it sharp? Does it have magical power?"

"That's a long story." Senno grinned. "But can I assume you like stories and adventures?"

"Now tell us, and don't keep us hanging here on tenterhooks," Lukas added impatiently. "You have at least made us curious." He wrapped himself up in his bearskin and settled down comfortably in front of the fire beside his sister and his closest friends.

Something told him that the rebuilding of the castle might take a while.

ABOUT THE AUTHOR

 Oliver Pötzsch spent years working for Bavarian Broadcasting and now devotes his time entirely to writing. He lives in Munich with his family. His historical novels for adults made him internationally famous. He is also the author of the children's novel *Knight Kyle and the Magic Silver Lance*.